Prince of Swords

Prince of Swords

Anne Stuart

Five Star
Unity, Maine

Five Star Romance.
Published in conjunction with Zebra Books, an imprint
of Kensington Publishing Corporation.

Cover photograph by Alan J. La Vallee.

July 1997
Standard Print Hardcover Edition.

Five Star Standard Print Romance Series.

The text of this edition is unabridged.

Set in 11 pt. Plantin by Rick Gundberg.

Printed in the United States on permanent paper.

Library of Congress Cataloging in Publication Data

Stuart, Anne (Anne Kristine)
    Prince of swords / Anne Stuart.
       p.   cm.
    ISBN 0-7862-1116-4 (hc : alk. paper)
    I. Title.
    [PS3569.T785P75   1997]
    813´.54—DC21   97-10482

Prince of Swords

One

London, 1775

Lady Plumworthy had magnificent jewels. All of society knew that — they'd been subjected to the sight of heavy, badly cut diamonds and emeralds draped around her bewattled neck far too often, ear bobs dragging down her lobes and grazing her dimpled shoulders. They were jewels fit for a courtesan, as Lady Plumworthy had once been. Now, however, she was an ancient, raddled hag with a soul even uglier than her aged face. She'd gone through three husbands, each one richer than the last, and amassed an impressive number of wealthy lovers during her lengthy career. She still kept impecunious young men at her beck and call, and she decked herself in her battle trophies.

In truth, she deserved to lose those trophies. And Alistair MacAlpin, the sixth Earl of Glenshiel, meant to see that she did.

Downstairs the night was lively. Lady Plumworthy's ball was a smashing success; a crush of people danced and gamed and ate with careless abandon. Several couples had already found their way to secluded bedrooms. Lady Plumworthy was known to be particularly benevolent about such matters. What few people realized was that she liked to observe.

Alistair knew far too much about Isolde Plumworthy, née Bridget Stives. She'd been casting out lures that were becoming increasingly more like threats, and if he hadn't found his current mode of occupation, he might well have been forced to succumb.

He scooped the heavy mass of emeralds from her dressing table, where she'd tossed them earlier. Arrogant old crones were always the best subjects for his particular attention — they never imagined someone would dare broach the sanctity of their bedroom unless specifically summoned.

Alistair had broached the sanctity of many bedrooms, for any number of reasons. He had come to the wry conclusion that nowadays he derived far more pleasure from stealing than from sex.

He slipped the jewels into the soft velvet pouch he'd brought with him for that purpose, flattening them so they wouldn't present an unsightly bulge beneath his gray silk jacket. Five minutes later he was sipping claret and ogling Miss Carstairs's cleavage. And the diamonds that danced above it.

"Are you going to come hear the fortune-teller, my lord?" she asked, pressing closer in the crowd. She smelled strongly of rose perfume and body heat. He smiled at her.

"There's a Gypsy here tonight? How enterprising of Lady Plumworthy."

"Not precisely a Gypsy. A card reader, one who can tell the past, present, and future by a turn of the cards. How can you resist?"

"Quite easily, my pet," he said, having had occasion to sample Miss Carstairs's cleavage firsthand. "I know my past, my present is obvious, and I make it a policy never to think about the future. It's far too morbid." He detached his hand from hers gingerly. "You go ahead and see this Gypsy, and if he happens to mention anything about me, you can come back and report."

"I told you, it's not a Gypsy. It's a young Englishwoman

8

Lady Plumworthy has hired for the occasion. Not of our class, of course, but she should prove a little less eccentric and a great deal less odorous than the usual."

"A cit fortune-teller? How singular." He wanted to leave. Now that he'd managed to fill his velvet pouch, the jewels weighed heavily against him, and he wanted to escape back to his tiny house on Clarges Street, where he could admire the huge, ugly jewels at his leisure and calculate how much money they would bring him. And whether he'd sink more of it into the rapidly decaying pile of stone known as Glenshiel Abbey, or simply scatter it at the gaming tables.

But he didn't dare leave yet — it would be too remarkable. At least a fortune-teller might manage to beguile him enough to bear the next two or three hours until he could escape.

Miss Carstairs caught his hand again. "Come with me, Alistair. I may need you for moral comfort if she tells me something depressing."

"Trust me, my love," he murmured, allowing her to draw him through the crowds of people toward one of his hostess's gaming rooms. "Morality is one thing I'm in short supply of."

The room was even more packed than the ballroom. He could see Isolde Plumworthy, her stately bulk ensconced on a chaise, her hand upon the satin-breeched thigh of young Calderwood. The boy was barely out of leading strings — twenty if he was a day — and he looked both terrified and flattered by Lady Plumworthy's attention. Pity, Alistair thought, turning away from them.

At first he couldn't see the clairvoyant through the crowds of people. Miss Carstairs lost her grip on his hand, for which he was devoutly grateful, and they were separated. He moved through the crush with his usual feline grace, slyly observant beneath half-lowered eyelids.

It took him a moment to realize that the quietly dressed

young woman who sat at the green baize table was, in fact, the fortune-teller. She was concentrating on the cards laid out in front of her, her head bowed, so his first impression was of a small, well-shaped head crowned with a neatly arranged cap of hair, light brown, ordinary enough. She was dressed in a sedate blue dress with a minimum of ornamentation, and the hands that held the pack of cards were devoid of even a plain silver ring. Pretty hands, though, he thought, and willed her to look up at him.

If she felt his silent summons, she managed to ignore it, a fact that amused him. He moved to the edge of the room, behind her, where he could watch the back of her head and his fellow guests' gullible reactions.

Her head lifted, and he could see her profile. Surprisingly delicate for a bourgeoise, he thought. He moved slightly, hoping for a better glimpse, but she managed to elude him. The longer he was unable to get a proper view of her, the more determined he became.

Her voice was soft but surprisingly clear, and no cit's voice. "I see a man, Lady Plumworthy," she murmured. "In your bedchamber."

Alistair didn't move as the crowd tittered. There was no reason why she should be referring to him, when there were far more obvious reasons for a man to be in Isolde's bedchamber. The leering smile she cast at young Calderwood suggested that Lady Plumworthy agreed.

"A lady doesn't admit to such things," Isolde announced in a voice subtly less cultured than her fortune-teller's. Isolde Plumworthy had risen in the world during her long and varied career. Alistair could guess that the fortune-teller, conversely, had fallen upon impecunious times.

He moved slightly, still frustrated by his inability to get a glimpse of her. "This man is not a friend or a suitor, my lady," the girl said quietly. "He is a thief."

Alistair grew very still indeed. The buzz of conversation increased, and Lady Plumworthy no longer seemed quite so sanguine. "You're telling me I shall be robbed?" she demanded, releasing her grip on Calderwood's thigh.

The young man took that moment to escape, wise child that he was. Alistair stayed watching. "I believe the robbery might already have occurred," the girl said.

"Nonsense!" Lady Plumworthy hissed. "No one would dare . . ."

"Perhaps the Cat has struck again," Freddie Arbuthnot said with a silly laugh. "It's been quite a time since he's been on the prowl."

"I do believe, Freddie," Alistair said lazily, "that the Cat has never been seen. How can you be sure it's a man?"

"Don't be daft," Freddie protested. "What else could it be? There's more than physical agility involved in these robberies. There's incredible daring and cunning as well. Don't expect me to believe a child could carry out such involved and outrageous schemes."

"I was thinking more along the lines of a young woman," Alistair said smoothly.

She turned then, as he knew she would, goaded by his subtle suggestion, and he was able to view her with lazy deliberation. He took his time doing so, lifting his quizzing glass with casual disdain.

She was past the first blush of youth, which relieved him. She wasn't astonishingly beautiful, though he could find no fault with her small nose, her generous mouth, her high cheekbones, or her stubborn chin. If there was anything unusual about her face, it was her eyes. They were far too wise for a woman only a bit past twenty, and their clear, translucent green-blue reminded him of distant seas. Her hair was streaked

11

with light, and what he could see of her form was trim and well shaped. But it was her eyes that held him. Dangerous eyes. Contemplating him with odd clarity.

He smiled at her. He had no faith whatsoever in fortune-telling, or in quiet young women being able to see past his indolent exterior. He knew perfectly well how such sharps worked — they took a combination of fact and conjecture and came up with a logical guess. The Cat hadn't made an appearance for quite a while; he was due to strike. And the fortune-teller was betting her reputation that it would be tonight.

"Don't intimidate the child, Glenshiel," Lady Plumworthy chided him. "I'm hardly likely to have given her the run of the house. If you like, we can have her searched for any missing trinkets before we leave."

"Only if you allow me to do the searching," he drawled, but his eyes were caught with hers, and he could see the wariness, and the sudden anger there.

"This is tedious," Lady Plumworthy announced. "I'm more interested in my love life. Come, Miss Brown, let's concentrate on the rest of my reading. I've been told remarkable things about you — I'd hate to think I was mistaken in hiring you for the evening."

If the old hag thought she could cow the mysterious Miss Brown, she was as deluded as she was about her irresistibility. The girl turned back to her with more dignity than Isolde had ever possessed. "Certainly, your ladyship. If there is a robbery, it would be only a temporary inconvenience. A more lasting influence would involve . . ."

Alistair stopped listening. He had no interest in the Page of Swords or the Knight of Cups, and he doubted the rest of the crowd did. He was interested only in Miss Brown, and if that were indeed her true name, then he was the Archbishop of Canterbury.

In truth, there was very little that had held Alistair's interest in months. Even his marked fondness for women and the pleasures of the flesh had begun to pall. Scented skin and pleasant sighs were all well and good, but the women all seemed much the same. He'd vaguely considered despoiling an innocent, but even among the new batch of young ladies he could scarcely find a virgin, and virgins were highly overrated anyway. Gaming was tedious — either you won or you lost, and relying on the fall of the card seemed a rather silly thing to do.

The only thing that brought him the slightest bit of pleasure was stealing. He no longer needed the money — he had a dislike of amassing too many possessions, and he'd managed to pay for temporary repairs to Glenshiel Abbey. Enough to keep it in one piece until his heir took over.

He expected it would be one of his prosy, distant cousins. The possibility that he might live long enough to marry and breed a son seemed both unpleasant and unlikely. At least he'd done his bit to keep the place going.

But Miss Brown entertained his interest far more than anyone or anything had since he could remember. He lounged against the damask-covered wall, surveying her. What would she do if he suddenly dropped the velvet bag on the table in front of her, proclaimed his guilt, and demanded how she knew the truth?

She'd probably faint dead away at her inadvertent luck. She knew nothing, absolutely nothing, and the look that had passed between them had merely been one of mutual curiosity, tinged with animosity on her part. She looked at him and saw nothing more than an indolent society creature.

He'd felt no animosity at all, just the predatory instincts of a hunter. It had been a long time since he'd been intrigued by a woman. He wasn't about to let the delicious sensation disappear into the night with the mysterious Miss Brown.

He could spike her guns quite effectively, of course. By choosing tonight of all nights for the Cat to make a new appearance, he'd played right into her hands. He could just as easily sneak back upstairs and return those oversized, gaudy jewels to their place amid the spilled powder. That in itself was an entertaining challenge, and he was half tempted to do so, before he considered the ramifications.

If Miss Brown were proven correct in her surmise, her reputation would be made. She would be the darling of the ton, invited to give readings at all the best parties. Sooner or later he would get her alone. And he intended to enjoy far more than a reading from her pale, generous mouth.

But were she to be proven the fake that she had to be, she would leave and he might never see her again. He wasn't going to let that happen.

The jewels were warm against his body through the layers of cloth. Miss Brown wore no jewels, and he idly considered what she might look best in. Blue topazes would bring out the color of her eyes, but they wouldn't be costly enough. Pearls, thick, creamy pearls draped around her body. And nothing else.

"What does that look signify, old man?" Freddie had sidled up to him, a curious expression on his vague, pleasant face.

"Boredom, Freddie, nothing more. Are you ready to lose this quarter's allowance?"

"You never know, Alistair. I might possibly win this time," he replied, leading the way toward the gaming room.

Alistair paused in the door, he wasn't quite certain why. He turned his head to glance back at the impeccably demure Miss Brown, only to find those magnificently strange eyes on him, sharp with doubt.

His smile was faint and infinitely challenging, and he sketched a formal little bow. She quickly turned away, pretending she hadn't been watching him. But Alistair's mood was

14

sanguine when he joined Freddie at the tables, and he even allowed him to win a few hands before he took to fleecing him in earnest.

Alistair MacAlpin, sixth Earl of Glenshiel, son of one of the oldest, most respectable families of England and Scotland, could pinpoint the exact moment he decided to become a jewel thief. It had been a night very much like this one, but in fact, most of his nights bore a tedious sameness. He had lain alone, naked, in the huge, high bed he'd recently shared with the energetic Lady Highgate, and he spied the diamond necklace lying beneath the dressing table. And he'd decided to take it.

He'd always had an eye for jewelry, indeed, for most pretty things. His nanny had called him a magpie in his youth, when he'd been attracted to the glitter of fine jewels in his mother's jewel case.

But his mother had died when he was twelve, and the jewels had been locked away for the time when they would be presented to his older brother James's wife. A younger son had no cause to be concerned with the MacAlpin family jewels, and he'd accepted their loss with his usual coolness.

They never made it to James's wife. James had never had a wife. He'd gambled and drank his life into complete and utter ruin in three short years, and when they buried him, there was nothing left of the estate but an ancient title, a ruined manor house in Scotland, and an empty jewel case.

That jewel case had come to symbolize all that Alistair lacked in his life. And when he'd left the damp, drafty halls of Glenshiel Abbey and traveled to the wicked city that had been his brother's downfall, he brought the empty case to remind him how empty life was. As if he needed reminding.

Even from his vantage point on the bed he recognized the necklace. It belonged to Lord Edgerstone's horse-faced daughter, the one with the pursed lips and the haughty manner. When

15

he and Clarissa Highgate had first tumbled into this darkened bedroom, Alistair had assumed, correctly, that they weren't the first to make use of its privacy, though he never would have suspected Miss Edgerstone would lift her skirts for anyone outside the marriage bed.

He lay in bed, lazy, sated, and contemplated his alternatives. He could take the necklace and present it to the heiress, preferably in public, in the presence of her cold stick of a father and the stiff young lordling who'd probably dared to lie between her legs.

Or he could simply pocket the piece. He had no money — he relied on the generosity of friends and the cachet of his empty title, but there was a limit to how far that would take him, and he was already finding certain demands to be uncomfortably pressing. The necklace would go a way toward meeting those demands, and provide him with a few elegancies. And he had a soul that took a fond delight in elegancies.

Not for one moment did he consider the third alternative as he lazily dressed once more. The proper thing would be to return the jewels to Miss Edgerstone privately, anonymously. But Alistair MacAlpin had never been interested in being proper. And he needed the money far more than she did.

He glanced back at the rumpled bed with a wry smile. Clarissa Highgate had been her usual energetic self — one benefit of having a mistress whose husband was more interested in young boys than in his luscious wife. He wondered what she'd think if she realized she'd taken Miss Edgerstone's place in bed.

Knowing Clarissa, it would probably amuse her. She was as unencumbered with morals as he was, which made them a perfect match. If she knew of his sudden entry into the world of larceny, she would throw back her head and laugh her rich, deep laugh.

16

But he had no intention of telling her. He'd learned young not to trust the female of the species, and Clarissa, for all her cheerful amorality, was capable of a certain ruthless dedication to her own well-being. She was more than likely to throw him to the wolves if she decided it would benefit her.

The necklace was heavy with the weight of exquisitely cut diamonds and deep topazes. The topazes made Miss Edgerstone look sallow — he was doing her a favor relieving her of the piece.

The ballroom was still a veritable crush of people when he strolled in a short while later. Miss Edgerstone was nowhere to be seen, but since her swain and her father had disappeared as well, he assumed she'd gone home. He wondered idly who would be blamed for the loss of her jewels. Silly creatures like Miss Edgerstone weren't the type to accept their own carelessness — she'd most likely turn off her maidservant in a rage.

Alistair accepted a glass of his host's excellent claret and examined his soul for any remnants of guilt. He was blissfully free of such a failing. Anyone forced to wait on Miss Edgerstone would be better off seeking a new position.

"There you are, Alistair!" Clarissa sauntered up to him, her color high, her mischievous eyes bright with lust. "You disappeared several hours ago, and I thought you might have left."

Since he'd disappeared with her, he knew perfectly well she had no such thought, but he smiled coolly. "I felt the need of air, Lady Highgate," he murmured, taking her slender hand in his. He'd noticed the overlarge diamond early that night, but he'd been far more interested in what her hand had been doing than in how it had been adorned.

It was a very fine diamond. Doubtless one of Lord Highgate's guilt presents.

He met Clarissa's eyes with a faint smile, and his fingers surreptitiously caressed the hand that bore the diamond. "Next time," he murmured, "I'll invite you into the garden with me."

Her voice trilled with laughter. "You know I could never do that, Alistair. I have my reputation to think of."

She had the reputation of an overeager bitch in heat, but he wasn't about to point that out to her. He brought her hand to his mouth and brushed his lips against the large, cold diamond.

A reasonable man would never have slipped it from her fingers. A good man would never have given in to the original temptation, taken a careless bitch's discarded jewels, and used the proceeds to keep body and soul together. A good man would have berated himself for his lack of honor if he'd even succumbed to temptation.

Ah, but then, he'd never made the mistake of considering himself a good man, a reasonable man. The ring slipped from her thin fingers without her even noticing it as she whirled off in search of fresh worlds to conquer. With a faint smile he tucked it into his pocket, and his fate was sealed.

He'd gotten away with it ever since.

The past two years had been entertaining ones. He had become more imaginative, rivaling the infamous Jack Shepperd with some of his daring robberies and escapes, and not for one moment had anyone connected the Cat, as the broadsheets had styled him, to his lordship the Earl of Glenshiel.

And now this quiet little creature with the clear, dangerous eyes had looked at him and managed to stir his latent energies. What had been behind that look? Contempt for an obviously frivolous creature such as he? Supernatural knowledge of his nefarious pastime? Love at first sight?

The last was almost as unlikely as the second possibility, more's the pity. The pseudonymous Miss Brown was obviously a young lady of breeding who'd fallen on hard times. His discerning eye had picked out numerous details in a matter of moments. The material of her dress was very fine, but showed signs of wear. It hadn't been made for a woman with her curves, and it strained across the top just slightly.

He leaned back in his chair and surveyed Freddie. He'd already lost the bulk of his quarterly allowance, and for some sentimental reason Alistair always chose to leave him with enough to get by on. Besides, he was far more interested in seeing exactly what Miss Brown was doing.

"That's all for now, Freddie. I'll leave you with your dignity intact." Alistair rose with his usual indolent grace.

"Good of you," Freddie mumbled. "You going after the Gypsy?"

"She hardly seemed like a Gypsy, did she? Much too pale, for one thing."

"All fortune-tellers are Gypsies," Freddie said wisely, well gone into his third bottle. "Wouldn't trifle with her if I were you. Her eyes were most peculiar. Gave me a decidedly eerie feeling."

"Ah, but you're not me, are you, Freddie? And I happen to like eerie feelings."

"Your funeral, old man," Freddie said morosely. And then he brightened. "If you meet your comeuppance, then you won't be around to clean out my allowance. I'll be rich."

"No, you won't, Freddie. Some Captain Sharp will do it for me, and they won't stop with your allowance. Be lucky I win your allowance and keep you from gambling too deeply."

"I'm all gratitude," Freddie said, turning back to his claret. "Watch out for the Gypsy. She'll ferret out all your secrets."

"I have no secrets, Freddie," Alistair said gently.

"Everyone has secrets. And I suspect you have more than your share. Go find the Gypsy before she runs away, old man. But watch your back."

Two

Jessamine Maitland was adept at keeping her emotions from displaying themselves. That man had unnerved her, and despite her best efforts, she was unable to put him from her mind. She had any number of reasonable explanations for his effect on her senses. For one thing, he'd caught her attention in the midst of a reading, a time when she was naturally more vulnerable. She'd been so lost in the cards that her customary defenses had abandoned her, leaving her easy prey to marauders.

She wasn't quite sure why she thought of him that way. She'd been surrounded by the silken, perfumed peacocks that composed some of the wealthiest of London society, and the man who'd stood behind her was one of the most elegant. She'd felt his eyes, watching her, boring into her back, but she'd managed to ignore them as she concentrated on the cards. They were all staring at her, and she'd be foolish indeed if she let them interfere with her work.

Ah, but his eyes were different. When he finally spoke, giving her a reason to turn around, she'd been astonished by what she'd seen.

She'd imagined someone dark and dangerous, though she wasn't quite certain why. Instead, he seemed a fairly common garden-variety dilettante, from the toes of his jeweled, high-heeled slippers to the top of his carefully curled wig. He held a lace handkerchief in one hand, no doubt properly scented, and he looked down at her as if she were the insect.

He immediately annoyed her. He was indolent, lazy, and far too cynical, and he looked at her as if he knew her to be a liar and an opportunist ready to cheat his friends from their hard-earned money. And instead of being outraged, he was amused by it all.

Except that none of them had earned their money, Jessamine thought with a grimace. They'd inherited it, as she would have as well had her father not been a hopeless wastrel.

And though she might be there under slightly false pretenses, she meant no harm. Indeed, if she could supplement the tiny family income with society readings, then so be it. It might cleanse her soul a bit.

She was a fool to berate herself for her work. Helping the police to catch criminals was surely a noble cause, beneficial to society and a godsend to her family's well-being.

If only it hadn't involved working with someone like Josiah Clegg.

She turned away again, concentrating once more on the cards, dismissing the fop as a worthless fribble. But the man Lady Plumworthy referred to as Glenshiel wasn't easily dismissed. Long after he left the room, and she knew immediately when he had, his presence lingered in her mind. Not a clear vision of him, just a sense of amused, elegant disdain.

Disdain was nothing new to her — there was no earthly reason she should be particularly incensed by his obvious contempt. If she had learned one thing in the few years since the Maitland family had fallen on such desperately hard times, it was that class and fortune were everything. And while the Maitlands, formerly of Maitland Hall, Landsheer, Northumberland, still possessed the requisite breeding, their complete destitution made them an embarrassment to all and sundry. They were shunned by former acquaintances, dear friends, and distant relatives, all of them, doubtless, terrified that either the

Maitlands' ill fortune was contagious or that they might request a loan.

The result was that Mrs. Maitland and her two daughters lived in lonely poverty near the silk weavers in Spitalfields, and even that straitened existence had been in jeopardy before Jessamine had determined to save them. Before fate had been belatedly repentant enough to provide her with a way to use the doubtful gift that had haunted her since childhood. Her well-nurtured gift with a wicked pack of fortune-telling cards.

She was having difficulty focusing on the cards in front of her. She usually tried to ration her energy — most of these shallow people were interested in three things: fortune, power, and sex. The young women wished to learn how they would go about marrying it, the young men wished to learn to acquire it, the older men wanted to learn how to keep it. It was simple enough to tell them what they wanted to know.

But that man had upset her equilibrium. She was reading the cards too clearly now — she could see one young woman's death in childbed, another at the hands of her deranged husband. She could see the madness of syphilis hovering over a young man's future, and finally she could stand it no longer, pushing the cards away from her and closing her eyes.

"I'm sorry," she murmured. "I can do no more." Her hands trembled slightly as she shuffled the pasteboard images back together, and from a seeming distance she heard grumbles of discontent. It was almost two in the morning, and she was exhausted. Most of these gilded creatures seemed eager to socialize all night long, but Jessamine had lost the knack for mindless frivolity. She needed quiet to soothe her aching head, and she needed her bed.

Lady Plumworthy's guests had already dismissed her, returning to other amusements, when Jessamine made her way down the wide marble staircase, clinging to the banister, the precious cards wrapped in velvet and tucked inside her reticule. The majordomo awaited her in the hallway, accompanied by two burly footmen, and she wondered if Lady Plumworthy had arranged for her to be escorted home.

She was shortsighted, and it wasn't until she reached the bottom step that she recognized the smug hostility in the man-servant's face.

"Her ladyship's emeralds are missing," he announced in accusing tones.

"I'm not surprised," Jessamine replied with deceptive calm.

"No, I'd say you ain't. And you won't be surprised that her ladyship has insisted we search you before you get away with the jewels."

He had a cruel, thin face with thick lips. Jessamine didn't move. "It wouldn't surprise me," she said. "But you aren't going to touch me."

She'd already noticed that all of Lady Plumworthy's servants were very large, healthy-looking men, something that filled her with unpleasant misgivings. The majordomo was not much above average height, but his shoulders were wide and hulking, and his hands were huge. "And who's going to stop me in doing my duty, miss?" he said with a sneer.

"I will."

She must have been more frightened than she realized. She hadn't even been aware of his approach. The man from the card room, Glenshiel, he of the elegant disdain, had come to her aid.

"Your lordship, this creature . . ." the majordomo began in a whine.

". . . hasn't left the card room all evening, Hawkins. There's no way she could filch her ladyship's jewels. And where do you suggest she's carrying them?"

"There are all sorts of places," Hawkins muttered, glaring

23

at her. The two footmen had already retreated.

"Hawkins, you shock me!" the man said, mocking. "I had no idea such depravity existed."

Jessamine allowed herself to look at him, almost wishing she didn't have to. Up close she could see his eyes — a clear light brown that was almost amber. He had a narrow, slightly beaked nose, high cheekbones, and a wide mouth curved in a mocking smile, as if he found the world both tiresome and amusing. He looked like a man who knew far too much about depravity, and Jessamine would have told him so except that he was, for whatever his reasons, coming to her rescue. It would behoove her to be gracious, at least for the moment.

Hawkins obviously knew he was defeated. He moved away from the door, grudgingly to be sure. "Very well, my lord. I'll tell her ladyship you judged it prudent not to interfere with the young lady."

"Tattler," the man said with a soft laugh. "And what about the money?"

"Money, sir?"

"Miss Brown was promised remuneration for her efforts tonight, was she not? And I imagine once you'd satisfied yourself that she hadn't taken Lady Plumworthy's jewel, you were planning to give it to her. Weren't you?"

She must have imagined the faint hint of steel beneath that elegant drawl. "I'm not satisfied . . ." Hawkins started to say, but something in the man's face must have stopped him, for he turned, picked up a small bag of coins, and tossed it at Jessamine's feet.

She started to stoop down to pick it up, rejoicing in the very heavy chunk of coin as it had landed, but her cynical Galahad moved too quickly. He put his pale, hard, elegant hands on her forearm, holding her still.

"The bag must have slipped," Glenshiel said with great

pleasantness. "Fetch it, will you, Hawkins, and present it to the young lady."

Jessamine half expected the majordomo to refuse, and she wanted that money in her hand quite desperately. But the deceptively light grip on her arm kept her from moving.

She could see him quite clearly now, and she realized he wasn't as young as she'd first thought. There was a hardness in his amber eyes, in his full mouth, that suggested a wealth of less than innocent experience.

Hawkins crossed the room, sank down in front of her, and scooped up the sack of coins. She resisted the impulse to kick him while he was down, then accepted the agreeably heavy bag with a murmured thanks.

"Well done, Hawkins," the man said. "Now you can have one of the footmen call a sedan chair for the young lady while you and I go have a little discussion with your employer."

He'd released her — dismissed her — and it took Jessamine a moment to realize she was alone in the vast hallway. She wanted desperately to take the time to see what the bag contained, but she didn't dare hesitate. She wasn't going home ensconced in the safety of a sedan chair. For one thing, she had no intention of spending her hard-earned money on such frivolity. For another, sedan chairs weren't seen in the environs of Spitalfields, and she had too much sense to make herself conspicuous.

The night was cool, but she didn't bother searching for her wrap. She simply wanted to escape, both from the overzealous Hawkins and the disturbing presence of the mysteriously mocking Glenshiel. She had learned how to keep herself safe on the nighttime streets of London, and most of the underworld were far too aware of her connection with Josiah Clegg to dare anything.

Like a shadow, she slipped into the night, thankful that

25

there were no eyes to watch her as she made her escape.

"Naughty boy!" Isolde Plumworthy batted him with her ivory fan, almost breaking the delicate sticks with the force of her little tap. "Interfering with my servants! Why, I might almost think you were in collusion with that creature."

Alistair managed a faint smile. "I've never seen the wench before in my life, Isolde. But I have a weakness for helpless infants, and I disliked seeing Hawkins put his meaty hands on her."

"So instead she escapes with my jewels! That is too bad of you, Alistair!"

"You know perfectly well she didn't steal your jewels, Isolde. The Cat did."

"There's no certainty . . ."

"Since when have you expected life to have any sort of certainty? Your choice is simple. You can let it be known that you were gulled by a slip of a girl who made up fortunes and stole your jewels, or . . ." He trailed off, and Isolde jumped to the bait.

"Or?"

"Or you could revel in your status as the Cat's newest victim. He hasn't been on the prowl in months — clearly your jewels were enough to coax him out of retirement. I would take that as a compliment if I were you, Isolde."

Lady Plumworthy smiled a plump smile. "Very true."

"And on top of that, you have discovered a true gem, a fortune-teller who can truly predict the future. You'll be the toast of society. Everyone will want to hear about your adventures with the Cat; everyone will want to know where you discovered Miss Brown."

"I don't seek to better my position in society — I am completely secure," Lady Plumworthy said with complete disregard for reality and her own somewhat tarnished lineage. "Still, you have a point, Alistair. Miss Brown has a real gift, hasn't she? And those eyes of hers — quite deliciously unnerving. As if she could see through to one's inner soul."

Alistair frankly doubted that Isolde Plumworthy even possessed a soul, but he forced himself to take one plump, beringed hand in his, pressing it meaningfully. "You are a very generous woman," he murmured without batting an eyelash.

Isolde smirked. "I never really liked those emeralds," she confided. "Too paltry by half. This will give me the excuse of acquiring some new ones."

Alistair thought of the ugly, oversized gems residing next to his skin and managed to keep his expression composed. "And Miss Brown?"

"Oh, you're absolutely right. I'll have her at my next soiree. It will all be very mysterious — I'll request all the guests wear black, there will be no gaming or music, and all will be very eerie and subdued."

"Wonderful," he said. "The rest of society will follow your lead."

"Of course."

"But where did you find such a fascinating creature?" he murmured with just the right amount of casual interest. "I've never seen cards like the ones she used. And it's rare to find an Englishwoman of common lineage so adept at the arcane arts."

"Common lineage?" Isolde echoed with a rough laugh. "That's what you think, my boy. Her family . . . well, that's none of your business. Nor is it any of your concern where I found her. She's my little secret, and I intend to use her most wisely."

"You might not have realized what a treasure you had if I hadn't pointed it out to you." Alistair let none of his irritation show through. He never let anyone be privy to his emotions. He even did his absolute best to avoid recognizing them himself. Emotions were foolish, weak, and tiresome. He disliked them intensely.

But Lady Plumworthy was a skilled reader of people. "There's no use trying to cozen me. She'll remain a secret. If you have some particular interest in her, then you'll simply have to exercise patience, a trait you're not overfamiliar with. You'll see her soon enough."

Alistair was not a man who believed in violence or in exerting himself unnecessarily. He simply stared at the smug, toadlike face of Lady Plumworthy and wished absently for a lightning bolt to strike her. But fate had always proven deaf to his desires.

He bowed low over her hand, brushing his lips against her diamond rings with true reverence. There was no chance in hell he could remove them — the flesh was swollen tightly over the gold bands. "Always the flirt, my lady," he said gently.

"I would do more than flirt, Alistair," she said with an arch laugh.

"And break young Calderwood's heart? I couldn't do it to him. He was looking for you in the gaming room."

In actuality he was hiding from her in the gaming room, but Alistair had no mercy when it came to saving his own hide. Isolde was far more interested in a perfect twenty-year-old than a jaded thirty-two-year-old, for which Alistair could only thank God. He watched as she hastened in search of her young prey, then cast a mocking glance at Hawkins.

"You see, Hawkins," he murmured. "Your conscience is clear. Not only did you do your best to obey your mistress's instructions, but you were saved the odious duty of hurting an innocent young lady."

"I rejoice, sir," Hawkins said in a sullen voice.

Alistair strolled past him. "I suppose you'll simply have to find some other young woman to hurt, won't you?"

"Yes, sir," Hawkins said, and his eyes shone with chilly malice. "It shouldn't be too difficult, my lord."

"Ah, yes," Alistair murmured, "but you might have to bed her as well, which wouldn't be half the fun."

"Not necessarily, sir. In London you can find anything for a price." He lifted his head, staring up at Alistair with cool effrontery.

With another man Alistair might have admired his substantial self-possession. But there was about Hawkins an air of evil so sour that it failed to entertain Glenshiel. "Very true," he said in his most gentle voice. "But if you go anywhere near Miss Brown again, I'll cut off your hands."

Hawkins's expression didn't change. "Yes, sir," he said politely.

She'd left, of course, and not in a sedan chair. He shouldn't have been surprised — Miss Brown was far too enterprising a creature to wait tamely while two aristocrats decided her future.

He supposed he should fear for her safety. The streets of London were scarcely safe for a decently bred young woman carrying a comfortable sum of money, particularly in the middle of an autumn night.

But Miss Brown of the fascinating eyes was far from an ordinary young woman, and he had no doubt whatsoever that she'd be able to get herself home safely. For all he knew, she might live just across the square, a governess in one of the grand houses nearby.

She didn't look like a governess. She didn't look like a witch either, apart from those eyes.

But she'd known far too much about Lady Plumworthy's emeralds. She hadn't seemed to connect him with their disappearance, but he was curious as to whether hers had simply

29

been the kind of educated guess most fortune-tellers employed or whether she really was gifted.

It was his safety and livelihood at stake. The sixth Earl of Glenshiel survived, nay, thrived, by taking the jewels of the wealthy and distributing the proceeds to the poor, just like Robin Hood of old.

The difference was that he characterized the poor as himself, and the proceeds went nowhere but into his own increasingly deep pockets.

And he really didn't give a damn whether Miss Brown could see into the future, into his past, could delve into his secrets. He simply wanted to delve beneath her skirts.

First, however, he had to find her.

It was just before dawn when Jessamine finally reached the safety of her bed. She could hear her mother's noisy snores echoing through the tiny house, while her sister, Fleur, lay in the big bed she shared with Jessamine, sleeping the sleep of the innocent.

Jessamine stripped down to her chemise before giving in to temptation and opening the pouch. It was all worth it — the stupid self-absorption of the guests, the threat of search and heaven knew what else from that evil majordomo. It was even worth the most unsettling part of the evening, the presence of that man, whoever he might be. He of the topaz eyes, the pale, hard hands, the faint air of mockery, and something else, something far more personal and an even greater threat than Hawkins's rough treatment.

There was enough to pay the butcher, the landlord, the greengrocer, and have quite a bit left over. Perhaps enough to hire a servant for the heavy work. And it might even run to a new dress for Fleur and Mrs. Maitland.

"Where were you?"

Fleur was sitting up in bed, her golden-blond hair tumbling around her perfect shoulders, her china-blue eyes dazed with sleep. Jessamine smiled at her affectionately, once again wondering how fate could have put together such a gorgeous creature as her sister. "Right here, dearest," she said, shoving the coins back into the little pouch.

"I woke several hours ago and the bed was empty."

"I couldn't sleep — I went for a cup of milk to help me," she said, the lies coming far too easily. She hated having to lie to Fleur and her mother, but she could see no other choice.

"Your side of the bed wasn't touched."

"I'm a neat sleeper," Jessamine said.

"You're a clever liar," Fleur murmured softly. "Won't you tell me what you're doing, Jess? You shouldn't have to bear the burden alone."

"Not that clever a liar," Jessamine said with a wry smile. "And no, I won't tell you what I'm doing. There's no need for you to know. Trust me enough to know that I would never do anything wrong."

"I know that!" Fleur said hotly. "I worry about you, Jess. I should be doing my part. . . ."

"Your part is waiting for you, dearling. You're only nineteen. As soon as we get enough together to make a small entry into society, you'll be bound to attract the attention of some fabulously wealthy, devastatingly handsome, astonishingly kind young man who'll marry you and make you deliriously happy. And he'll be more than willing to take care of your indigent sister and mother as well."

It was an old story, one she wasn't sure she had much faith in anymore, but Fleur managed to produce a dutiful smile. "It would be nice, wouldn't it?" She sighed, leaning back against the pillows.

"It will be heaven, Fleur," she said firmly, willing herself to

31

believe it. She climbed into bed beside her sister, sinking down on the soft feather bed.

"But what about you, Jess? Will you change your mind after all? Shall we find you a handsome, rich young man as well?" Fleur murmured, drifting off toward sleep again.

Unbidden, the memory of Glenshiel came to her, he of the cool eyes and hard hands. She struggled for something to say, then realized it was unnecessary. Fleur had fallen asleep, untroubled by the cares of the world.

Jessamine lay awake, wide-eyed, as she thought about the events of the previous evening.

She didn't need the cards in front of her to do a reading. In truth, she was too bone-weary to even attempt such a thing, but in her worn-out state the pictures danced in her mind even as she tried to banish them.

Marilla had warned her that would happen. Marilla had warned her of the many ways she would have to pay the price for nurturing her gift, not the least of which was abandoning any hope for a happy future, a family, a man to love, or the children she wanted so dearly.

She had made her choice, years ago, and she would make do with Fleur's children. She would be the best sister, the best aunt, that had ever lived. She would know worlds that most people could seldom even begin to comprehend. But she would be locked out of what most people took for granted.

She'd been too young to make such a life-altering decision. Scarcely eleven years old, trusting, gifted, and not wise enough to run when Marilla had given her the choice. And in the end they'd both known she'd really had no choice at all.

Who would have thought the comfortable nursemaid from Berkshire would have more talents than the wildest Gypsy? Who would have thought the dark arts were alive in one wicked pack of cards that told too much?

And who would have thought Jessamine Maitland of Maitland Hall would be inexorably drawn to those cards, with a gift for divination that put her mentor in the shade?

It was too late now. Marilla's cards were hers and Marilla's gift was hers as well, tenfold. She could look at the cards and see the past, the future, and the present. She could see things she never wanted to glimpse — death and disaster. Though she could see joy as well, there were times when she wished she could simply toss the well-worn pack with its velvet wrapping into the fire.

But the cards would haunt her. As they did then. She closed her eyes, willing sleep to come, but the cards floated in her head, shifting, spilling outward. And every face resembled Glenshiel's.

She didn't want to attempt to understand. Why this man should haunt her sleep was a question too threatening to contemplate. She squeezed her eyes more tightly, trying to think of the audacious burglar and the cards that had told her of his presence in Lady Plumworthy's house.

But all she saw was Glenshiel.

Three

Robert Brennan was a thief-taker. One of Sir John Fielding's men, more often known as a Bow Street runner, he was uncommonly reliable, honorable, and compassionate despite his sternness. Sir John himself counted him among the best of all his men and the majority of his fellow runners considered him a very good soul indeed.

Except for Josiah Clegg. If Brennan was Fielding's right-hand man, then Clegg was his left. Clegg's success at tracking down thieves and pickpockets surpassed even Brennan's, and his thief-taker's share enabled him to live in surprising luxury. If anyone had doubts about Clegg's scruples, or the number of thieves who died while trying to escape, then they kept those concerns to themselves. After all, a thief was inevitably sentenced to hang. If Clegg dispatched him more promptly, then who was to complain?

Robert Brennan kept his eye on things as best he could, but his path seldom crossed Clegg's. Perhaps Sir John knew of his misgivings, or perhaps Clegg himself was wise enough to steer clear of the one man who distrusted him. All Brennan could do was watch from a distance when his own duties allowed him the time.

Right now his duties were particularly tasking. He was determined to find the latest scourge of lawful harmony. The Cat, that daring thief who insinuated himself into the very heights of society and sauntered off with a fortune in jewels, had transformed from an irritation to an obsession for Brennan. No one had the faintest idea who the criminal might be, and none of his elegant victims seemed particularly eager to help a member of the lower classes bring the perpetrator to justice.

Silly, stupid, useless twits, Brennan thought with more annoyance than his phlegmatic temperament usually allowed him. They'd rather be robbed blind by one of their own than do anything that would brand them a traitor to their class.

Brennan had very strong feelings about class, none of them particularly sanguine. He'd grown up in the Yorkshire dales, and his broad accent proclaimed his yeoman status as much as his large, untidy body, his shaggy hair, and his big workman's hands. He was no gentleman, not even a bourgeois, and there was no way he would ever aspire to be one. He'd been put on this earth to make the place a little bit safer for the innocents of the world, and he had accounted himself well pleased if he could make even a bit of a difference.

But things had changed recently. He was thirty years old, he'd been in the business of thief-taking for a good eight years, and there were times when he longed for the peace and straightforward hard work of his parents' farm near Robin Hood Bay. He was mortally tired of twelve-year-old prostitutes being murdered by their pimps, weary of fourteen-year-old apprentices hanged for running off from their masters with a few pieces of silver in their knapsacks, and worn to the soul knowing that he couldn't save the twelve-year-olds, and that his efforts sometimes brought the fourteen-year-olds to the gallows.

The Cat was a different matter. There was no question in Brennan's mind that he was a gentleman born to wealth and privilege. There was no way a lesser soul could get away with such outrageous crimes, could mingle with the aristocracy, and no one would even blink. For the Cat, Brennan had no sympathy, just a steely determination to bring him to justice.

35

The thief-taker's share on such a felon was high indeed. Brennan could take that moiety, along with the rest of the money he'd husbanded so carefully over the years, and leave the wretched city he'd come to a mere decade earlier, filled with ambition and dreams. He'd go back to Yorkshire, to his parents' farm perhaps, or buy a place of his own, and sooner or later wash the stink and horror of the city from his soul.

Of course, he wasn't the only thief-taker in London who planned on apprchending the Cat. Every Bow Street runner had just that goal in mind, including Josiah Clegg. And Robert Brennan knew that if he were the decent man his parents brought him up to be, he would simply rejoice that the villain had been apprehended, never mind who took him.

But Robert Brennan was far from perfect, as well he knew. He was as troubled as the next man by lust, envy, and desire. He just fought harder against those all-too-human sins.

With a man like Josiah Clegg, Brennan couldn't seem to rise above his base feelings. It had little to do with Clegg's recent string of astonishing luck in apprehending a record number of felons. Instead, it seemed more connected to Brennan's deep misgivings about Clegg's way of doing things. There were times when Brennan wondered whether Clegg wasn't worse than some of the villains he apprehended. But Clegg was no more than a distraction, and Brennan wasn't a man to be distracted easily. Not when Sir John himself had recently brought a most interesting piece of information to his attention.

The robbery at Lady Plumworthy's was almost a duplicate of similar robberies perpetrated by the Cat over the last two years. Sometime during the evening someone had made himself free with his hostess's bedroom and jewelry.

As expected, the victim refused to divulge her guest list to Brennan, offended that official suspicion might fall upon one of the upper levels of society. "It had to have been one of the servants," the old harridan had insisted, eyeing him as if he were some creature crawled up out of the gutter. "Do you think I number thieves among my acquaintance?"

"I think you must, your ladyship. You say there were no strangers here last night," Brennan had said politely.

"Insufferable," her ladyship had muttered, and Brennan had little doubt she was referring to his studiedly polite manner and not the robbery.

If he weren't already certain it was the Cat, he would have been more than happy to blame Lady Plumworthy's major-domo. The haughty creature who ushered him out of her ladyship's august presence was everything Brennan despised, from his small, cruel eyes to his malicious tongue. Robert Brennan had a real gift for summing up a person in just a glance, and Hawkins was a bad 'un through and through.

"Her ladyship must have forgotten the Gypsy," Hawkins said as he opened the front door for Brennan. Robert had little doubt the man would have showed him to the servants' entrance, but there were occasional gestures of respect that he insisted on. He was not about to use the servants' entrance like a dustman.

"The Gypsy?" Brennan murmured. An upper servant such as Hawkins would want a fair amount of blunt for his information, more than Brennan usually had available. "There was a Gypsy here last night?"

For some reason Hawkins didn't seem more than casually interested in remuneration, and when Brennan's hand didn't dip toward his pocket, he simply shrugged and continued. " 'Course, she didn't call herself a Gypsy. Acted more like she thought she was a real lady, but if someone nabbed the sparklers, it must have been her."

Hawkins's knowledge of thieves' cant was even more interesting. Brennan nodded encouragingly. "And who was she?"

"Some old acquaintance of her ladyship's, I think, fallen on hard times."

"Then she could hardly be a Gypsy, could she? Not the sort to mingle with the aristocracy."

"Lady Plumworthy ain't exactly aristocratic, if you know what I mean," Hawkins said with a coarse laugh. "She's risen high, she has, but that doesn't mean she doesn't still know where she came from."

"What was the Gypsy doing here?"

"What else do Gypsies do? Tell fortunes and rob you blind," Hawkins said with a sneer.

Brennan reached into the pocket of his greatcoat, pulling out a sheaf of paper and a carbon pen. "And what is the name and direction of this Gypsy?"

"What's it worth to you?"

"Absolutely nothing," Brennan said calmly. "It's your responsibility as a citizen and an employee of her ladyship's to see that justice is done. I'm certain I can rely on your sense of duty, can't I?"

"Not likely," Hawkins muttered, starting to turn away.

Brennan was not in the mood to be trifled with. He towered over the servant, and it was a simple matter to catch him by the scruff of the neck and shove him up against the heavy oak door. "I would appreciate your cooperation, Hawkins," he said smoothly.

Hawkins's protruding eyes bulged out farther. "Maitland," he gasped. "Miss Jessamine Maitland. Called herself Miss Brown, but her ladyship confided in me, seeing as how I was supposed to make sure she arrived safely. She lives in Spitalfields, near the Five Diamonds pub."

Brennan released him, and Hawkins sagged against the door with a muffled curse. "I appreciate your help, Hawkins," he said smoothly. "Give my thanks to her ladyship."

Spitalfields. It was the first break he'd had in more than a year of frustration. Many of the more adventurous thieves employed a moll to distract the victim while his pocket was picked. What better distraction than a lovely young Gypsy telling fortunes?

And yet, as far as he knew, no pockets were picked, and the Cat always worked alone. Perhaps he'd changed his ways.

Still and all, Jessamine Maitland was an odd name for a Gypsy.

"Here's your share of the proceeds, my girl."

Jessamine looked at the small pile of silver coins Josiah Clegg pushed in her direction, doing her best to control her shiver of distaste both for the money itself and the man giving it to her. It was early afternoon, and the Fives Diamonds was sparsely filled. No one paid any attention to the somberly dressed young woman and the Bow Street runner in the darkened corner.

"Did they have to hang him?" she asked, making no move to touch the coins.

Josiah Clegg laughed with that cheerful braying sound that set Jessamine's teeth on edge. "He ran away from his master, stole three silver tea spoons and an ell of watered silk. What else would they do with him?"

"He was fifteen years old!"

"Old enough to know better," Clegg said with his usual lack of concern. He was a heartless man but far from stupid, and he must have sensed Jessamine's distress. "Now, now, Miss Maitland, there's no need for you to get all sentimental over the lad. He would have just done it again and again, and well you know it, and sooner or later some poor innocent would have gotten killed. You stopped that from happening. You should be proud of yourself, doing your duty to society."

She raised her eyes to look at Clegg. He was not unhandsome in a thick-lipped, swarthy fashion, and he fancied himself a bit of a lady's man. He'd never attempted any liberties with her, presumably because he knew her gift was of more value to him than her rather ordinary physical attributes. Their unlikely partnership had stood him well, assisting in the rise in his fortunes, and he wasn't about to endanger that.

"I don't like it," she said quietly.

"You came to me in the first place, miss," he reminded her. "You were the one who wanted to help."

"I couldn't ignore what I saw in the cards," she said in a small voice. "That man . . . that creature murdered nine children. He had to be stopped."

"And so he was. With your help and mine. And you ended up with a generous share of the reward for capturing him, didn't you? You can't say that's come amiss."

"I didn't do it for the money."

"Of course not," Clegg said smoothly. "You're a lady fallen on hard times, but a lady nonetheless, and we all know ladies do nothing for money. Still and all, your charitable work with the Bow Street runners has made your purse just a bit heavier, hasn't it? And doubtless that pleases your mother and pretty little sister. What was her name . . . Fleur? Taking little thing. Quite a delectable little handful, I would think."

Jessamine froze. The very thought of Clegg even knowing Fleur's name frightened her. It shouldn't have. Clegg made it his business to know everything, and what eluded him he chased after until he discovered the answer.

She was afraid of the man. She had no proof of his evil, just an instinctive feeling that came to her at odd moments, through the cards, and through her dreams. "You'll leave her alone," she said fiercely.

There was a glint of smug amusement in Clegg's dark face. "Of course I will, Miss Maitland. I wouldn't want anything to upset you, now, would I? And if something happened to your sister, it might distress you so much, you'd have trouble concentrating on the cards. As long as you're so very helpful to me and to society, I'll make it my duty to be sure your sister is safe and unmolested."

"And if I'm no longer so helpful?" She shouldn't have asked the question. Subtle threats were safer, more easily swallowed. But she couldn't ignore a threat to Fleur.

Clegg smiled, and his gold tooth flashed in the afternoon light. "Why then, I'm afraid she might be fair game. You make my work easier, Miss Maitland. Without your help I'd have to work a lot harder in finding and apprehending criminals, and I couldn't be counted on to protect your little family. You'd be on your own."

At least he wasn't threatening to touch Fleur himself. She was their only hope — a safe, wealthy marriage would mean the end of their never-ceasing cycle of misfortune, but no one would take damaged goods, even someone wrapped in as exquisite a package as her sister, Fleur.

"I understand," she said in a dull voice.

"I thought you might," he said. "Take your money, Miss Maitland."

She reached out and put the worn silver coins in her reticule. Her chest was tight, and she felt as if she would suffocate if she didn't get away from this man into the dubiously clean air of the London streets, but when she started to push away from the table, his hand shot out and clamped around her wrist.

Too many men were getting in the habit of doing that, she thought absently, holding herself still for the moment. First Lady Plumworthy's manservant with his thick hands, then the mysterious Glenshiel, who'd haunted her dreams and her waking hours as well. Clegg's grip was the final straw. "Let go of me," she said in a deceptively pleasant voice with just the right

41

amount of hauteur left from her more secure days.

His instinctive reaction was gratifying, if dangerous, as he released her wrist, then glared at her. "There's a little problem that's been plaguing me, and I've decided to do something about it. I want you to do a reading about the Cat."

"The Cat?" she echoed, carefully keeping her face devoid of reaction. "What is that?"

"*Who* is that, you might say," Clegg corrected her, leaning back in his chair. "It's a thief, that's what it is. A creature who sneaks into people's houses and robs them blind."

"A burglar?"

"But not your common garden-variety burglar. This one preys only on the very wealthy, stealing their jewels and fancy trinkets. And he's one of them. A bloody aristocrat, robbing his own kind, and he's been doing it for more than a year."

She clutched her reticule in her lap, concentrating all her tension into her unseen hands as she gazed at Clegg. "Why haven't you asked me before now?"

"I didn't give a rat's ass, begging your pardon, miss, what the bloody ton does to one another. Besides, he'll be a sight trickier to catch, much less bring to justice. I prefer the easy cases."

"The fifteen-year-old apprentices?"

"Exactly." Clegg showed no remorse. "But Sir John has entrusted me with the case, and it's in my best interest to convince him I can handle it better than that country oaf."

"What country oaf?"

"Never you mind. It's none of your concern — it's the Cat who should entertain your interest, and no one else. Where are your cards?"

"I didn't bring them."

"Why not?"

He'd made it clear that she couldn't tell him the truth: that

42

she'd decided not to help him anymore. The money Lady Plumworthy had grudgingly given her was five times the amount Clegg paid her, and the work didn't stain her soul. She was promised to her ladyship that afternoon as well, and all sorts of possibilities were opening up.

Her eyes met Clegg's small, dark ones. "I haven't been sleeping well. The cards don't speak to me if I'm not well rested."

Clegg snorted, but there was no way he could refute her statement. "Go home, then. Take a nap. And come back to me tomorrow at the same time — and bring your cards." He grinned at her benignly. "Unless you'd rather have me call on you? This place might be a little rude for the likes of you."

"This place is fine," she said quietly, barely able to suppress her shudder of horror at the thought of her vague, aristocratic mother coming face-to-face with Josiah Clegg. Not that it was likely — Mrs. Maitland enjoyed ill health and a fondness for ratafia. She kept to her bedroom most of the time, mourning her lost position in society. She probably assumed her self-reliant older daughter was out shopping, and indeed, the basket full of slightly wilted cabbage sat under the table at Jess's feet. She rose, and this time he let her escape.

She could feel his eyes on her as she left the public house, squinting as she stepped out into the autumn-damp streets of Spitalfields and wrapping her heavy shawl around her. At least Clegg, who knew everything, seemed unaware of her newfound sideline, or the fact that she had already enjoyed a vicarious encounter with his latest quarry. For the time being she could balance her society readings against Clegg's demands, and the money would pile up faster than ever, enabling the Maitlands to regain their place in society.

At least some of the Maitlands. Fleur would be the toast of society even without a dowry, and if she were decently dressed she could attract any number of wealthy suitors. With Mrs. Maitland as a benevolent, graceful chaperon, all was assured.

But not for Jessamine. Unlike the other members of her family, she preferred to look at the truth squarely. Her reputation could survive her collusion with Clegg — once she escaped from his clutches, it was unlikely anyone else would even hear about it. And she would survive one late-night party, reading cards and telling fortunes.

But a repeat would doom her. Lady Plumworthy had already informed her that polite society was agog at her talents, and this afternoon's tea and reading promised to be a crush. The guests had ignored her the other night, all but that mocking, mysterious creature who had come to her rescue so unexpectedly. They would ignore her no more, and there would be no way she could show her face in society once Fleur was launched.

It was no matter. She had no great love for the city or for society. Fleur would simply need to find a husband wealthy enough to maintain several country estates, and his reclusive sister-in-law could retire to a graceful pattern of rural living. Solitary rural living.

She made a moue of self-disgust. Her mother was possessed of enough self-pity to supply the entire Maitland family, and Jessamine had no intention of falling prey to such a failing. She had made her choice long before, calmly, rationally, and she would live with the consequences. Alone.

She'd lied to Clegg, something she didn't regret for one moment. She knew perfectly well who the Cat was — his visit to Lady Plumworthy the night before had haunted her dreams almost as much as the man who had rescued her. Taunted her.

She reached down to pat her reticule, and she could feel the solid bulk of the cards, seemingly warm to the touch. And dancing through her mind, the Prince of Swords, with the golden eyes of a cat, staring back at her.

Four

It was a compact house in Clarges Street, but more than ample for a man of Alistair MacAlpin's elegant tastes. He entertained in small numbers, usually other bachelors, merely for the sake of gaming. The public rooms were not overlarge but well appointed, the bedroom sybaritic and sufficient for his habits. He was seldom called upon to offer hospitality — his family was dead, and few of his friends were in the habit of drinking so deeply that they couldn't find their way home at the end of an evening.

He cherished his solitude and his little house. He'd moved from cramped, drafty rooms near St. Paul's, and if his pied-à-terre held no resemblance to the lost splendor of MacAlpin House, he didn't mind. MacAlpin House had never been his — his brother had inherited it, along with everything else, and had died there, poisoned by drink and despair. It now belonged to a nabob's family, suitably renamed, and Alistair told himself he'd even forgotten its direction.

His current abode had cost the worth of Miss Edgerstone's jewels, plus the proceeds of a rather nice collection of yellow diamonds he'd liberated from the Earl of Pemberton's extremely nasty wife. The money had lasted a surprising amount of time, augmented by his habitual luck at the gaming tables, and it was boredom rather than necessity that had sent the Cat on the prowl again.

It was late afternoon of the following day, and he sat in front of a fire, staring into it thoughtfully, an unusual occurrence for him. He'd been a moody child, and it had availed him nothing, not a father's attention nor a brother's time. Self-pity was an annoying waste, and he'd learned to eschew it, but this late autumn day he was melancholy, when he should have been elated at the stash of ugly stones secreted upstairs where no one would ever find them. And he knew exactly who to blame.

The mysterious Miss Brown, who'd vanished without a trace, leaving him with no alternative but to possess himself in patience, had had a most unsettling effect on his usual indolence. She would reappear again, he made no doubt. He'd sent enough lures Isolde's way to assure himself of that. But he'd never been a particularly patient man, and he wanted to see her eyes again, to discover whether they were really as eerily translucent as he remembered. And whether she could take her strange cards and tell his fortune as well.

"Personage to see you, my lord," his manservant announced in that tone of voice reserved for Nicodemus Bottom. Malkin disapproved of Nicodemus, as any right-thinking servant would, but he dutifully turned a blind eye and a deaf ear to Alistair's business dealings. Alistair had little doubt that Malkin knew exactly what business he conducted with a sinister-looking little man like Nicodemus, but he managed to hide his disapproval valiantly.

Indeed, it was often hard for Alistair to suppress a shudder, more at the strange and disconcerting odor that often accompanied his accomplice than the peculiar appearance. Nicodemus had once been a chimney sweep, and his feet and hands still bore the scars and doubtless some of the soot he'd collected years earlier. He was a small man with a ferret face, a random selection of dark teeth, gaudy taste in clothing, and an intense dislike of bathing. He also knew how to dispense with stolen diamonds to their best advantage, and if Alistair hadn't had

46

the dubious fortune of catching Nicodemus Bottom's hand in his pocket, a famous alliance might never had come about, and his first night's proceeds might still be sitting, untouched, in his old rooms.

"You work fast," Alistair said lazily, careful not to breathe too deeply. "I didn't know you were so eager."

"I figgered you were about due for a little exercise, yer worship," Nicodemus said. "But I'm not in that much of a hurry for the sparklers. Haven't made arrangements yet, so they can sit pretty for the time being."

"Not that I don't delight in your company, dear friend, but if you haven't come for the jewels, why are you here?" he asked, still giving him only half his attention.

"I came to warn you."

Alistair lifted his eyes lazily. "About what, pray tell?"

"The runners are after you."

"That's hardly a surprise. I haven't been concerned before — I see no reason to be concerned now."

"That's because Sir John hadn't put his best men on to you. Brennan's bad enough — he looks like he's half asleep, but that man's as sharp as a needle. But it's Clegg you need to keep your eyes peeled for."

"Clegg?"

"Josiah Clegg. He's always been a bad 'un, and most of us does our best to steer clear of him. He makes more money informing on runaway apprentices than bothering with the more dangerous types."

"Then I shouldn't have to worry. Considering I'm one of the more dangerous types," Alistair murmured.

"Word has it that he's got a little extra help. Sort of an unfair advantage, if you know what I mean."

"Explain yourself," Alistair suggested.

"He's got some woman to help him."

"I doubt I'd be likely to bare all my secrets to some creature allied to a Bow Street runner."

"You won't have to. She's part witch, they say. She uses dark powers to help Clegg, in return for money. Reads these funny-looking cards and then tells Clegg where to find things. Gives me the creeps, it does, just thinking about it."

Alistair was startled enough to move closer to Nicodemus, an act he immediately regretted. "Who is she?" he demanded. "What does she look like?"

"Ah, so now you're interested in what old Nic has to say," the man said smugly. "Don't know as many people have seen her. She keeps low, she does. Someone thought she was French. One of them Huguenots."

Alistair had schooled himself to keep all expression from his face. The mesmerizing creature from the previous night had been no more French than he was. "And this French woman proposes a danger to me with her cards and magic tricks? Somehow I doubt it."

"Jim Stebbins didn't think he had nothing to worry about till Clegg came calling. Knew exactly where he'd buried his wife, and brother as well, and no one knew but Jim."

Alistair allowed himself a faint shudder. "I hardly think I'd be as interesting as a man who slaughters his family."

"That's where you're wrong, guv'nor. The moiety on you is much higher."

"Moiety?"

"Thief-taker's share. You're worth a lot, yer honor."

"How gratifying. Then why don't you turn me in?"

Nicodemus's grin would have daunted a less hardy soul. "I've been tempted, yer worship. Fact of the matter is, though, people who inform to Clegg have a bad habit of disappearing before they can claim their share of the reward. And I reasons that you're worth more to me while you're actively pursuing your interests, so to speak."

"So to speak," Alistair echoed, amused. "What about Clegg's young woman? Why does he allow her to live?"

"I imagine she'll outlive her usefulness as well. Pretty girl, from what I've heard. She has strange eyes."

Alistair jerked. "I thought you said no one had seen her?"

"You must have misheard me, guv. I said not many have seen her. I happen to be one of the few."

"I could strangle you," Alistair said musingly. "If I could bear to get that close to you . . ."

"Why are you so interested in her, yer worship?"

"Shouldn't I be interested in someone who poses a threat to my well-being?" he countered.

"But you don't give a damn about Clegg."

"True enough," Alistair admitted. "I was ever a fanciful creature, Nicodemus. I'm far more interested in beautiful young witches with strange eyes than Bow Street runners. Where do I find this mysterious woman?"

"Normally I charge for such information. However, in your case . . ."

"In my case you'll tell me before I drag it out of you," he said in a pleasant voice.

"Where else would you find Frenchwomen but Spitalfields? I followed her one night after she met with Clegg. Secretive little thing, she was. Crept in the back door like a servant, but the people who live in those houses can't afford servants. 'S'matter of fact, maybe that's why I thought she was French. I never heard her speak, but that's where all the émigrés live, so I just assumed she was one of them."

"Perhaps," Alistair murmured. "And perhaps her dark talents have absolutely nothing to do with me and a great deal to do with the fact that your friend Mr. Clegg has to pay for his pleasures."

49

"Mebbe," Nicodemus allowed. "But she didn't look like no piece of muslin. And Clegg wouldn't have to pay — he's got half of Covent Garden terrified of him. Most doxies would be happy to lift their skirts for free if he left them alone. Besides, she didn't look like a doxy, despite them strange eyes. Dressed very neat and soberlike." He squinted at Alistair doubtfully. "What are you doing?"

Alistair had already stripped off his velvet dressing gown. "Preparing for an evening stroll. Spitalfields sounds like a fascinating section of town. Care to join me, Nicodemus?"

"Do I have a choice, yer worship?" he grumbled.

"Not much. Besides, I may need you to protect me from wandering Mohocks and the like."

Nicodemus Bottom smirked. "Not likely. You're a man who can take care of himself. But I'll show you where the girl lives, if that's what you have in mind."

"That's what I have in mind, Nicodemus," Alistair said gently. And he drained his brandy and headed for the door.

Alistair had a strange passing fondness for London at night, even the rudest sections. The modest little building that Nicodemus assured him contained the elusive Miss Brown was no different from any of the other small, cramped quarters that housed the majority of the vast city's French Protestant population. With one interesting difference.

He and Nicodemus were not alone in their perusal of the building. Two other men were just as interested.

He had cat's eyes — he could see in the dark, and he was almost preternaturally observant. In his chosen line of work he had no choice but to be unnaturally watchful. One man stood on the far corner, blending in with the shadows, but Alistair could discern an ample height, a large, loose-knit body, and eyes almost as observant as his own.

However, that watcher's eyes were focused on the building, and he seemed unaware that he was not alone that chill autumn night.

The other man walked slowly by, seemingly caught up in his own concerns, but Nicodemus's swift hiss of indrawn breath disabused Alistair of the notion that this might be a casual passerby. "Clegg," Bottom whispered. "What the hell is he doing around here?"

"I thought you said she worked with him?" Alistair responded in a hushed voice.

"Not at night, I wouldn't think. Not so's her family might know. He must be keeping watch on her. Most like he doesn't trust her. But then, Clegg doesn't trust anyone."

"The man shows some wisdom."

"He's smart as a whip, more's the pity," Nicodemus muttered. "That's what makes him so dangerous. You watch out, yer worship. Take a close look at the likes of him. He'll be your downfall if he can manage it."

"And what about the other man?"

"What other man?" Nicodemus demanded.

Alistair glanced back to the shadowy corner, but the large man had disappeared, fading back into the shadows. "He's gone," he said abruptly.

"You're seeing things, gov'nor. Best concentrate on the danger at hand, and not start looking for ghosts in the shadows."

He looked back at the building. An occasional female figure passed by a dimly lit window, but he was unable to discern whether or not it was Miss Brown. Not that he had any real doubt. How many ladylike card readers with strange eyes could there be in London? The fact that she worked for his natural enemy only made the temptation more delightful. "I don't suppose you know her name, do you?"

51

"I can make it my business to find out. I'll have to be careful though — I don't want Clegg knowing I'm interested. I don't want Clegg to even remember my existence."

"Find out for me, Nicodemus," he said, still intent on the window. "And I'll double your share of last night's work."

"You're a good man, haven't I always said so?" Nicodemus demanded of the night.

"An absolute paragon of virtues," Alistair murmured, faintly amused, still staring at the small house. "If you say so, old son. If you say so."

"You're quite the talk of society, my dear," Lady Plumworthy cooed from across a plate of tiny cakes. It was late afternoon the next day, and Jessamine hadn't eaten since early that morning, and the porridge had been thin and tasteless at that.

It had been months since she'd had a truly decent cup of tea served in fine bone china. She hadn't realized how very much she missed the small elegancies of life. She'd trained herself to concentrate on more important matters, such as life and death, yet there she was, seduced by an elegant cup of tea. "Am I?" she murmured in polite response, managing not to devour the cake in one gulp.

"It appears that your readings were amazingly accurate. I've had all manner of notes and visits, with people inquiring about you and regaling me with tales of the veracity of your forecasts. Of course, some say you're a witch, but fortunately we no longer burn witches in England." Lady Plumworthy's honk of laughter would have been unnerving, but Jessamine didn't even blink.

"I have a gift," she said. "I have no idea where it comes from, but I assure you, I've made no pact with the devil." There was a pact with fate, she added to herself. A cold bargain that was no one's concern but her own. "I simply see things others don't."

"You have a gift for telling the future, but your taste in clothes is boring beyond comprehension." Lady Plumworthy gave a theatrical shudder as she surveyed Jessamine's attire. Jessamine knew full well how she appeared, and she had no interest in changing. She was an average young woman with the normal requisite of curves, unremarkable features except for her dratted eyes, and plain brown hair. Her wardrobe was limited by finance, and she still dressed in the plain day dresses of her youth. They'd been made by the finest seamstresses, of excellent cloth, and even if they strained a bit over her lately acquired curves, they were serviceable enough.

"They suit me," she murmured, helping herself to another cake. It was her fourth, and she devoutly hoped Lady Plumworthy wouldn't notice.

"You look so ordinary! A fortune-teller shouldn't look ordinary," Lady Plumworthy complained. "I'm going to arrange for my dressmaker to come up with something suitable. No need to thank me, my dear. I'll simply subtract it from the money I'd pay you."

Jessamine took a fifth cake, not bothering to argue. It was going to make her sick, but the alternative, shoving it in Lady Plumworthy's smug face, was unacceptable no matter how tempting.

"But now my guests are waiting, and quite impatiently," her ladyship continued, rising. "If you can wipe the crumbs off your face, then we can join them and commence with the reading. You're prepared, aren't you?"

"Of course." In actuality it was a lie. Jessamine did far better on an empty stomach, but then, she had no intention of giving these flighty social butterflies her best work. Some of the things she saw in the cards were too disturbing for such people to handle.

He was there in the room. She must have known it — it

53

explained the unnatural tightening in her stomach, the high pitch of her nerves. He stood apart from the various groups of people, watching her with a lazy intensity that made her want to turn back and slam the wide double door behind her.

It was impossible, of course. For one thing, the unpleasant majordomo kept hold of the door, and she would never be able to wrest it from him. For another, she wasn't a coward, and she had no intention of displaying her uneasiness to anyone, particularly to him.

She simply ignored him, sitting down quietly at the side of the same green baize table she'd used before, pulling her velvet-wrapped pack of cards from her reticule and preparing to do her job.

At first it was quite simple. She could steer Miss Ocain in the direction of an eager young lordling who would make her quite happy. She could reassure Lady Barnett that her daughter would make a fine match. Signorina Varvello would spend an enjoyable season on the Continent, where she would find the answer to her dreams, and elderly Miss Hamilton would rediscover her missing locket.

Throughout the safe, happy futures she could feel him watching her, his slanted amber eyes sliding over her ordinary little body like his bold, elegant hands. She didn't like him. He upset her in ways far different than Josiah Clegg did.

Clegg she simply despised, for the venal, bullying, dangerous creature that he was.

The man who watched her was dangerous as well, in far different ways. He unnerved her, pulled her attention away from the cards and toward him, and she found herself fiddling with a stray curl that had come loose from her tightly coiled mane of hair.

"My turn," a young woman said gaily, throwing herself into the vacated seat. "Tell me my fortune, O mysterious one!"

She was astonishingly fair, almost as beautiful as Fleur. Her eyes were bright with joy and good health and the knowledge that she was well loved.

Jessamine took the cards in her hand slowly. "And you don't need to tell me whom I'll marry," the lady said. "I'm already married. I want to know how many children I'll have."

"Besides the one you're carrying?" Jessamine asked softly, flipping the cards.

"But I'm not —" The woman stopped. "That is, I didn't know . . ."

Jessamine looked up and smiled. "A healthy boy, Lady Grant, for you and your husband, in eight months' time."

The clamor that arose after that pronouncement was deafening, and Jessamine cursed her flapping tongue. She should have kept her mouth shut, offered some vague, conventional hopes, and left it at that. Lady Grant would discover soon enough that she was pregnant — she didn't need Jessamine to impart that information.

Her head was pounding, her stomach was knotted, and her hands were shaking from the strain of the afternoon. There were at least half a dozen more young women eager to hear their future, and the very thought made Jessamine drop the cards in a clumsy pile.

She reached down to pick them up, but a hand covered hers. She already knew that hand too well.

"Miss Brown is exhausted," he said. "I'm sure the rest of you will excuse her." He already had his hand under her arm, helping her to her feet, and she was too tired and bemused to protest.

"Glenshiel, you are a bad man!" Lady Plumworthy said. "I promised my guests that they would have their fortunes told."

"And so they shall. On some other occasion." He was leading her from the room, and she had no choice but to go with

55

him. She couldn't bring herself to look up at him; it was all she could do to regulate her uneven heartbeat.

A few moments later she found herself sitting in a small, quiet salon. A glass of wine had appeared out of nowhere, and the door was closed against the intruders — except that the intruder she most dreaded was already there, leaning against that very door, watching her.

"Who are you, Miss Brown?" he asked in deceptively polite tones. At another time she might have admired his voice — it was deep, elegant, and undeniably soothing. Like the purr of a great cat.

She was slowly regaining her composure and her defenses. "No one of any consequence, sir."

"Just an ordinary witch, is that it?"

"I'm not a witch!" she shot back, still unnerved by the suggestion.

"No, of course you're not," he said, pushing away from the door and coming closer. He was much taller than she'd realized — his wiry grace minimized his height. He leaned down so that he was close, dangerously close, and his voice was soft and seductive. "You're Miss Jessamine Maitland, formerly of Maitland Park. Aren't you?"

She looked up at him in absolute horror. "You're the one who's the witch," she said.

56

Five

Miss Jessamine Maitland, late of Maitland Park, was looking quite deliciously indignant. Alistair was a man who lounged and reclined rather than stormed into a situation, so he simply sat on the damask chaise opposite her, stretched out his long legs, and bestowed a faint smile on her.

She looked back at him stonily, clutching the glass of wine in one hand. He was rather taken with her hands. He'd had plenty of time to observe them as she shuffled the cards, and he'd found himself weaving the most absurdly erotic fantasies about them. Her fingers were long, graceful, and the very lack of even the plainest of silver rings fed his fantasies. She didn't have soft white hands with no other use than adornment. She had hands that when properly encouraged could drive a man to sweet oblivion.

"Why are you looking at me like that?" she demanded in an irritable voice.

"Like what?" he murmured lazily.

"Like a cat who's discovered a juicy mouse."

It took all his concentration not to show how startled he was. Clearly she had no idea what she'd said — his connection with a certain notorious feline seemed to have eluded her fortune-telling gifts. Or at least eluded the more conscious part of them. He had the suspicion that even though she hadn't realized it, it wouldn't be long before she knew quite well who and what he was.

"You are rather mouselike in that dull gray dress," he agreed lazily. "But quite quivering and delicious, for all that."

She started to rise, took one look at his face, and clearly thought better of it. A wise decision on her part. If she'd surged to her feet, he would have been required to rise also, and it would have put him in very close proximity to her. He would have had no choice but to touch her, and if he were to touch her, he had every intention of kissing her quite thoroughly. And not stopping there.

"How did you find out my name?" she demanded.

"Quite easily. I simply asked the right person," he murmured.

"And why should you care?"

"Dear girl, you fascinate me," he said frankly. "I've never known a cross between a proper young English girl and a Gypsy. Your talents are quite remarkable. Usually I find young virgins to be deadly dull, but in your case I find myself absolutely drawn to you."

"Draw back," she snapped, her color high. "I assure you my talents are paltry at best, and mostly consist of lies and lucky guesses. I'm scarcely the sort of creature to hold your interest. I'm no longer of your class."

"I didn't say I was interested in marrying you, child," he said.

She managed not to flush at the deliberate taunt. "Then what do you want from me? And don't call me child! I'm no longer in the schoolroom, and you can't be that much older than I am."

"In years I'd surmise about a decade, but in more important matters I'm old in the ways of sin and the world, and you're still an infant. And I should think it would be quite clear what I want from you."

She sighed quite loudly, and began to untie the silk strings of her reticule. "I can't promise that the cards will tell me much. I'm tired, and I don't do well with —"

He leaned forward and placed his hand over hers, stopping her as she fumbled for her cards. His own hands were long, graceful, pale, and strong, and they covered hers as they rested on her lap. Even beneath all those layers of clothing he could sense her skin, her warmth, and he knew his touch shocked her.

"I don't want you to tell me my fortune, Jessamine," he said softly, "and I have no interest in making use of your dubious talents."

She tried to pull her hands from under his, but he simply pressed harder, the strength and the heat of his hand against her legs. "Then what do you want?" she demanded.

She really didn't know. It astonished and delighted him. How a woman with her subtle, delicious charms could be so oblivious was a wonder.

"I want your body," he purred.

She blinked those magnificent eyes at him. "What for?"

He was becoming less charmed and more irritated. "I want to seduce you, my pet," he said in a cooler voice that she couldn't fail to understand.

Her reaction was gratifying. She didn't turn pale, or flush, or giggle like a simpleton. She simply stared at him. "Oh," she said flatly. "You're a rake."

"I'm not denying it. What made you come to that particular conclusion?"

"Rakes like to seduce every female they come across, do they not? My mother warned me that men like you existed, but our fortunes changed before I ever actually met one."

"Curse all mothers," he muttered. "And I don't seduce every female I come across. Only the ones who interest me."

She looked at him with a calculating eye, clearly unmoved.

59

"Do you live in London, Mr. . . . ? I'm afraid I don't know your name — we've never been properly introduced. You can't seduce me if we haven't been introduced."

"That's what you think," he said half to himself. "And actually I'm not technically a mister. I'm the sixth Earl of Glenshiel. You may call me Lord Glenshiel, but I'd prefer you call me Alistair."

"A title," she said approvingly. "Even better. Does that title come with a convenient fortune?"

"I said I wanted to seduce you, not buy you," he drawled. "Cooperation is so much more enjoyable than commerce."

"I wasn't thinking of me," she said sharply.

"Oh, you've become an abbess?" he inquired politely.

The color flared in her pale cheeks then, most gratifyingly. The longer he resisted touching her, the more powerful the need became. Her ridiculous arguments should have made him lose interest. Instead, they merely increased his determination.

"Matchmaker," she said in a severe voice. "You aren't married, are you?"

"Fortunately, no."

She positively beamed at him. "Excellent. And you're a very handsome man. I'm certain you'd want a beautiful wife as well, one who could give you equally lovely children — a good, talented, docile girl who —"

"What in God's name are you talking about?"

"My sister."

"You want me to seduce your sister?" he echoed, momentarily diverted.

"Of course not. I want you to marry her."

"Why in God's name would I want to do that?"

"All men need heirs. And I told you, my sister is without question the most beautiful girl in London. Men only have to see her to fall in love with her."

He surveyed her calmly. "Then why hasn't someone married her already?"

"Because I don't let anyone see her. I'm saving her. Our unfortunate reversal of fortune has kept us in retirement, but as soon as I . . . as we regain our proper circumstances, she'll make her bow in society, and I have no doubt whatsoever that a splendid marriage will ensue."

"You *are* an abbess," he said dryly. "I'm sorry, child, but I have no intention of marrying, now or in the future. I prefer my pleasures unshackled. Besides, I have no interest in your sister, no matter how lovely and docile and talented she is. Those aren't the qualities that interest me."

"They're not?" she said, clearly surprised.

"I'm far more interested in women who are adventuresome, imaginative, and not in the ordinary way. I prefer women with strange eyes to those of classic perfection. In fact, dear girl, I want to bed you, not marry your sister."

She blinked at his plain speaking, but still managed to keep her composure. "You have very uncommon tastes, my lord."

"Yes," he said. "I suppose I do."

She really did have the most extraordinary eyes. They were sea green, translucent, witch's eyes, and they stared at him with sudden dismay, as if she finally realized the danger she was in. She scrambled out of her chair, clutching her reticule, backing away from him and knocking the chair over as she went.

He didn't move from his spot on the chaise, merely reclined there, watching her. The poor innocent thought she could escape — she didn't know how quickly he could move.

"This has been most entertaining, my lord," she said, and he could hear the breathless anxiety in her voice. "But I'm afraid I need to be getting home."

"To that incomparable sister of yours? This time you'd best take a sedan chair. Spitalfields is a fair distance from Mayfair."

"You know where I live?" she demanded, aghast.

"It's a very drab little house."

"It's only temporary."

He'd lulled her into a false security. If she had any sense at all, she'd escape quickly, but she was lingering, still several feet from the door, and he had more than enough time to reach her.

"You don't want to go back there tonight, do you? Wouldn't you rather eat roast quail and drink fine claret? Wouldn't you rather spend the night in my bed?"

"Absolutely not," she said sternly. "And I don't believe you have the faintest interest in taking me there."

She made the mistake of turning her back as she crossed to the doorway. By the time she put her hand on the knob, he was behind her, looming over her, moving with total silence as his hand covered hers.

He turned her around swiftly, and she uttered a little shriek, more of surprise than real fear, and she looked up at him with disapproving eyes.

"You think not, Jessamine? You underestimate your charms." He used his body to press her up against the door, exerting just enough strength to pin her there without hurting her. He cupped her face with his hands, and her skin was smooth and soft beneath his fingers. Her mouth trembled as she stared up at him in utter fierceness, and her eyes dared him.

He never could resist a dare. He set his mouth against hers, tasting her lips, the wine that she'd drunk, the fear she tried so hard to hide. She made no effort to fight him or resist him, she simply held very still, like a trapped animal, like a tiny, cowering mouse trapped by a big black cat.

The notion amused him, and he tipped her head back, moving his lips across hers lightly, dampening them. She seemed to be having trouble breathing, and he decided to make things even more difficult. He put just the right amount of pressure on her jaw, and she opened her mouth to him.

The sound she made when he used his tongue was soft, distressed, and longing. For a moment she pushed against him, but when she realized that nothing short of an earthquake could dislodge him, she started to drop her arms in defeat.

He didn't want her defeat. He caught her arms and pulled them around his neck, and she shuddered. But her body pressed up against his, and he could feel the sweet swell of her breasts against his chest, and the stirring of a need that mirrored his own.

She wouldn't know much about that kind of need, and she would doubtless deny it if she could. He wanted to take her far enough along that she couldn't pretend, and he moved one hand between their bodies, up her plain, stiffened bodice to the curve of her breast, claiming it with his long fingers.

"Alistair!" Lady Plumworthy's less than genteel bellow was unmistakable echoing through the town house, and Alistair's immediate thought was murderous indeed. He didn't want to stop. He wanted her to kiss him back. He wanted to unlace the back of her decent, boring dress, and bare her breasts for his eyes, his hands, his mouth.

"Alistair!" Isolde bellowed again, once more displaying the manners of her youth. She was getting closer.

With a sigh of regret Alistair released Jessamine's mouth, her breast, her body, stepping back, surveying her out of hooded eyes.

She was leaning against the door, breathless, panting slightly, her eyes shut. Her mouth was damp and reddened from his, her face was pale, and she looked as if her safe little world had just tipped on end. He could only hope it had.

The sight was so delicious, he almost reached for her again,

63

but the doorknob turned and Jessamine was thrust toward him unceremoniously as Lady Plumworthy barged into the room.

He caught her arms, careful to keep her face away from Isolde's until she recovered some of her wonderfully disordered senses. She glanced up at him, and there was such confusion, pain, and longing in her mysterious eyes that he felt the first pang of guilt he'd experienced in years. He reached out an involuntary hand to touch her, reassure her, but she had already swept around, away from him, brushing past Lady Plumworthy with no more than a murmured farewell.

Isolde surveyed him with grim humor. "You've been a naughty boy again, Alistair," she chided him, her arch tones making his skin crawl. "Don't you know better than to interfere with the bourgeoisie?"

"I thought she was a Gypsy," he drawled.

"You know perfectly well she's not. She's a decent, unimaginative English maiden whose father was a wastrel."

"So I gather."

Isolde blinked. "You mean she told you?"

"Of course not. I have my own sources of information, Isolde, as do you. I'm perfectly aware of Miss Maitland's background."

"Then you should know better than to try your wiles with her."

"I know better, Isolde. I just don't choose to act on that knowledge. She's a bit too delectable to pass by. You know I could never resist a challenge."

"Silly boy. Experience is always preferable to awkwardness." She batted her creped eyelids in a grotesque attempt at flirtation.

Alistair was not in the mood for this. Now that he knew who Jessamine was, he no longer relied on Isolde Plumworthy for his connection, but common sense told him that she would

64

be a dangerous enemy to make. "Come now, Isolde," he said. "Had you the choice between an aging roué like Castleton and a young, untried buck such as Calderwood, it's more than clear which one you'd choose. You enjoy a challenge just as much as I do."

"I suppose I do," she said with a sigh. "Still and all, Alistair, you've always managed to elude me."

"It makes me far more interesting," he murmured, moving toward the door. "Forgive me if I take my leave of you, my lady."

Isolde sank heavily into a chair, waving him away with her plump, beringed hand. There was a particularly fine emerald on her fat little finger, and Alistair wondered if he ought to break the Cat's unwritten code and make a return visit to one of his victims. If anyone deserved it, Isolde did. "Go away, go away," she said crankily. "But first tell me, what do you intend to do about the girl?"

"Seduce and abandon her, of course. What else would you expect?"

"You're an evil soul, Alistair. I've always liked that about you. You remind me of me."

Alistair managed a faint smile that was just this side of a sneer. "You flatter me, Isolde. No one can even approach you for sheer malice." And her laugh echoed in his ears as he made his escape.

A weaker, more vulnerable soul might be close to tears, Jessamine thought as she hurried through the darkening streets of late afternoon. Another female, less certain of her lot in life, might feel shaken, overset, disturbed. But not Jessamine.

"You have a rare gift," Marilla had told her years before. "You see the cards more clearly than anyone I have ever known. But there is a price to be paid. To keep that gift you need to remain pure. Untouched, unsoiled by the hands of men. You can never marry, never lie with a man. If you do, your talent will vanish and the cards will be no more than pretty pictures. Let a man touch you and kiss you, let him lie between your legs, and I will have taught you for nothing. You must choose, love, and you must choose wisely, for there will be no going back."

And Jessamine Maitland, who at the tender age of eleven considered the male of the species nothing more than an annoyance, and the act of procreation utterly disgusting, agreed without hesitation.

She was doubly glad of her choice now, she told herself, wrapping her shawl around her body even more tightly, and reaching up a surreptitious hand to scrub at her mouth. Never had another person touched her in such a way. His mouth had been hot, hard, damp, his tongue an intrusion that made her shudder in horrified memory. His hands were hard as well, with narrow, strong fingers that had held her prisoner. She would have bruises, she was certain of it. He was a monster, a depraved, cowardly villain. . . .

She realized absently that her fingertips were stroking her mouth. She pulled her hand away with a horrified gasp, ducking her head and moving onward down the crowded streets.

In truth, now that she had time to think about it, it hadn't been that awful. She could see why most women wouldn't mind such importunities. Why, some of them might even welcome such a languorous assault.

But not Jessamine. She had made her solitary bed, and she would lie in it. And milord Glenshiel would find someone else to play his cat-and-mouse games with.

The phrase rang uncomfortably in her head, and she could see his golden cat's eyes in her memory. If she had any sense at all, she would do a reading when she got home. She tried to keep the cards away from Fleur and her mother — they worried too much, and Mrs. Maitland had been jealous of Marilla's influence even after Marilla had died of old age. She could closet herself in the bedroom and lay them out.

Except that she already knew what she would discover. The cards danced in her head quite clearly, and she shook the memory away. She didn't want answers to her unspoken question. She didn't want Alistair MacAlpin in her mind, in her life, teasing her, touching her. What dark secrets lay beyond his indolent exterior was none of her concern. And so she would tell Clegg if he made any more demands.

Once again knowledge was coming uncomfortably close, knowledge that angered and frightened her. She would keep her distance from Lady Plumworthy. The heavy purses she offered were no match for the harsh behavior of her hulking servants.

Or the demoralizing effect of the Earl of Glenshiel when he put his mouth on hers.

Six

The Cat was on the prowl again. It was a cool, dark night, a few short weeks after his last wicked visitation, but Alistair was restless, and he had no illusions as to what caused his current frustrated state.

Miss Maitland had proven herself to be annoyingly reclusive. Nicodemus had managed to get a goodly sum for Isolde's ugly gems, more than enough to keep Alistair in reasonable luxury, but he was bored. If he couldn't have Jessamine of the translucent eyes and the most delicious mouth he'd tasted in memory, then he'd simply have to distract himself with the pleasures of felony.

As it was, he was far more interested in Jessamine than he should have been. A careful man would have been determined to keep his distance from those too-observant eyes.

Ah, but when had he ever considered himself a careful man? Besides, she was simply too damned tempting. He wanted to see how long it would take her to realize who and what he was. Not that he believed in her particular gift, but he was too wise to discount any possibility, no matter how farfetched.

Besides, it would be a simple enough matter to distract her from her unfortunate alliance with the constabulary. He simply had to seduce her.

Somehow he wasn't finding the notion of such a sacrifice to be unduly arduous.

The Cat had two disparate styles of thievery, and Alistair

could never decide which he preferred. The sheer effrontery of simply strolling into one of his host's private rooms and helping himself to jewelry had a certain charm, just as his adeptness at relieving unpleasant women of their baubles amused him. That occasionally led to an error in judgment, one he found himself forced to correct. His code of honor, his sense of morality, was elastic indeed, nonexistent to most observers. But to him it was clear: One didn't rob those who couldn't afford it and didn't deserve it. He was interested in relieving only some of the wealthier, less pleasant members of society of their extraneous gewgaws. The same sort of people who'd had no qualms about helping his brother James in his downward spiral of drink and ruinous gaming.

Not that anything so noble as revenge lay behind Alistair's little journey into a life of crime. He preferred to think it was caused by nothing more than a combination of financial necessity and boredom.

That, however, precluded robbing innocent, pleasant women of their jewelry. He'd been forced to go to great lengths to return the young Duchess of Denver's pink pearl necklace. It was far from her most valuable piece, and her older husband could afford to replace it by the gross, but he discovered it had been given to her by her now-deceased mother, and the loss of it had sent the pretty young duchess into absolute despair.

He'd found the return even more challenging than the actual taking, and for a brief while he'd considered returning all the baubles he'd stolen. Practicality had soon taken hold though. Most of the stuff had already been converted into cash and spent. And besides, most of them didn't deserve to have it returned.

Miss Beauchamp had been a different matter. The gaudy Beauchamp diamonds were well known, and her father, Sir Reginald, had been one of Alistair's brother's chief cronies.

69

Together they'd gone through their various fortunes, with Sir Reginald following James in death at a discreet interval. Alistair had considered the diamonds fair game and only fitting recompense, until he discovered that they were simply all Miss Beauchamp and her mother had left of the once-notable Beauchamp fortune. And she had no idea that the magnificent things were a glass-and-paste substitute.

Alistair's amusement at having been gulled into stealing worthless baubles had paled when it came to the Beauchamps' despair. Returning them had been simple enough, done with the help of Nicodemus Bottom's expert assistance. Replacing the false gems with real ones had proven more difficult, but Alistair had been up to the challenge. And the Beauchamps had never realized their recovered jewels had once been totally worthless.

It was during that incident that Alistair had discovered his alternative form of thievery. The Beauchamps could not afford to entertain, and there was simply no way Alistair could casually find his way to the upper floors of the house, short of seducing Miss Beauchamp. And while that notion was far from repugnant, she was in love with a young lordling who adored her, and Alistair allowed himself enough sentiment to keep from putting a rub in the way of their upcoming nuptials.

Nicodemus and his cohorts had been more than helpful. Close-fitting black clothes, a moonless night, and a certain agility in scaling fences, buildings, and windows were all that it took.

He nearly broke his blasted neck the first time he tried it. By the third time, he achieved the fastness of Miss Beauchamp's virgin bedroom, tucked the refurbished diamonds into a spot where they'd be likely to be discovered with just the right amount of difficulty, and made his escape, feeling well pleased with himself. Like a black cat, he'd scaled the London rooftops, the moonless night overhead, and felt cool and free with ties to no one and nothing.

It was by far the way he preferred his reiving. There were times he simply took to the rooftops with no aim in mind. Tonight, however, he knew exactly where he was going. First to the Renfields' town house. The servants would be abed, the large and graceful rubies would be in Lady Barbara's jewelry box. If by any chance she'd decided to wear her ornate rubies to the less formal ridotto he knew they were attending, he'd console himself with her diamonds and pearls.

And then he would wander farther afield. To Spitalfields, where he would blend into the shadows. He had no intention of breaching the Maitland stronghold. He merely wanted to observe both Jessamine and whoever else happened to be watching the place. That other shadow still haunted him, and he wasn't a man who liked unanswered questions.

He didn't pay much attention to Nicodemus Bottom's warnings about the infamous Josiah Clegg. Nicodemus had a tendency to worry excessively, and he still couldn't quite believe that a member of the gentry was proving to be as adept a thief as ever he'd known. Alistair had little doubt he could outwit a dozen Cleggs, just as he outwitted everyone else.

With the possible exception of Jessamine Maitland. It might have been a trick of her strange eyes, but she seemed to see through him with no difficulty at all. He doubted she knew he was the Cat. If, as Nicodemus assured him, she was actually assisting Clegg, then she should have no hesitation in informing on him to her cohort and collecting the prize money. It could make a start in getting them out of that dark hovel in Spitalfields. Yet she'd done no such thing. If the cards had told her he was the Cat, she was keeping it to herself.

He didn't think it had gone that far yet. She might suspect he wasn't the lazy, rutting fop he carefully presented to society.

When he looked at her he felt neither lazy nor foppish. The strong desire to rut was a different matter entirely.

He should keep his distance, let her be. Put a temporary halt to his larcenous activities. But he had no intention of doing either of those boring things.

Lady Barbara had sensibly left her rubies behind. They didn't become her rather florid complexion, and he could only hope she replaced them with something a little more tasteful.

He seldom ventured into the more dangerous parts of the city during his nightly prowls, and the rooftops of Spitalfields were a far cry from those of Mayfair. Tiles were loose, chimney pots were smoking, and the sky seemed somehow darker.

The roof of Miss Maitland's house was in equally bad shape. It must have leaked in several spots whenever London was blessed with a soaking rain, he thought. The scent of dampness clung to the place, mixing with soot and ancient odors even less pleasant.

He could hear their voices drifting upward, the soft murmur of well-bred British women, and he wondered what they found to talk about. Did she tell them she'd been thoroughly kissed for what had undoubtedly been the first time in her life? Did she tell them about her fortune-telling cards?

The houses in Spitalfields were plain and unadorned, and there was nothing he could use to climb down and peer inside one of the windows, much as he would have sold his soul to do so. But then, he'd lost his soul long ago — it could hardly have been worth bartering over.

He stretched out flat on the rooftop, pressing his face against the broken tiles. He shut his eyes, letting the cool night air press down around him.

And he listened for her voice.

Fleur Maitland loved her sister Jessamine more than anyone else in the world. She loved her sister, and she hated lies. And yet, for some reason she hadn't told Jess of the man she'd met. The man who teased her impossible dreams.

It had been only a few short weeks earlier, and yet she couldn't remember what life had been like before she'd seen him. She didn't even know his full name. Perhaps it was better that way.

It had been a fine autumn afternoon with a warm sun beating down, giving lie to the approaching winter. Fleur sat back and stared at the watercolor she'd just labored over. It was not one of her best efforts, due, no doubt, to the excess haste she'd used in painting it. Her mother had been prostrate, as she was far too often, Jessamine was off somewhere, and Fleur had been unable to resist the clear afternoon light. She'd taken her paints and escaped the house, walking down to the canals to capture the late colors of autumn against the gray backdrop of Spitalfields, but she'd been ever mindful of her circumstances.

She'd had to grow used to being alone. The first fifteen years of her life had been spent cosseted and protected, with scarcely a minute left to her own devices, but since the Disaster, as she'd come to think of it, there'd been no maids, no footmen, not even much of a mother to look out for her. She went to the market stalls alone, she took solitary walks when need be. Surely she would be safe enough in broad daylight?

Someone was watching her. It wasn't an uncommon experience — she was used to having eyes follow her wherever she went. She found her pleasing appearance to be a mixed blessing. Ever since she could remember, young men had importuned her, old women had doted on her, the world seemed eager to please her for no more reward than her smile. It had always seemed a bit unfair to Fleur, and she tried not to use it, but that sense of being watched had become a second nature to her.

The colors she'd used were dark and drab, too suggestive of her troubled state of mind. She stared at her picture in dismay, so intent on it that she didn't realize someone had approached until a shadow crossed the canvas.

"Very nice, miss," he said in a voice that was broad and country. She looked up, blinded by the sun for a moment, aware only of immense height. She put up her hand and squinted, knowing she should ignore him, but somehow the broad Yorkshire voice brought her lost home back to her so forcefully that she couldn't help but turn to him.

He looked safe enough. He was dressed rather untidily in sober clothes, and his light hair was long and in need of a trim. But the untidiness seemed the result of having more important things on his mind rather than actual carelessness. He had a strong face — broad features, clear eyes, an overstrong jaw, and a generous mouth. He looked down at her quite kindly, and for one brief, dangerous moment she wanted to smile back at him.

"It's a hopeless daub," she said uncertainly, taking it from the easel and preparing to rip it up.

He caught it from her hand quite easily. "Don't do that, lass. It's far too pretty."

She'd never been called lass in her entire life. During her childhood no one would have dared, and in the big, filthy city of London, people were more likely to call her "ducks." There was something about his voice, the gentleness when he said "lass" that warmed her even on a cool autumn day.

And then suddenly she realized what she was doing, having a conversation with a strange man. She glanced around her, but the area around them was empty. She was alone, and he could be a dangerous madman, an abductor of helpless females, a rake and an unprincipled . . .

"Nay, lass, don't look so frightened. I'm not going to harm you. Do I look like an evildoer?"

"My sister told me I couldn't judge people by their looks."

"Your sister's very wise," he said gently. "Just as you're wise not to trust a stranger just because he seems harmless enough. But I promise you, you have nothing to fear. I'm one of Sir John's men."

Fleur looked up at him blankly. "I don't understand."

"I'm a member of the police. A Bow Street runner. I'm what passes for law around here."

"Oh," Fleur murmured, vastly relieved. "I was afraid — that is, I thought . . ." She could feel the blush mounting to her cheeks.

"I won't harm you, lass. But there are others who aren't what they should be. You shouldn't be here alone, so caught up in your painting. You didn't even realize I'd come up on you."

"I do get rather lost in my work," she said breathlessly. He was so very big, he should have been frightening. But she wasn't frightened. For the first time since the Disaster, she felt safe.

"I'll keep a watch out for you," he said, "but I can't always be there. You need to watch out for yourself as well, lass."

For a moment she didn't say anything. He was standing very close, and for a moment she felt as if they were alone in this vast, crowded, noisy city. The people and the filth faded away, and it was green all around, and she was home, in a place she'd never known.

"Miss?" he questioned, staring at her oddly, and the spell was broken.

"I have to go," she said, catching up her paints.

She half expected him to stop her, but he made no effort to do so, simply stepping back politely. "Take care, Miss Maitland," he said in his deep, country voice.

It wasn't until she reached the safety of her home that she realized he'd known her name. And he still possessed her watercolor of the nearby canals.

She'd seen him again during the next few weeks, mostly from a distance, watching over her as she went about her errands. He wouldn't come close enough to speak, and the first time she smiled at him from across the crowded square, he pretended not to notice.

But she persisted, to be rewarded with a faint, acknowledging smile in return. And Fleur kept the memory of his smile in her heart, and said not a word to her older sister.

"What do you do when you go out?" Fleur asked in a deliberately casual voice.

Jessamine looked up from her mending, startled. The light was growing too dim to work by, and the open window, while it let in comparatively fresh night air, also let in a chill draft. "Why would you ask such a question?" she countered, setting the torn sheet down and peering at her sister.

"Just curious. There's little enough to occupy my thoughts during the day when you're gone. Mama stays in her bedroom, bemoaning her fate, and we can't afford the amount of paints and paper it would require to keep me busy the entire time."

Jessamine looked stricken. "I'm sorry, pet. Soon we'll be able to afford all the art supplies you could possibly want, but in the meantime . . ."

"In the meantime I could do something as well to help out. You know my watercolors are much admired."

"They always have been," Jess agreed warily.

"Our friends always said so, but you can't trust their kindness. They're hardly likely to tell me I'm a talentless waster of good paint. But the people around here who watch me when

76

I'm working have assured me I could make a small amount of money if I chose to sell my artwork. Enough to pay for my supplies and a bit left over to go toward the household expenses. There's no reason you should take on the entire burden of keeping us afloat, and if what I take such pleasure in could bring us some much-needed money then I see no reason why I couldn't do it. I could set up a stall near Covent Garden and —"

"No!" Jess cried in horror. In a moment she'd modulated her voice. "You cannot possibly do such a thing. Not in Covent Garden, where'd you be mistaken for a high-class doxy if you aren't carried off by procurers. If anyone should see you, or realize you sold your paintings, your chances of a proper marriage would be flown away."

"By proper you mean wealthy," Fleur said carefully.

"Isn't that what you want as well? A kind, caring man who'll take care of you? A man who won't waste his money, leaving his wife and daughters penniless? Wouldn't it be utterly splendid never to have to worry about where our next meal is coming from? Whether we'll be tossed out of even this awful hovel and left to beg on the streets?" Her voice was tight with strain. "Surely nothing would be too great a sacrifice to be spared that."

"Has it really been that bad, Jess?" Fleur asked quietly. She had never worried where the food had come from. Jess had always provided, and told her not to concern herself.

She watched with amazement as Jessamine gave herself a little shake, seeming to toss off the anxiety that had settled around her. She smiled at her younger sister. "I'm being melodramatic, silly goose," she said in a lighter voice. "I won't pretend things haven't been difficult since Father died, but we've made it this far, and things are definitely looking better. I've just got a case of the megrims."

"You've had it for days," Fleur said. "Why?"

Jessamine lowered her eyes, but Fleur didn't miss the sudden staining of color on her smooth cheeks. "It's nothing. An importunate gentleman, and I failed to deal him the setdown he richly deserves. It doesn't matter in the least — I'm unlikely to see him again, thank goodness. But I admit it's . . . disturbed me slightly."

"A gentleman? You've always insisted you didn't have any interest in men whatsoever," Fleur said. "Who is he?"

"Just some worthless aristocrat. An acquaintance or relative of Lady Plumworthy's. It's no great matter, darling. He was a bit overeager in demonstrating his appreciation of my card-reading abilities."

"I doubt your card-reading abilities had anything to do with it," she said wisely. "Did he kiss you?"

"It's none of your concern. It's past, and it doesn't matter. . . ."

"More than once? What was it like? Was it unbearably awful? Was he horrid and ugly and old?"

Jessamine hesitated, and a faint, reluctant smile played around the corners of her full mouth. "No," she said.

"No, he didn't kiss you more than once? Or no, he wasn't horrid and ugly and old? What was it like?"

"Quite . . . pleasant."

"Pleasant?" Fleur shrieked. "How very disappointing! I expected it would be life-shattering at the very least. Your first kiss and it was merely *pleasant?*"

"What makes you think it was my first kiss?"

"Wasn't it?"

"I've been kissed before."

"I don't believe you. You've never had the least use for men. Besides, if you're so experienced, then why do you have the megrims?"

"I'd never been kissed . . . in quite that manner," she confessed. "It was rather unnerving."

"Oh, how delicious. I wish someone would kiss me like that. I should so adore to be unnerved," Fleur said with a mischievous smile. And for some reason the vision of the large, untidy policeman danced into her memory and her humor faded.

"You're too young," Jess said sternly. "Wait for your husband to unnerve you. It's far safer."

"Do you want him to kiss you again?"

"Whether I do or not hardly matters, since I won't be seeing him again. I'm certain I can manage to avoid him, and if I can't, I shall simply have to give up my society readings."

"Which reminds me. What is the difference between my selling my paintings and your accepting money for reading the cards? Surely it puts you beyond the pale as well?"

"Ah, but I have no intention of marrying well, or at all. I don't possess the natural attributes you do, dearest."

"You're ridiculous, Jess!"

Jessamine shrugged her narrow shoulders. "One takes the path given one, Fleur. Just rest assured that you won't have to marry anyone you don't want to. I have trust in your good sense. I know you'll manage to fall in love with a very wealthy man," she said cheerfully.

"Oh, I'm most sensible, sister dear," Fleur replied evenly. "I still want to know where you go when you leave here for the day."

"I don't walk the streets looking for customers, love," she said lightly. "I do card readings."

"But that's fairly recent, isn't it? Lady Plumworthy heard of your existence only a few weeks ago."

Jess hesitated. "I . . . I've been doing readings for others as well," she said finally.

Fleur simply waited.

79

"For the Bow Street runners," Jess admitted.

"The Bow Street runners?" she echoed in a hollow voice, but Jess was too guilty to notice her sister's reaction.

"I know it's *not done,* Fleur," she said hurriedly. "And that's why I haven't told you or Mama. But it's helped support us, and it's been a force for good in society. At least, sometimes," she added with a trace of bitterness.

"I'm certain the police are quite estimable," Fleur said faintly.

"Not the ones I've met." Her voice was dark. "You keep away from the runners, Fleur. They're a bad lot, not much better than the criminals they arrest."

"I keep away from everyone, Jess."

Jessamine stared at her, suddenly troubled. "You haven't been bothered, have you? No one has accosted you, asked you questions, taken liberties?"

"You're the one who was kissed, Jessie. Not me. Though I expect I'm bored enough that I would have enjoyed it more than you did," she added with a forced smile.

"You'd be wrong," Jessamine said firmly. "Now, off to bed, my pet, or Mama will hear us talking."

"Yes, sister dear. I promise to dream chaste dreams. I wonder if the same could be said of you. What was your wicked seducer's name, by the way?"

"He didn't seduce me," Jess said sternly. "And I don't know his name."

"And you taught me never to lie!" Fleur said with a hollow laugh. "Promise me one thing. It wasn't your Bow Street runner, was it?"

Jessamine shuddered. "It wasn't, Fleur. And it never will be."

Alistair rolled over onto his back, staring up into the inky blue velvet of the London night. He'd grown used to the smells that surrounded him. In truth, the country was full of less than flowery scents as well, and yet, if he'd had his choice, he'd be far away from this damnable city that ate its children whole.

He'd heard almost every word with gratifying clarity. He counted excellent hearing among his many gifts, and the two Maitland sisters had made little effort to keep their voices down. After all, no one could hear them unless a cat happened to be prowling on the rooftops and stopped just above an open window.

Unnerving. Bless the girl. He'd managed to shake her equilibrium as soundly as she'd shaken his. Of course, in her case it wasn't much of a challenge. An untouched virgin would be easy prey for an experienced scoundrel. He frowned, remembering her words. What other men had she kissed? Whoever they were, they were far too polite and respectful. They probably had nothing but the most honorable of intentions toward her. Whereas his were nothing short of lascivious.

She couldn't get him out of her mind. He would have to do his best to remind her, should she have more success at dismissing his memory. She and her impoverished little family were obviously quite desperately in need of money, and he had little doubt the right offer from a respectable source could lure her into society once more. An evening performance, perhaps. She could read the cards for a few select couples, and he would stay well out of sight so as not to alarm her. And then he would be the perfect gentleman and escort her back to this dreary little hovel.

The thought of that long carriage ride cheered him immensely, and he started back across the rooftops, silent as a cat, moving between the closely packed buildings with his usual dexterity. Down below, the streets were deceptively quiet — too much so. At that time of night even areas like Spitalfields

81

should see some signs of life. A whore or two, perhaps a costermonger, or at least a stray four-footed cat.

On impulse he scrambled down a roof, then dropped to the ground on silent feet. It was a back alleyway, not two streets over from the Maitlands' abode, and it was a simple enough matter to blend with the shadows in his dark clothes. He hadn't bothered to blacken his face, but the night was a cape to cover him as he moved through the streets like his feline counterpart.

The lights were out in the Maitlands' house. He stood there, looking up, wondering if the haphazard windows would provide enough of a foothold for him to climb up to Jessamine's bedroom, when he sensed the presence of someone nearby.

"Nice night for a walk, isn't it?" said a man's voice, thick, plummy, with an unmistakable London accent.

And Alistair turned around slowly to meet Josiah Clegg's soulless eyes.

Seven

Josiah Clegg didn't appear to be that formidable a foe when observed up close. He was an ordinary-looking man, a bit vain, with a wide, thick-lipped mouth and a surprisingly pleasant smile. A warm smile, the kind to inspire confidence.

Alistair wasn't inspired. Nor was he particularly troubled by the appearance of a man who could be his nemesis. Apart from the interesting revelations he'd overheard beneath the Maitlands' roof, the night had been far too uneventful.

"*Qu'est-ce que c'est?*" he demanded in his passable French.

"Odd," said Clegg. "I wouldn't have thought you'd be one of these damned Frenchy émigrés. You don't have the face for it."

"*Pourquoi?*" Alistair said, looking vague.

"You don't look British, either," Clegg continued in a musing voice. "I'd say you were a Scot by the look of you."

"*Je ne comprends pas,*" Alistair murmured, about to run out of French phrases.

"Most people who are out at this hour are up to no good," Clegg went on, gazing at him thoughtfully. *Including you,* Alistair thought. "I wouldn't be doing my duty if I didn't make certain you were on the up-and-up. Hold out your hands."

"*Pardon?*"

"Your hands, man!" Clegg said impatiently, thrusting his own hands out in demonstration. They were thick, hamlike hands, the nails lined with filth.

83

Alistair immediately offered his hands. They were equally grimy from his sojourn over the rooftops, grimy enough to disguise his lack of calluses in the darkness of the night.

"You're not a weaver," Clegg said, more to himself. "You haven't got the hands for it. What do you do, live off your womenfolk?" The notion seemed to amuse him.

"Je suis un voleur," Alistair murmured sweetly. *"Je suis le Chat."*

"Voleur, eh? What the hell is that?" Clegg demanded. "Let me give you a warning, my friend. This is my territory. Clegg's, you understand? If you haven't heard of me by now, you should have. I'm a dangerous man. You have any interesting little sidelines, then you pay me to let you be. If you don't, you get hauled in before the Justice, and he doesn't like Frenchies any more than he likes criminals. I'm a little more broad-minded, if you get my drift. I'm willing to look the other way this time." His thick London accent was deceptively affable. "That is, if you'll tell me what you were doing sniffing around that house back there. I have a personal interest in the young lady there. You think you're going to crawl between her legs and you'll find you don't have anything to put there. You've a pretty face and she probably likes it well enough, but I've got her staked out for me. You understand?"

Alistair looked at him blankly, seething.

"Half-wit," Clegg said to himself. "Just keep away from them. You understand that much, don't you? I need to keep the older sister on my side for the time being, but when I'm through with her, I'm going after the young one. And I won't take kindly to anyone who's been there ahead of me."

"Bâtard," Alistair murmured politely, backing away from him.

"Yeah, *bâtard* to you too," Clegg muttered, dismissing him. "Just remember she's mine, Frenchy."

Alistair had never killed a man. He knew how to use pistols and a sword, he'd even fought the requisite number of polite duels. Usually he preferred to use his wits and his cunning, not brute force. But looking at Clegg, he found himself filled with a sudden longing to smash the man's teeth down his throat.

"Get out of here," Clegg said irritably. "Your idiot face is beginning to annoy me."

"Baisez mon cul," he said, bowing low. And before Clegg could decide to come closer, he disappeared into the shadows of the dark London night.

"But, my dear Jessamine, I had no idea you possessed such talents! You've been hiding your light under a bushel."

Jessamine stared at Miss Ermintrude Winters's pale, puglike face with ill-concealed dismay. She would have been much happier if she had been able to hide her entire self under a bushel. At least Mama was still abed, suffering from the megrims and a surfeit of ratafia, and wasn't there to witness the reentry of one of Jessamine's childhood acquaintances into their lives.

Ermintrude had never been more than that. She had always been an unpleasant child, holding herself aloof from the ramshackle Maitlands. Mr. Maitland's descent into poverty and death had set the seal on her disapproval, and the last time Jessamine had crossed her path, Ermintrude had given her the cut direct.

Not today, however. Ermintrude was all fat smiles and oozing charm, murmuring remembrances of a shared past which, in truth, they hadn't shared at all. To be sure, they had both attended the Christmas routs at Lady Andrews's estate. But Ermintrude had been with her group, Jessamine with hers.

"They say you have an extraordinary gift," Ermintrude continued. "I can't say that I'm surprised. You always seemed a bit different from the rest of us. It must be those lovely eyes."

Jessamine kept a pleasant expression on her face as she listened to these bald-faced lies. Ermintrude must have learned tact during the last few years. She had always made cutting comments about Jessamine's witch's eyes.

Jessamine herself wasn't feeling particularly diplomatic. "Who says I have an extraordinary gift?"

Ermintrude blinked. "Why, everyone. Everyone that matters, that is. You're quite the *on-dit* of society. Everyone wants you at their parties, everyone is dying to know more about you."

"Including you?" Jessamine said coolly.

Ermintrude may have learned tact, but sensitivity still eluded her. "I thought you might like to come to a small house-party my married sister is holding out in Kent. I'm certain you remember Sally — she married Mr. Blaine, who was quite a catch, as I'm sure you realize. There will be just a dozen or so guests, and it should all be quite gay. I imagine it's been quite a while since you've been in the country. You were always such a charmingly rural soul."

"Quite a while," Jessamine echoed. "But I'm afraid I must decline your so-charming invitation. My mother isn't at all well, and I couldn't leave my sister without adequate protection."

"Surely the servants could look after your mother," Ermintrude protested, patently ignoring the fact that she had seen no sign of servants during her damnably long visit that afternoon. "And you could bring your little sister with you. I remember her well — such a pretty child. I'm certain we'll find other children to entertain her."

Jessamine looked at her childhood nemesis. "Let us be frank, Ermintrude. You are not inviting me to your sister's house party for the pleasure of my company. You wish me to entertain the guests with parlor tricks, do you not? Reading their cards, telling their fortunes?"

"It's no less than you have done for Lady Plumworthy, if rumor can be relied upon."

"Let me give you a little hint, Ermintrude. Never believe rumors. How I choose to use my talents and for what rewards is simply none of your business."

"My sister said I was to offer you fifty pounds."

Jessamine didn't even blink. Ermintrude's sister Sally had married a nabob, and she'd obviously lost track of things she could spend her money on. Fifty pounds was a very great deal of money. Almost tempting.

"I'm sorry," Jessamine said. "I have my reputation to consider. As well as my sister's."

"One hundred pounds, and you and your sister shall be honored guests," Ermintrude said hastily.

"I doubt your other guests will view us as such."

"Don't be so starchy, Jessamine," Ermintrude said in an irritable voice that sounded much more natural than her forced amiability. "Your lineage is impeccable, even if your father was a wastrel. Lack of money, while to be deplored, shouldn't put you beyond the pale. Besides, there will be any number of eligible partis. You're a great deal older than I am, but you're not necessarily at your last prayers. If you were lucky, you could manage to attract a gentleman of independent means and secure your future. Perhaps an elderly widower."

Ermintrude was exactly two months younger than Jessamine's twenty-three years, but Jess was tactful enough not to mention that fact. The offer, fraught as it was with disaster, held too many possibilities to be dismissed out of hand. At the rate she was going, it would be another year before Fleur could make her debut. A year of living on the edge of squalor, a year of isolation and potential danger. A year where anything could happen, where temptation would be fatal. She needed to make her escape, to settle her family and then fade into graceful retirement, away from Clegg, away from the city. Far away from the disturbing Earl of Glenshiel.

"What do you say?" Ermintrude persisted.

Jessamine closed her eyes for a moment, letting her mind run free, open, seeking. The card that formed in front of her mind's eye was immediate and gratifying. The Nine of Cups. It would be well.

She opened her eyes to survey her erstwhile acquaintance's avid face. "Fleur and I will accept your gracious invitation," she said smoothly. "It's been too long since we've had the pleasure of a house party in the country. And we will be more than happy to add what small entertainment we can offer. Fleur has quite a gift with her paints, and I have no aversion to a playful reading of the cards to while away the time."

"A wise choice," Ermintrude said. "My sister's banker will draw you a draft on her account —"

"No," Jessamine said. "We will come only if this is a social invitation, between friends, and not a financial transaction."

"You don't receive money for what you do?" Ermintrude asked bluntly.

To admit that she did would put her on the level of dressmakers and shopkeepers. To lie would be even worse. "I do what I deem necessary, Ermintrude," she said sweetly. "Your companionship and hospitality will be ample reward."

Ermintrude looked as if she'd rather be a companion to a snake, but she pursed her plump lips into a sour smile. "I imagine you'll need transportation. My sister would be more than happy to send her carriage for you on Wednesday next. . . ."

"That would be lovely."

Ermintrude glanced down at Jessamine's plain, outmoded

dress. "I trust you'll be better dressed?"

Typical of Ermintrude, Jessamine thought wearily. Once she'd gotten her way, her overbearing nature came forth. In response she simply smiled. "I'm looking forward to the house party, Ermy."

Ermintrude hated being called Ermy. Particularly since her obnoxious boy cousins had always referred to her as Ermy-Wormy. Up until then Jessamine had resisted the impulse to use the nickname, but there was something in Ermintrude's smug blue eyes that brought out the worst in her.

Ermintrude rose majestically. "And you needn't worry about highwaymen and the like. My sister has made special arrangements for the Bow Street runners to provide protection. The Cat himself wouldn't dare make an appearance!"

"The Cat?" Jess echoed with perfect innocence.

"Oh, that's right, you've been out of society for so long, you probably haven't even heard of him. He's a most daring and remorseless thief. He steals his way into the finest houses in the city and relieves the owners of their jewels. Sometimes he commits his wicked deeds when the houses are deserted, sometimes he has the effrontery to rob when the house is ablaze with a party. No one quite knows how he does it. He's as sneaky and silent as a cat." Ermintrude's small eyes narrowed in sudden suspicion. "I thought you were at Lady Plumworthy's when one such a robbery occurred?" she said sharply.

"Perhaps I was. No one bothered to inform me of it," she lied blithely.

"I should think not. It could hardly be your concern," Ermintrude said with a sniff. She rose and bestowed a gracious kiss on the unwilling Jessamine. "If there's a problem with your wardrobe, let me know and I'll see if I can contrive something. I wouldn't want you to shame my sister."

Jessamine stumbled, treading sharply on Ermintrude's instep, then fell back. "I beg your pardon, Ermy," she said with breathless innocence. "I am so clumsy on occasion."

Ermintrude allowed herself the luxury of a glare. "Till next week."

Jessamine nodded and proceeded to accompany Miss Winters to the door. "I can't imagine where the servants could have gone to," she said vaguely.

Ermintrude cast a suspicious look around the place. If she suspected the impoverished Maitlands couldn't afford so much as a daily maid, her horror would be complete, and the social offer might be rescinded.

Ermintrude's carriage waited outside the Maitlands' front door, the liveried coachman guarding it from the curious denizens of Spitalfields. Jessamine stood in the open doorway until it pulled away, then slowly shut the door and leaned against it.

She had probably made a very grave mistake. Her plans were well and carefully made: once she amassed a certain amount of money from her work with the despised Clegg, she could afford to move to better quarters and manage a small, discreet launch into society for her beloved Fleur. Once she contracted a reasonable marriage, the future would be assured. Jessamine had learned to make do on very little indeed. Fleur didn't need to attract a Croesus — any decently landed gentleman with a kind soul would do.

But this was dangerous indeed. There was no guarantee that any eligible parti would be present at Sally Blaine's house party, and if the Maitland sisters appeared and then disappeared, questions would be asked.

She would have to take some of the carefully hoarded money and make new clothes for Fleur, not to mention something decent and discreet for herself. Her mother still had her extensive wardrobe, however, and there might very well be gowns that could be modified, modernized, cut down to fit Jessamine's slighter figure.

It would also make her identity clear. The Gypsy fortune-teller would be unmasked, and certain sticklers might not approve of such a creature for a sister-in-law.

Still, it was a risk she had to take. Josiah Clegg was beginning to frighten her. She'd always been uneasy around him, though she'd lessened her misgivings by assuring herself she was helping the almost lost cause of law and order in the wretched streets of London.

But lately she could no longer believe that, or believe that Clegg cared one whit for justice. He wanted his thief-taker's share, and it didn't matter to him if it came from the neck of a hardened criminal or an innocent child.

She could help him this one last time. She could enable him to ensnare the notorious Cat, and then she could call it quits. A criminal of such daring would doubtless be worth a generous portion. She could even eschew her own share of it if Clegg would relinquish his hold on her.

It seemed reasonable enough, and yet she knew it wasn't. The answer lay in her cards, and she was afraid to read them. Afraid to ask the questions that would place her in an impossible situation.

The Cat was the least of her worries, she reminded herself firmly. The elegant Earl of Glenshiel was similarly only a troubling distraction. With any luck he had already forgotten her very existence, and if she just managed to avoid crossing paths with him, she would be fine.

It was her family that worried her. She needed to get Fleur safely and wealthily wed to a decent man who'd accept his responsibilities, including a difficult mother-in-law.

And then Jessamine would be safe. The house party, despite its dangers, could provide the start of a new, more acceptable life for all of them. It was a chance she had to take. And even if it all came to naught, and they came away from the house party further impoverished with their reputations questionable, she couldn't regret the chance to get out of the stink and filth of London.

But she couldn't help but wonder if the Earl of Glenshiel was one of Sally Blaine's invited guests.

It had been a simple enough matter, in the end, for Alistair to secure an invitation. While he had no particular interest in traveling down to Sevenoaks for a house party of unremarkable men and women who would doubtless game poorly and indulge in tedious flirtations, the presence of Miss Jessamine Maitland and her younger sister would go a great way toward making up for any inconvenience. He didn't have to thank a lucky providence for coming by that information — the ever-useful Nicodemus Bottom imparted that juicy tidbit in the dark hours before dawn, along with other, more dubious warnings.

"You ought to keep away from her, yer worship," he said, pocketing Lady Barbara's rubies. "You'll have nothing to fear from her exposing you to Clegg, at least not for the next week or so. She'll be safely in the country, doing the pretty with the other nobs."

"I hardly think she suspects me of nefarious doings," Alistair said lazily.

"She's a sharp one. Clegg wouldn't be using her if she wasn't, and you know it. If you keep sniffing after her, she'll see right through you. Have a care. You're the best thing that's happened to my pockets in years — I'd hate to see you take a dance at the end of a rope."

"Do they hang peers?" Alistair murmured, unmoved at the prospect.

"They'd hang you, me boy, have no doubt of it. And that

92

girl would have a hand in doing so."

"Then I think it behooves me to throw her off the scent, don't you think? Besides, I'm in the mood to rusticate. A week in the country sounds like just the thing. And Kent is so conveniently close to London."

Nicodemus stared at him suspiciously. "What's going on in that fiendish mind of yours, yer honor?"

"That nothing would please me more than to spend some time with Miss Maitland in a social situation. And if, during my period of rustication, the Cat chooses to strike again in the heart of the city, then it would surely absolve me of any culpability."

"And how will you manage that?" Bottom demanded suspiciously.

"With a fast horse and a great deal of daring, my dear Nicodemus. Do you think I can't carry it off?"

"I think you're too wild for my good," he said gloomily. "Have a care. Clegg wants you badly."

"Fortunately he has no idea it's me he wants."

"Not unless Miss Maitland manages to put two and two together."

"In which case I'll simply have to take steps to make sure she doesn't divulge her prowess in sums," Alistair said gently.

"I can make the arrangements," Nicodemus said unhappily. "It wouldn't cost much, and the body would never be found. It's not the kind of work I like to take care of, but . . ."

"I don't want to kill her, my dear fellow," Alistair said. "There are much easier ways to silence a woman."

"Yes, but you have to keep her silent."

"Trust me. Miss Jessamine Maitland is the least of our worries. With a little energy and invention I intend to enchant her with my charms and convince her there's no way on earth I could be a notorious felon. And if Clegg has been relying on

93

information she's given him, then he too will be convinced."

"For the time being," Nicodemus grumbled.

"Nothing lasts forever. I can't see myself as a fifty-year-old burglar, climbing over walls. We'll end with a final, triumphant theft, something so extraordinary that everything afterward would seem unbearably tepid."

"I can't imagine it, yer lordship."

Alistair smiled, his eyes half closed as visions of jewel-encrusted gold glowed in his mind.

"I can," he said softly.

Eight

When Jessamine Maitland looked out the window on that gray November day, it was all she could do to ignore the air of foreboding that settled down over her.

"Do you suppose we'll be riding in a crested carriage?" Fleur asked, peering out the window beside her.

Jessamine allowed herself a maternal glance at her younger sister. There was very little money left now — almost everything had gone into Fleur's new wardrobe. There was enough to keep the small household for a few weeks, enough to pay for a maid-companion to keep the reclusive Mrs. Maitland company while her daughters enjoyed a visit in the country. But when they returned, if Fleur was still unattached, their situation would be dire indeed.

If worse came to worst, Josiah Clegg would be waiting.

"I can't imagine why we should. Ermy's sister didn't marry anyone with a title," Jessamine replied, smoothing the gray silk of her altered dress with a nervous hand. It had been one of her mother's, and it had taken the dressmaker's best efforts to transform the large, stately gown into something resembling a young woman's dress à la mode. Her efforts hadn't been an entire success. To be sure, at least Jessamine's breasts weren't crushed flat beneath a too-tight bodice. But with the drab color, high neck, and modest skirts, she looked like a boring governess.

It was just as well — it made her a perfect foil for Fleur.

They'd managed to afford three new day dresses of flowered silk, two evening dresses, and a new bonnet. Their finances hadn't lent themselves to a riding habit, but Fleur cheerfully announced that she'd simply say she didn't ride. And if an occasion called for a different sort of clothing, she would plead a headache and retire to her room.

Jessamine peered back into the rainy morning. "I didn't think you cared about crested carriages," she said, trying to shake off the peculiar edgy feeling that assailed her. She hated premonitions. Her gift with the cards was a gift and a burden, enough to fill her life. The odd feelings that sometimes crept in were almost more than she could bear.

"I've decided I ought to enjoy the finer things in life, since I intend to marry them."

There was a faint troubling note beneath Fleur's carefree voice, though when Jessamine turned, Fleur flashed her a dazzling smile. "You don't have to," Jessamine said soberly.

"If I don't want to spend the rest of my life in Spitalfields, I do," Fleur said cheerfully. "Besides, didn't Marilla always tell me it was just as easy to love a rich man as a poor man? I'm a practical creature — I intend to fall in love with a very wealthy man with all due haste. Making certain, of course, that he's equally enamored of me."

Jessamine managed a faint smile. "That sounds most convenient. I can only hope fate decides to cooperate." She turned her gaze back into the dark London street as a carriage pulled up in front of the house.

"We have a week to make it happen, Jess," Fleur said with a confidence that was almost believable.

"I believe our carriage is here, Fleur." Jess pulled away from the window. "We should —" She stopped, perplexed. "Who in heaven's name is that man?"

Fleur peered out the window beside her, then drew back in

sudden shock. "I — I don't know," she stammered, her face pale.

Fleur had no talent for lying. She seldom even attempted it, particularly with Jessamine, and it made the failure all the more apparent. Jessamine didn't say a word, she simply looked hard at her younger sister for a moment. "Then we'd best see who it is," she said calmly enough as a firm rap was sounded on the front door.

"You do it," Fleur said breathlessly, racing for the narrow stairs. "I'm going to see that Mama has everything she needs before her companion arrives."

She disappeared up the stairs in a flurry of skirts before Jess could utter a protest. The knock sounded again, firm but not peremptory, and Jessamine moved to open it, steeling herself for what she might find.

The tall, loose-limbed man who stood there looked vaguely familiar, though she couldn't quite remember where she might have seen him. He was quietly dressed in plain dark clothes, he held his hat in his hand, and his hair tumbled above his clean, rumpled collar. "Miss Maitland?"

It was a northern accent, a country one, that conjured up memories of hay fields and horses and bright hot sunshine. But the man in front of her had the city in his eyes. "Yes?"

"I'm here to escort you to Blaine Manor. My name's Brennan. Robert Brennan."

He hardly seemed the type to socialize with Ermintrude, but he was, on closer examination, an extremely handsome man in a rough-hewn sort of way. She'd seldom seen such clear blue eyes. "Are you one of the guests, Mr. Brennan?" she asked.

"No, miss. I'm a Bow Street runner. Hired for the occasion, to provide protection for the guests."

She couldn't control her little start of shock, but she hoped he wasn't sharp-eyed enough to notice her discomfort. "Are the wilds of Kent that dangerous, Mr. Brennan, that we need a bodyguard?" she asked lightly.

"Not likely, miss. Most of the highwaymen in the area are an incompetent lot, and they're unlikely to be out and about in such nasty weather. Mrs. Blaine is concerned about thieves. In particular, the Cat."

"Then why did she invite him, Mr. Brennan?" she asked innocently.

She expected annoyance. Instead, a gleam of amusement lightened his clear blue eyes, and the faintest trace of a smile tilted his mouth. "If anyone knew who the Cat was, Miss Maitland, then he wouldn't be free to accept invitations and continue his thieving." He glanced around the empty hallway. "Where's your sister?"

Jessamine didn't need the cards in front of her to see the truth. Indeed, Fleur's sudden appearance at the top of the stairs, the narrowing of Brennan's eyes as he caught sight of her, told her far more than she particularly wanted to know.

"I'm here," Fleur said breathlessly, descending the stairs.

"This is Mr. Robert Brennan. My sister, Fleur Maitland. Mr. Brennan is a Bow Street runner who's been hired to protect Mrs. Blaine's house party from stray felons. We're lucky enough to have his protection for our trip to Kent."

She watched as her sister lifted her clear, lovely eyes to meet the solid blue ones of the man who towered over her. "Miss Fleur," he said politely, seemingly impervious to her astonishing beauty. If he really had no reaction to it, he would be the first man to prove resistant. "Miss Maitland, I realize this is an imposition. If you would rather, I could ride outside with the coachman."

"Oh, no, Mr. Brennan," Fleur broke in, breathless. "It's a wretched day, and Jess and I would be glad for your company. Wouldn't we, Jess?"

98

Jess would have been entirely glad for Robert Brennan to have fallen into the Thames and stayed there, but she said nothing, summoning a faint smile as she felt her world and her plans begin to crumble around her. "Of course, Mr. Brennan," she said. "We would have it no other way."

Brennan was a very large man indeed. When he climbed in opposite the two sisters, the carriage seemed unbearably crowded. The huge man sat across from them, his greatcoat damp with cold rain, his untrimmed hair sodden. Jessamine wondered if there was any way she could change her mind about this ill-advised journey. It was too late to turn her ankle climbing up into the carriage — perhaps a sudden convincing indisposition . . . ?

The carriage started with a jerk, flinging them back against the thinly cushioned squabs, and the die was cast. She glanced over at Fleur, horrified to see the faint, hopeful smile that flitted around her perfect mouth. At least Brennan seemed impervious to Fleur's perfection. His expression was bland, polite, everything that it should be. And yet Jessamine didn't believe it.

He settled his large body into a corner of the carriage, obviously trying to make himself inconspicuous. A goal that was doomed to failure, given the sheer size of him. It took Jessamine a moment to realize that he wasn't going to intrude on them, wasn't going to speak unless spoken to, and she knew she should breathe a sigh of relief.

But she'd been in Spitalfields too long, and Robert Brennan, for all that he represented a greater threat to their future than Clegg himself, reminded her of decent people and the countryside, two things she missed very dearly, and she couldn't bring herself to snub him as she knew she should.

"Have you lived in London long, Mr. Brennan?" she murmured with all the manners Marilla had drummed into her.

Brennan smiled, and Jessamine could have cursed herself. The man was attractive enough in a rough sort of way when he was looking stern. When he smiled, even Jessamine could feel an answering warmth. As for Fleur, she was sitting in her own corner, peeking at him, obviously besotted.

"How could tha' tell I'm nought from around these parts, miss?" he said, letting his Yorkshire accent broaden even further. "After twelve years in this city I would have thought I'd sound like a native."

"I doubt you'll ever sound like a Cockney, Mr. Brennan," Jessamine said.

"It was foolishness that brought me here," said Brennan wryly. "A boy's desire to do good and make a difference. When you're nineteen you don't realize you can do just as much good on your father's farm by Robin Hood Bay as you can chasing criminals in London."

"Your parents were farmers?"

"Aye," Brennan said. "They had their own land, and a place big enough to support a growing family. But I was too wise to realize how little I knew. As for my parents, I expect they thought I'd be dead in a matter of weeks. But here I am, twelve years later, hale and hearty."

"Don't you miss the countryside, Mr. Brennan?" Fleur asked in her soft voice, her eyes not quite meeting his. "I know I do. I would give anything to return."

"Aye, I miss it," he said, and Jessamine realized with a sinking feeling that he couldn't bring himself to look directly at her sister either. But he'd had no trouble whatsoever meeting her gaze. "I'll go back, I expect, sooner or later. Once I finish what I've set out to do."

"And what's that, Mr. Brennan?" Fleur asked softly.

"No *Mister*, lass," he said, looking somewhere past Fleur's shoulder. "Just Brennan will suit me fine."

100

"Do you plan to rid London of crime before your return to your bucolic existence?" Jessamine murmured.

"Hardly, miss," he said with a wry grimace. "I'd be here till doomsday. No, I've set myself a task, and once I've completed that, I'm free to leave. I want to catch the Cat himself. Once he's brought to justice, I'll return to Yorkshire. Find myself a good country lass to marry and raise children." He deliberately looked away from Fleur. "A simple life but a good one, that's all I ask."

"Well, then," Jessamine said in a deceptively quiet voice, "we'll simply have to hope you find your master thief as quickly as possible. Won't we, Fleur?"

"Of course," Fleur murmured instantly, her voice lacking the ring of enthusiasm.

A trail of alarm danced down Jessamine's backbone. The danger was all around, but her first thought, as always, was to protect her family, and the rest could sort itself out. "And we'll do our best to help you, Mr. Brennan," she added generously. She would deal with Clegg when the time came.

Fleur was staring at her, openmouthed in shock. "But, Jess, what about. . . . ?" Her voice trailed off before Jessamine's fiercely silencing glare.

"I'd be most grateful, miss, though I can't imagine how you'd be able to help. I mean to catch him, and I'm not about to let anyone stand in my way. Not the Cat himself, not his accomplices, not the people he's bribed or the thief-takers who want him themselves. I'll catch him in the act, present him to Sir Robert, and turn in my pikestaff and pistol for boots and a pitchfork."

"I used to love it when they harvested the corn near our house," Fleur said soulfully.

"That's not all you use a pitchfork for, miss," Brennan said wryly. "There's nothing to love about manure."

101

"Not so, Mr. Brennan. You'd have a poor crop without it," she shot back.

"True enough, miss. You might make a farmer after all."

The words fell into the carriage with shocking force. "I don't think that's what my sister aspires to," Jessamine said in a deceptively calm voice.

Again there was that easy, polite smile. "I wouldn't think so, Miss Maitland. When she marries a wealthy landowner, she'll have more understanding for the tenants though."

Jess relaxed slightly — only slightly. "And what about you, Mr. Brennan? Will you be able to look back on your time in London with pride? Knowing you kept the city safe from twelve-year-old felons?" She couldn't keep the faint hint of acid from her voice. Robert Brennan seemed a far cry from the odious Josiah Clegg, but if she had learned one thing over the last few difficult years, it was that looks could be deceiving, and she would be a fool to trust anyone.

"No, miss," he said. "But I'll feel right pleased when the Cat comes to the end he deserves. Dancing at the end of Tyburn's rope."

Alistair was not in a dancing mood at that particular moment. It was a dank, miserable day, he was up before noon, and he was soundly regretting his rash decision to spend the next week in company with an entirely odious bunch of brainless matrons and their docile spouses. He had to have been mad to come up with this latest notion. For all Miss Jessamine Maitland's bizarre attractions, she was surely not worth the trouble he was setting himself. He could always blame it on his inability to resist a challenge. She'd set herself up as a woman who could see past masks and charades, who looked into her cards and divined the truth. If she had any talent at all, she clearly hadn't bothered to ask the cards about him. He wanted to see how far he could push her. Whether she would stay oblivious, or whether she really had some supernatural talent beneath those witch's eyes?

And he wanted to bed her quite desperately. Desperation was not an emotion he was used to entertaining.

He didn't like to think himself ruled by his passions. The fact that he had a strong desire to tumble Miss Maitland of the mysterious eyes was nothing to worry about; the fact that he was willing to go to such lengths to do so was decidedly unsettling. He could tell himself her presence at this dratted house party was the least of his concerns, but he made it a point of honor never to lie to himself.

At least Freddie Arbuthnot would accompany him on the rain-soaked journey, and they could while away the trip with a few hands of cards. Of course, he'd have to let Freddie win enough to continue gaming, but subterfuge was hardly beyond Alistair's capabilities. As long as Freddie didn't go on too much about his intended's dubious virtues.

It wasn't as if Freddie were truly enamored of the very wealthy Miss Ermintrude Winters. He was madly in love with her sixty thousand pounds a year, however, and by extolling her attractions, he obviously hoped to convince himself of the felicity of his hoped-for union. This house party was to put the seal on his ongoing courtship — Ermintrude's father had looked upon his suit with favor, and the exacting heiress seemed to consider Freddie's witless charm appealing.

Which would leave Alistair free to pursue Jessamine. Whether he would simply endeavor to convince her of his guileless innocence, or seduce her into not caring, was a question still to be decided. The second tack was preferable, but fraught with danger. And Alistair knew himself well enough to realize it was the danger that appealed almost as greatly as Miss Maitland herself.

103

There was a damp chill in the small, elegant house, brought on by the rain and the fact that he'd dismissed his servants for the week, knowing he'd be gone. It reminded him of his childhood. The drafty halls of Glenshiel Abbey, the damp loneliness of the east wing with only his tutor for company. A sudden sweep of pain rushed over him, and he shivered, clenching his hands so tightly they broke the delicate chicken-skin fan he used for comic effect. At the moment he didn't feel particularly comic.

The anger that flared up deep inside him was almost painful. He wasn't ready to consider where that anger came from, but he knew where he could direct it. Toward the busybody, entrancing Miss Maitland, who would deserve the very thorough seduction she was about to receive. And would, in her dotage, look back upon the memory with fond pleasure.

He seldom spent his time seducing virtuous young women, but he had little doubt he could accomplish the task. Particularly since she'd shown herself such an apt pupil when he'd kissed her in Isolde Plumworthy's parlor. The memory, the taste of that kiss, immediately made him hard, and he found his anger had fled, replaced with a wry smile. The thought of Miss Maitland continued to have that decidedly adolescent effect on his anatomy. If he didn't take pains to render himself resistant, the house party could prove quite an embarrassment.

"Halloo? Anyone home?" Freddie called from the hallway. He spied Alistair through the gloom. "What in God's name are you doing, moping around in the darkness, Alistair? It's not like you. Where are the servants?"

Alistair donned his indolent charm like a discarded cloak, crossing the dark room into the pool of light. "They've abandoned me, Freddie," he murmured. "You're late."

"Demme, it's an indecent hour," Freddie protested. "I don't

see why we can't drive at a leisurely pace, stop along the way, and arrive there tomorrow."

"You'd best get used to the parson's mousetrap, Freddie. If you want all of Miss Winters's lovely money to play with, you're going to have to let her call the tune. And she wants you there today."

Freddie snorted, obviously not sure the heiress's tidy portion was worth an early rising. "Well, let's not stand about discussing it. If we have to go at such a godforsaken hour, let's be off." He looked suddenly abashed. "Beg pardon, Alistair. I forgot you were doing this for me. It was demmed kind of you to offer to keep me company. Not quite sure of Ermintrude yet, and I could use your support."

Alistair smiled faintly, forebearing to mention the irresistible presence of Jessamine Maitland. Not that Freddie would have the faintest idea that Alistair would be interested. She was hardly Alistair's usual sort of inamorata. "Glad to be of assistance, Freddie," he said. "Besides, I could use a little rustication."

Freddie, never a lover of rural pleasures, looked even more gloomy. "Quite so," he said under his breath. "And if Ermintrude turns down my suit, we could always leave early." He looked marginally more cheerful at the notion.

"Leaving you with Lady Elizabeth Marshall as your only other marital possibility," Alistair pointed out.

Freddie shuddered. The sour and portly Lady Elizabeth made Ermintrude Winters appear to be a diamond of the first water. "Kent isn't that countrified," he said hopefully. "She'll have me, won't she, Alistair?"

"She'd be a fool not to," he said gently. Freddie was an exceedingly feckless, foolish young man, in many ways reminding Alistair of his brother. So far Freddie had resisted the lure of heavy drinking, but his gaming was already dangerously deep, and he needed a wife to settle him, a rich wife to keep him, and a horde of noisy children to distract him.

If only everyone's life could be so easily settled, Alistair thought grimly, none of his thoughts showing in his cool, detached expression. "The sooner you come up to scratch, Freddie, the sooner you can cease worrying," he pointed out. "Shall we to Kent?"

"To Kent!" Freddie said, reaching for enthusiasm but falling sadly short.

"To Kent," Alistair murmured. "And all the pleasures that there await us."

Nine

The weather didn't improve during the seemingly endless trip to Sevenoaks. Fleur was fortunate enough to fall asleep, Robert Brennan leaned back and closed his eyes, but Jessamine wasn't fooled. In his own way, he was as alert as Josiah Clegg. Perhaps that was a necessity for thief-takers. It made sense — if you were ever alert, no one could sneak up behind you.

The poorly sprung carriage went over a bump, and Jessamine found herself tossed against the thin cushions with a resounding thump. Fleur slept on, the sleep of the innocent, but Brennan opened his eyes.

"It was kind of Mrs. Blaine to send us the coach," he observed pleasantly in a voice pitched low so as not to wake her sister.

Jess looked around her. It was, in truth, a horrid coach, made for transporting servants and poor relations. The squabs were thin, and the wind and rain blasted through the windows. Either Sally Blaine was less well-to-do than Ermintrude had suggested, or the coach was a deliberate snub. Jessamine had the melancholy suspicion it was the latter, and her dread of the upcoming visit grew.

"Very kind," she said absently, stroking the cheap material.

Silence filled the carriage once more, broken only by the sound of their breathing and the clop of the horses in the heavy rain. For a moment Jessamine thought she too might sleep, until Robert Brennan cleared his throat.

107

"I'm a man who prefers plain speaking, miss," he said calmly enough. "And you're a lady who's more observant than most. I'd say you've guessed that your sister and I were previously acquainted."

It was only a slight knot in her stomach, Jessamine thought, keeping a calm expression on her face. She'd survive. "I suspected as much," she replied, surreptitiously putting a hand on her stomach.

"I wouldn't want you to get the wrong impression," he continued in a soft voice as Fleur slept on. "I know my place, Miss Maitland. You needn't fear anything from me."

She looked at him steadily. "What is your place, Mr. Brennan?"

"I'm a thief-taker, Miss Maitland. Born a farmer, and I'll die a farmer, but in the middle I've spent a few years seeing things you couldn't even imagine. Your sister is a lady. She'll marry well and have a good life, and I wish her the best."

"Mr. Brennan —" she began, uncertain what to say.

"Pay me no mind, Miss Maitland. I just didn't want you to worry about something that will never, ever happen. I'm from another world, and I know that. I was sent to keep you and others safe. And you are safe, miss. Have no fear of that."

She looked into his strong, calm face. He was a good man, far more worthy than a thousand Cleggs put together. More decent than the undoubtedly decadent Earl of Glenshiel, kinder than anyone she'd met in years.

"Mr. Brennan," she said gently, "I hope and pray my sister marries a wealthy, titled gentleman who is exactly like you."

He smiled at her kindly. "I do too, miss."

Their arrival at Blaine Manor confirmed Jessamine's worst fears. Sally Blaine's coachman deposited them at a side entrance, with no covering from the heavy rain. They found their way into a dank, ill-lit hallway, only to be met by a sour-looking woman who could only be the housekeeper.

She looked at the rain-bedraggled trio and sniffed. "You there," she said to Brennan. "One of the footmen will show you to the kitchen. Your colleagues are there, eating up cook's best tea cakes." Her disapproving gaze slid over Jessamine and her sister, and instinctively Jess put her arm around Fleur, feeling her faint shiver. "I'll show you to your room." There was no missing the grudging tone in her voice.

Jessamine steeled herself. "And where is Mrs. Blaine? I should like to greet my hostess."

"She's busy with her guests," the woman said shortly, making it abundantly clear that that category did not include the Maitlands. "She'll see you when she has time. Follow me." She started up a narrow flight of stairs.

Jessamine managed a soothing smile for her sister as she tucked her arm through hers. "Don't worry, Fleur," she said softly, "I'll sort everything out. In the meantime, I think we want to get out of our wet clothes, don't we?"

"Yes, Jess," Fleur said. She glanced back toward Brennan, who stood waiting in the hallway, a troubled expression on his face. "Thank you for your company, Mr. Brennan," she said in her soft, lovely voice.

"My pleasure, miss," he said stolidly.

"Come along!" The voice that floated from down the narrow stairs sounded more like a schoolmarm's than a housekeeper's. With a fleeting smile in Brennan's direction, the two sisters began to climb the narrow stairs.

By that time Jessamine had lost most of her illusions, so it came as no surprise to find the chilly, uncarpeted hallway stretching out before them.

The woman was standing outside one plain, dark door. "I'm Mrs. Jolly," she informed them, and it was all Jessamine could do to keep a straight face at the ill-fitting name. "Housekeeper to Mrs. Blaine. My room's right down the hall from this one, and I'll thank you not to disturb me. I work hard and I need my rest." Her mean eyes narrowed. "Where are your bags?"

"In the hallway," Jess said serenely. "Waiting for a servant to bring them up."

"Saucy," Mrs. Jolly muttered under her breath.

"And we'll need hot baths, and someone to help us unpack," Jessamine continued smoothly, determined not to be cowed.

The housekeeper pushed open the door, exposing a small, cold room with one narrow bed, a washstand, and not much else. There were no hangings on the window, and the bedlinen lay folded neatly on the bare mattress. "I wouldn't be counting on it, miss. This is a busy household this week — we don't have time for any extra work." She started away from them, but to Jess's surprise, Fleur spoke up, her soft voice firm.

"And when shall we be joining Mrs. Blaine?"

"That's up to her. You'll be having dinner brought to your room for the time being. You'll be informed when you're needed." Without another word she left them, sodden, angry, standing in the drafty hallway.

"I suspect," Fleur said quietly, "that I'm not about to meet my future husband this week."

"I'm going to kill Ermintrude Winters," Jessamine said fiercely. "I'm going to strangle her with my bare hands, and then I'm going to strangle her sister as well."

"I'd really prefer you didn't, darling," Fleur said in a weak attempt at humor. "I wouldn't want Mr. Brennan to arrest you."

"It would be quite convenient for him," Jessamine replied. "The culprit would be caught red-handed, and there wouldn't even be a need for a chase."

"But I wouldn't like it. I was awake, you know, when you were talking about me."

"I suspected as much," Jessamine said. "You aren't very good at fooling me. Do you have any . . . feelings for Mr. Brennan?"

"Feelings?" Fleur echoed with an airy laugh, stepping into the small, dank room. "Don't be ridiculous, Jess."

"He's very handsome in a rough-hewn sort of way," Jessamine offered, closing the door behind them.

"Is he? I hadn't noticed. I'm grateful for his company, as I'm sure you are. And I have the morbid suspicion that he's going to be the last friendly face we see all week. Nevertheless, he's not of our world," she said firmly. "And apart from gratitude, I have no feelings for him whatsoever."

It was a flat-out, bald-faced lie, but Jessamine made the wise decision not to call her on it. She looked around the pitiful little bedroom. "I doubt his world can be that far removed from our current circumstances," she said gloomily, dropping down on the bed. The mattress was thin and hard and gave off a peculiar odor. "I'm sorry I brought you here, Fleur. Sorry I got you full of hopes."

Fleur sank down beside her and put her arm around Jessamine's waist. "It's not your fault, Jess," she said fiercely. "Couldn't we just leave? Say we were called back to London by our ailing mother?"

"They would know we'd received no such message. And if this is any example of Sally Blaine's hospitality, I imagine we'd be lucky to catch a ride in the back of a farmer's wagon."

"You know," Fleur confessed, "I've always wanted to ride in a farmer's wagon. When I was little I wanted to be a farmer's wife."

And Jessamine, who thought her spirits couldn't sink any lower, burst into tears.

The Cat was on the prowl. Not that Alistair had the slightest intention of helping himself to any of Sally Blaine's tawdry jewels. For one thing, they were not only hideous, but second rate, the gemstones flawed and poorly hued. For another, it would have set his plan awry. He had come to this wretched little house party with the sole intention of diverting any possible suspicion away from himself.

He merely liked to know the lay of the land, so to speak, in case he was called upon to make a quick escape.

And, he had to admit, it wasn't quite his sole purpose. He was still awaiting, with growing impatience, the arrival of Jessamine Maitland. He had every intention of whiling away his time flirting with her, of stripping her of her doubts, her wariness, her inhibitions, and her clothing in short order. He couldn't remember when he'd last wanted a woman so badly, and her very lack of pretension to matchless beauty seemed only to fire him more.

In the meantime, though, he was restless and irritable. Sally Blaine's guests had nothing to talk of but horses and hunting, subjects that grew stale quickly. Freddie was doing his damnedest to fix his interest with Ermintrude Winters, a task that filled Alistair with sympathetic horror, and his hostess herself had a tendency to place her hand on his knee when her husband was oblivious, which seemed to be most of the time.

If things grew any more tedious, he was tempted to say the hell with it and make his way back to London no matter how Nicodemus Bottom would scold him. Tyburn Tree was preferable to boredom any day.

Blaine Manor was singularly lacking in challenge. It was an ell-shaped building, the public and family rooms in the main section of the house, including his own ornate bedchamber, the kitchens and servants' quarters in the ell. He'd already managed to delve through all the main bedrooms, and the narrow, dimly lit back quarters were small, depressing, and unoccupied. Or at least, most of them were. He could hear the murmur of voices behind one narrow door, and he was ready to beat a hasty retreat, armed with an ingenuous smile and the excuse that he'd gotten lost, when the door opened into the hallway and a vision stepped out, closing it carefully behind her.

Actually, *vision* wasn't quite the word. Jessamine Maitland looked like a drowned rat. Her hair drooped around her pale face, her plain dark dress was sodden, though he could see that it clung quite nicely to her breasts. Her eyes were red from weeping, and for the moment she didn't realize that he stood there, watching her. When she looked up and spied him, her expression was one of such horror that it was comical.

"Oh, God," she cried, and he wasn't sure if it was a curse or a cry for help. "It only needed this!"

"This, I gather, is me?" he replied, moving closer. It was a very narrow hallway, and there was no way she could pass him. She could only turn around and run.

"What are you doing here?" she demanded in tones of deepest loathing.

"Here as in what am I doing outside what I presume is your bedroom, or here as in Blaine Manor?"

"Both." She no longer looked so woebegone, despite the general dampness of her appearance. There was color in her cheeks and a snap in her iridescent eyes, and Alistair realized with distant amusement that he was physically aroused just by her proximity.

"Why don't you answer my question first. Who's in that room? Your lover?" The notion, once entertained, was decidedly unpleasant.

"Don't be insulting. My sister. And keep your voice down,"

she added in an angry hiss, ignoring the fact that her own tone had been charmingly strident. "We've had a long journey and she's just fallen asleep. I don't want you to wake her up."

"I wouldn't think of it," he said in a soft, low voice like a cat's purr. "But why is she in a servant's room?"

"Clearly because Sally Blaine considers us to be servants," Jessamine said bitterly. She glanced up at him, backing away slightly. It didn't take much effort to follow her. "Stop looking at me like that," she said in an angry undertone.

"Like what?" he murmured, wondering which part of her body he'd touch first. He wanted to put his mouth against the damp material that covered her breast. He wanted to put his mouth between her legs.

"Like I was a sweetmeat and you a starving man," she snapped.

"You have it about right," he said. "Though I liked your cat-and-mouse analogy even better."

"I suppose I'm not certain whether you want to eat me or kill me," she shot back.

"So innocent," he murmured. "I want to eat you, Miss Maitland. I want to put my mouth all over your body."

She backed away from him, startled, some of her annoyance replaced by wariness. He followed her. The hall was dark and deserted, and it had been too long since he'd touched her. "My lord . . ." she began to say in a tight, furious voice.

"Call me Alistair," he said. "You remember what we did the last time we met?"

"I remember you insulted me gravely," she shot back, edging away.

"Prepare yourself, Jessamine," he whispered. "I'm about to insult you again."

He was unprepared for her slap. It was no gentle tap — the force of her blow was impressive, whipping his head back. She looked absolutely horrified at what she had done, and she stared at her hand as if it were an alien part of her body.

"I beg your pardon," she stammered. "I didn't mean . . ."

"Don't apologize. You meant to do just that. You'll probably hit me again. After I kiss you."

This time he didn't give her the opportunity to slap him. He simply pulled her against him, pinning her arms with his, and set his mouth against hers.

She didn't struggle, but he couldn't congratulate himself on winning her over. She was still too astonished at herself for hitting him to realize that he was, as usual, taking advantage. By the time her disordered senses could reassert themselves, he'd already managed to strip them away again simply by pulling her tightly against him and using his mouth.

She was bemused enough to open her mouth to him without protest. She was cold, shivering slightly, and the dampness of her clothing plastered against his made him want to shiver as well.

She didn't kiss him back, but then, she hadn't the other time. She simply stood in his arms, as if enduring the insult, and he wondered how many other kisses she'd suffered. How many other gropings in a dark hallway.

The notion was disturbing enough that he released her, and she leaned back against the wall, staring up at him. Her mouth was damp and reddened from his, and he expected to see cool hatred in her eyes.

Ah, but he'd forgotten her eyes. Bewitching, they stared up at him with reluctant longing and confusion, and it was all he could do not to push her up against the wall and pull up her full, damp skirts.

"Come to my room," he said, his voice husky. "You're cold and damp. Let me warm you up."

"No, thank you, my lord." She was jarringly polite despite

those vibrant eyes. "If you'll let me pass, I'll see to finding our baggage."

"The servants should be bringing them up."

"I've been informed by the housekeeper that servants don't wait on servants," she said stiffly.

He just looked at her. "Go back to your sister," he said.

"As you pointed out, I'm damp and cold, and so is she. There's no fire in our room, and I really don't fancy either of us getting pneumonia. We have no money for a doctor. Oh, I beg your pardon — we're not supposed to mention anything as crass as money," she said bitterly.

"You'd best make your escape while I'm still inclined to let you. Go back to your room," he said again, keeping his volatile temper under control. "Or I'll take you to mine."

She was wise enough not to call his bluff. He'd gone through a bewildering torrent of . . . he wouldn't call them emotions, but reactions seemed a less-threatening word. Annoyance, irritation, outrage, grudging admiration. All underlaid with the worst case of lust he'd suffered since he'd first lost his virginity with a randy dairy maid.

Maybe this even outdid his passion for the buxom Rose. It took him a moment to realize Jessamine had disappeared back into her room, closing the door tightly behind her. He almost changed his mind and went after her, when he remembered the annoying presence of a sister.

First things first. He went in search of his hostess.

Fleur opened her eyes drowsily. "Did you find our baggage?" she murmured.

"Not yet, sweeting. Go back to sleep."

The room was dark, and Jessamine leaned against the door, grateful for the protection of the shadows. She had no idea what she looked like, but she had little doubt it would be

116

damning. Just as she could see through her sister's weak attempts at subterfuge, so could Fleur see to Jessamine's troubled heart.

Not that her heart had anything to do with it, she reminded herself fiercely, scrubbing at her mouth with the back of her hand. Despite the upheaval of the last few years, she was still a relative innocent. She had witnessed things, known things, seen things in the cards that horrified and astounded and yes, even fascinated her, but she hadn't *done* any of those things, and she never would. Had never wanted to — until he put his hands on her.

In truth, it was a good thing they were segregated from the other guests. While it would surely prevent Fleur from forming a suitable attachment, it would also keep Jessamine away from Glenshiel.

And what if he should happen to spy Fleur? He seemed positively enamored of her own dubious attractions. When presented with a diamond of the first water like Fleur, there might be no stopping him.

And how could Fleur resist such a wicked, beautiful, dangerous gentleman? Jessamine was made of much sterner stuff, and yet even she ended up odiously helpless in her response to him.

Fleur would be ruined, and Jessamine wasn't about to let that happen. The fast-fading plans for a secure future were the least of her worries. He would break Fleur's gentle heart, and that Jessamine would not allow.

Her own heart and spirit were made of sturdier material. She could survive anything. Her sister was far more vulnerable.

She glanced over at Fleur's sleeping form. So delicate, so lovely, and so very sweet. It was that sweetness of nature Jessamine envied far more than her celestial beauty. Fleur would never have slapped that man's elegant, beautiful face so hard that the outline of her hand was imprinted on his skin. Fleur would have shamed him with her goodness.

There was one rickety chair in the dismal room, and Jessamine sank down on it, hearing its ominous creak with true dismay.

It was going to be a truly wretched week, and she had no one to blame but herself.

118

Ten

It was going to be a truly splendid week, Alistair MacAlpin thought as he bestowed his most Machiavellian smile upon his shallow hostess.

"Really, Lord Glenshiel?" Sally fluttered. "The Maitlands . . . ?"

"I'm so looking forward to seeing them again," he continued smoothly. "Few people were aware of the fact that my father stood as godparent to the two of them, and my late brother's attachment to Miss Maitland hadn't been made public before his untimely death, but I still consider them to be family."

Sally turned bright pink. "Your brother was engaged to Jessamine Maitland?" she said with a little shriek of astonishment.

A lie was a lie, and a convenient tool to be used when needed, but for some reason Alistair was loath to let his brother have any claim on Jessamine, fictional or otherwise, even in death. "No, Miss Fleur Maitland."

Sally looked even more horrified. "She could have been no more than sixteen when your brother died!"

"It was a family arrangement," he said smoothly. He was almost as adept a liar as he was a thief, a talent that provided him with a wry amusement. "We were waiting until she left the schoolroom before we announced it."

"How very sad," Sally said, placing a sympathetic hand above his knee and kneading slightly. She had thin, grasping fingers, and each time she touched him, her fingertips climbed higher. He'd resigned himself to the fact that sooner or later he'd have to bed her, a prospect he had viewed with lazy acceptance. However, one look at the bedraggled Jessamine Maitland and his mild enthusiasm for his hostess had vanished.

"You're extremely fortunate they've agreed to come to you for your party. Miss Jessamine is in great demand, you realize. Her rare combination of breeding and esoteric abilities make her much sought after."

"Er . . . yes," Sally muttered.

"I believe she's even been consulted by the royal family." He wondered if he had gone overboard, but Sally drank it up like a scraggly kitten at a bowl of milk.

She rose abruptly. "We're very lucky indeed to have such a distinguished guest," she said breathlessly. "As a matter of fact, I'd best make sure they'll be comfortably settled when they arrive." She disappeared in a flurry of puce skirts, heading toward her unpleasant sister. Whatever she whispered in her ear was not well received, and Alistair tried to summon up an ounce of pity for Freddie Arbuthnot, sitting obediently by her side. Freddie cast him a look of glazed despair, and Alistair simply shrugged, leaning back against the fussy, overstuffed chair, a faint smile playing around his mouth.

In fact, he was prepared to enjoy himself immensely.

It was going to be a hellish week, Robert Brennan thought miserably, looking across the scrubbed kitchen table at his two compatriots. Samuel Welch was a wiry little man, neither worse nor better than most of Sir John's men. Brennan had tipped a few with him, and found him congenial enough company, if a bit too willing to take a bribe. He was busy crowing about the ease and pleasure of their current assignment, guarding a bunch of nobs and enjoying themselves without having to exert the slightest bit of energy. Welch was no more ambitious than most of his type, and if he'd be lacking his thief-taker's share during the next week, at least he'd live better than he'd ever expected to.

It was the third man at the table who gave Brennan pause. He was busy flirting with one of the housemaids, his swarthily handsome face creased in a reassuring smile, his gold front tooth glinting in the firelight. He must have felt Brennan's thoughtful gaze on him, for he turned back to look at him, his eyes narrowing.

"Enjoying yourself, Brennan?" Josiah Clegg demanded, draining his mug of ale. "Or do you prefer life out on the streets, catching criminals?"

"I prefer to be where I'm needed," Brennan said.

"Such a little schoolboy. But no, you're a farm boy, ain't you?" he said. "Did you like your ride here? Got to cuddle up with two ladies. One of them's right pretty, I hear."

"I know my place, Josiah," he said.

"I know my place as well," Clegg said with a wheezy laugh. "And it's underneath Miss Fleur's skirts. . . ."

Brennan didn't launch himself across the table and wrap his huge hands around Clegg's throat, much as he longed to. He didn't allow even the slightest change of expression to mar his cool demeanor. Clegg would use any weakness he could find in his enemies, and to Clegg, all men were enemies, particularly those in competition for the same thief-taker's share.

"I'm with Sammy here," Clegg continued. "I intend to live well while I have the chance. When we get back, it'll be time enough for me to catch the Cat. In the meantime, let him prowl all he wants. His days are numbered."

"What makes you think you'll be the one to catch the Cat, Josiah?" Welch demanded. "With that price on him, you've got some strong competition. I for one intend to be the man to

121

catch him. I 'spect Brennan does as well."

Josiah's smile would have been positively beatific if it weren't for the cunning in his small eyes. "Intend all you want, boys. The Cat's mine, and nothing and no one is going to stand in my way of a thousand pounds."

"I thought it was five hundred?" Welch murmured. "For a thousand pounds I'd turn in me own father."

"If you happened to know who he was," Josiah replied. "Don't get in my way, Sammy. I'll cut your throat if you try." And he smiled pleasantly, the gold tooth flashing.

Brennan didn't move, his razor-sharp memory taunting him. It had been years earlier, before Sammy Welch's time. A Bow Street runner on the trail of notorious Flash Robbins had been found in bed with a whore, his throat slashed. The whore was dead as well, and no one had seen anything suspicious. And two days later Clegg had run Robbins to ground and collected the moiety on him.

It had been a curious coincidence, one that had troubled Brennan. He'd been drinking with Martin, the hapless runner, the evening before he was killed, and Martin had boasted that he'd set a trap for Robbins that no one could possibly escape.

But it had been Clegg who'd sprung the trap. And Martin who'd been buried in a pauper's grave a few days before Flash Robbins followed him.

"Good with a knife, are you?" Brennan asked casually, reaching for his own mug of beer.

"Fair to middling," Clegg replied with heretofore unobserved modesty. "But I wouldn't hurt my old friend Sammy. I was just joking, is all. We're brothers, the three of us. Comrades in arms."

"Brothers," Brennan said, keeping the irony out of his voice.

It was going to be a hellish week.

122

* * * * *

"I don't understand how such a dreadful mistake could have been made," Sally Winters, now Sally Blaine, was saying as she tucked a confiding arm through Jessamine's. "I gave strict orders to Mrs. Jolly that you and your sister were to share the blue and gold room. It's the most elegant room in the house, usually reserved for visiting dignitaries, but it's been so long since we've had a chance to have a comfortable coze that I thought you deserved to be pampered. I was in alt when Ermintrude told me you'd agree to come to our little party, and I cannot think how such a misunderstanding could have come about. I'm much distressed."

Jessamine had spent the last two years of her life in circumstances that would have curled Sally's artfully arranged hair. She had no doubt whatsoever how they'd come to be put in such a wretched little room, and Ermintrude's sour expression as she accompanied them to their new rooms was a far more honest testimonial than Sally's flutterings. What puzzled Jessamine was the fact that Sally had obviously thought better of her shabby treatment.

"Don't give it a thought," Jessamine said sweetly, casting a cursory glance around their new rooms. Four times the size of the little cul-de-sac they'd originally been allotted, the room was ornate to the point of garishness. Marriage hadn't improved Sally Blaine's taste. "I'm certain we'll be extremely comfortable here."

Sally's smile slipped for a moment, and she glanced around the room with anxious pride. "We do hope you'll be refreshed enough to join us for dinner. My guests are most eager to meet you — I've told them all about my dear childhood friends."

I'm certain you have, Jessamine thought coolly. For some reason their value had increased dramatically, and she had no idea why.

123

"We have all sorts of entertaining people," Sally chattered on brainlessly. "Mr. Arbuthnot has come, and the Earl of Glenshiel as well, though I suppose you know that. Such a tragic history, poor man, losing his brother like that. He manages to bear up so well."

"His brother died?" Jessamine murmured.

"But of course you know that as well, since your sister was engaged to the poor man. If only he'd been able to control his fatal addiction to gaming and drink. Fortunately milord Glenshiel seems far more temperate."

Temperate was the last word Jessamine would have used for Glenshiel, and Sally's light prattle made no sense whatsoever. "Indeed," she murmured helplessly.

"Such a sad case. When Alistair arrived in London, people were quite fearful he might harbor a grudge. Not that there was any cause, of course. No one put the glass in James's hand. No one forced him to game away most of the family resources. But Alistair has proven to be the most charming of companions, if not precisely marriage material. Not that you would be thinking of such a thing, dear Jessamine. You've always had a delightfully pragmatic view of your circumstances."

"Indeed," Jessamine said again, inwardly seething.

"So I know you won't mind if I monopolize his lordship, considering your connection with him is so distant."

"Practically nonexistent," Jessamine said through gritted teeth.

Sally bestowed a condescending kiss on Jessamine's stony cheek. "I knew you were a sensible girl. We'll see you shortly."

"We'll look forward to it," she said, dismissing her hostess with a cool air. Sally practically raced her way out of the room, Ermintrude beside her, making no effort at graciousness.

"What do you suppose that was all about?" Jessamine murmured, staring at the closed door.

124

"I don't care!" Fleur replied, tossing herself on the huge bed. "Perhaps it was simply a mistake."

"I wouldn't count on it if I were you. Sally had every intention of treating us like upper servants, until something, or someone, happened to change her mind. Someone told her a pack of outrageous lies, and it doesn't take much to guess who that person was. The Earl of Glenshiel. And if he's nursing a broken heart due to a family tragedy, I'd be very much astonished."

"Why worry?" Fleur said, flinging herself back amid the billowy coverings. "At least we're going to get the week we hoped for. Let that suffice for the time being."

"I suppose I should," Jessamine said uneasily.

"You worry too much, Jess. You'll get wrinkles."

"Better me than you."

"For the worry? Or the wrinkles?" Fleur shot back.

"Both," Jess said firmly. "I'm used to worrying, and we're not counting on my face to save the family fortune."

It was only the faintest shadow darkening Fleur's beautiful eyes. A moment later it was gone, as if it never existed. "Have no fear, Jess. If there's a wealthy prospective suitor, I'll have him eating out of my hand in a matter of days. I just need to practice my feminine wiles."

"You don't have any," Jess said flatly. "And you don't need any. Just be your sweet self, and you'll enchant anyone who sees you."

"There speaks a doting older sister," Fleur said wryly.

"Who always knows best."

Jessamine's sanguine mood lasted a remarkably long time. It survived a dinner that was only slightly better than her worst nightmare. She was ensconced between an elderly bachelor who dribbled food on his lavender satin waistcoat and a long-married squire whose conversation seemed limited to hunting

125

and port. Fleur was sitting dangerously close to the Earl of Glenshiel, but for some reason he seemed impervious to her remarkable beauty. Almost every man in the room seemed enchanted by her younger sister, Jessamine thought with gratification, except Alistair MacAlpin. He seemed far more interested in watching *her*.

It was covert enough, which was small comfort. She doubted if anyone else at the huge expanse of table would have noticed. But there was no way she could avoid it — every time she glanced up she could feel his cool gaze on her.

After dinner wasn't a great improvement — while they were spared the presence of the gentlemen, who lingered over the squire's beloved port, most of the young ladies and hopeful mothers viewed Fleur and her sister with justifiable hostility.

Fleur took her leave early, pleading exhaustion, and Jessamine wished she could do the same. But she knew perfectly well why they'd been invited, and if Sally had suddenly chosen to be gracious, that warmth could vanish just as abruptly as it had appeared.

At least Glenshiel came nowhere near her. He was in the room once more, watching, but for some reason he had no interest in her card readings. He was probably as skeptical of her abilities as most of the gentlemen, a fact that disturbed her not in the slightest. It was easy enough to read the cards for the women who surrounded her, now friendly with avid curiosity. Their futures were serene; they were all satisfied with the same thing.

In fact, Jessamine was feeling as serene as the rest of them when she made her way back toward the bedroom she shared with Fleur. There was no servant to light her way, so she held the candelabrum herself, catching up her full skirts with her other hand as she climbed the broad staircase. She saw the shadow out of the corner of her eye, but not for a moment did she consider her danger. Glenshiel had been ensconced in a cozy tête-à-tête with Sally Blaine, seemingly unaware of her departure.

She smelled the thick odor of garlic and beer, covered imperfectly with mint, and a moment later the candelabrum was dashed from her hand, plunging the stairs into darkness, the only light coming from the candles in the hall above.

A hand clamped over her mouth before she could scream, and a thick body shoved her against the marble banister. She let herself go limp, waiting for a chance to fight back. She was more than a match for any randy gentleman — her time in Spitalfields had taught her how to keep herself safe — but the voice that whispered hoarsely in her ear stripped away all her furious determination.

"All alone, my dear?" Josiah Clegg whispered in her ear. "Where's the pretty little sister of yours, mmm? Gone off with one of those rich boys? Or has she gone sniffing after Brennan? He's got a soft spot for her, I can see it in his eyes no matter how hard he tries to hide it. Maybe she likes it rough and tumble as well. I can oblige her far better than a man like Brennan."

"What are you doing here?" she demanded in a fierce whisper when he removed his hand from her mouth. "And take your hands off me!"

"Ah, now, miss, I wouldn't be so fast with my orders if I were you. How do you think your fine, aristocratic friends would like to hear you've been helping the likes of me? Think you'd still be considered fit company, or would they send you down to the kitchens with Brennan and me? That may be where Brennan belongs, if it's not in a sty, but Josiah Clegg is made for better things in this world."

"Take your hands off me," she said again, standing cold and still within his grasp. "I don't give a damn about your threats, and if you ever expect me to read the cards for you

127

again, you'll go away and leave me alone."

"I dunno, miss," he said, his gold tooth flashing in the dim light. "You haven't helped me find the Cat, and I'm beginning to doubt what you've told me before. It might just be coincidence, and I've no fancy to share my moiety with a down-on-her-luck *lady*." He said the word like a foul curse. "Maybe we'll just call off our little arrangement."

She yanked herself free from him, but she had no illusions that she could have done so if he hadn't been willing to let her go. "That sounds perfectly agreeable to me, Mr. Clegg."

"And that way I can see whether your sister has any of your talent."

"No!" She lunged after him as he started up the stairs.

"No, miss? Then why don't we stop all this foolishness? You give me what I want, and I'll leave your sister alone. But I'm tired of waiting."

"Waiting for what?"

"I want the Cat, miss. And you're the only one who can find him for me. I'm tired of waiting, and making sure no one else gets the jump on me. I wouldn't take it kindly if someone like Brennan were to nab him first. You know that, don't you, miss?"

She stared at him dully, feeling the trap close around her as surely as it would close around the Cat. Not that he mattered — whoever he was, he was one felon who deserved Clegg's tender mercies. "I know that," she said. "Do you want me to come back to London?"

"No need for that, miss. I have my informants, and word has come to me that the Cat is going to make his appearance at this very house party. You don't suppose a man of my reputation and standing would agree to this sort of work if there wasn't good reason? He's going to try for one last theft, and I'll be waiting for him."

"You and Brennan."

"No, miss. No one's getting in my way. I'll see to that, and I suspect you know me well enough to believe I'll do just that. When the Cat arrives by the dark of moon, he'll find he's made a fatal mistake."

"What if he's already here?" The moment the words popped out of her mouth she could have kicked herself. She had no idea where such a thought came from; she knew only that Clegg was far too dangerous a man to volunteer information to.

"What do you mean?" His eyes narrowed. "You've seen something in those bloody cards of yours? You know who he is?"

She shook her head. "I don't know anything," she said with perfect truthfulness. "I just wondered. It's been rumored he's a gentleman, else how could he simply wander throughout the great houses of London picking up jewels?"

"You'll find out for me, won't you, my sweet?" Clegg cooed in a repulsive voice. "I know you're here to read the cards for these toffs, same as you do for me. You read them for each gentleman and tell me what you find."

"It's not usually the gentlemen who will sit for a reading. They deem it claptrap."

"Ah, but you and I know different, don't we, miss?" Clegg's gold tooth flashed. "You wheedle them, and if that fails, get your sister to work on them. Can't imagine anyone saying no to that pretty sister of yours."

"Keep away from her!"

"Certainly, miss. As long as you give me what I want, I'll leave her strictly alone."

"What about Brennan?"

"Oh, he won't go anywhere near her if I know Robert Brennan. He has a code of honor, he does. One of his many flaws."

"One you're not troubled with," Jessamine said in an acid voice faint with fear.

"That's one thing I have in common with the Cat. You find him for me, miss, or you'll be sorry the day you met me."

"I already am."

Clegg's unholy grin was complacent. "Most people are. It don't bother me none. I likes people to be afraid of me. It makes 'em do what I want. I'm getting a mite bit impatient. You meet me and tell me what you've discovered, and maybe your job will be over."

"And what if he isn't already here?"

"Then that just makes things a bit more complicated, doesn't it? But I'm counting on you and your witching cards, miss. If he isn't here, you'll figure out when and how he's coming, won't you? For your old friend Clegg?"

Jessamine eyed her old friend Clegg with unmitigated hatred. "Where and when do you want me to meet you?" she asked coldly.

"Never you fear, miss. I'll find you." And without another word he vanished into the shadowed hallway, leaving Jess standing alone, shivering in the sudden draft.

Eleven

The bedroom was empty. Jessamine slammed the door behind her, leaning against it, out of breath, panting, her heart pounding from her panicked dash down the hallway. Where in God's name had Fleur gotten to? Was there more behind Clegg's veiled threats than she supposed?

She took a deep breath, trying to calm herself. He would scarcely have come after her, taunting her, and not mentioned that he had her sister stashed somewhere.

But where was she? Surely she knew better than to wander around without proper protection. Unless she was in search of a man who made protection his profession.

Jessamine pushed away from the door, shaking her head. Fleur wouldn't do that no matter how tempted. She knew the family was counting on her to make an advantageous match — she wouldn't throw away their only chance at security on a handsome Bow Street runner.

Perhaps she'd simply gone in search of something improving to read, or to eat. Perhaps she'd gone back to the gathering, feeling suddenly lonely.

Except that Jessamine would have run into her if she'd been heading toward any of the public areas of the house.

She sat down in the comfortable chair and leaned back, feeling the pain pound through her head. She was always like this: shaken, exhausted, full of megrims, after she'd done readings, even the shallow ones she'd offered that night. She needed

131

her sister's soothing hands on her temples, she needed a tisane. She didn't need to worry about Josiah Clegg's threats, or where exactly her young sister was at that very moment.

Ah, but when had life been kindly enough to cater to her needs, much less her wants? If she'd learned one thing over the last few years, it was that it was up to her. Everything. She couldn't count on fate or a fairy godmother or a deus ex machina to appear and solve her problems.

She needed to go in search of her sister immediately. Even if it meant running into Clegg again, even if it meant the far more dangerous risk of running into Glenshiel. She wasn't quite certain why that would be the more frightening of the options. Clegg was evil, Glenshiel was neither bad nor good. He simply was.

Maybe it was what they wanted. Clegg wanted money plain and simple, a need Jessamine could understand and anticipate.

Glenshiel, for some odd reason, seemed to want her. A far more dangerous proposition.

It made no difference — she had to go in search of Fleur. She couldn't leave her sister unprotected.

She would rise from this wickedly comfortable chair, ignore her headache, and find her. In just a moment. Just a brief moment while she closed her eyes and tried to banish the pain and exhaustion. Just a brief moment . . .

The pounding rain had stopped at last. It was late, and the temperature had dropped sharply. Fleur wrapped her shawl around her slight frame more tightly as she stepped onto the damp grass and took a deep breath of the cool night air.

Country air. She filled her lungs with it, tipping her head back to view the stars overhead. She seldom saw the stars in London. The wood smoke from a thousand fires filled the city air like a dark curtain, and the tightly packed houses of Spitalfields left little room to look for the stars. There was no way she could step out into the street after dark to peer upward — it would be to court death and disaster.

But out here, in the kitchen garden beyond the stone mass of Blaine Manor, she could stare out into the sky and listen to the night birds calling, sounds she hadn't heard in years. She could walk among the neat rows of cabbages and carrots, hear the distant mutter of the chickens, and feel at peace.

Jessamine would have a fit if she knew she was out here. Fleur could only hope she'd make it back to the room before her sister retired — there was no need for Jess to worry needlessly.

Indeed, Fleur had avoided the formal gardens on purpose, to make certain she wouldn't run into any of the other guests. To do so might be to invite importunities, and that would sour her chances for the marriage Jess was counting on.

She didn't want to marry any of the men cluttering up Sally's drawing room in their silks and satins, their snuffboxes and their dripping laces. They were either witless, like Freddie Arbuthnot, enamored of themselves, like the majority of the guests, or completely terrifying, like my lord Glenshiel.

She wasn't quite sure why he frightened her. He was drawlingly, mockingly polite, even charming. His clothes were elegant to the point of foppishness, and if one didn't look too closely, one would assume he was as harmless and shallow as the others.

But Fleur was used to looking more closely, with an artist's eye. And what she saw in the Earl of Glenshiel's catlike eyes frightened her.

She ought to warn Jessamine, though she doubted her sister would thank her. If anything, Jessamine would deny any interest in the enigmatic earl, a denial that would ring false to both of them.

She lifted her skirts, stepping carefully down the neatly

planted rows. There was a half-moon that night, providing a fitful illumination, and from the house she could hear the vibrant sound of laughter from the servants' hall.

Suddenly she felt cold, lonely, she who usually reveled in her solitude. She'd felt miserably out of place in the drawing room. To be sure, she'd manage to disguise it well enough so that not even her sister realized her discomfort. She'd smiled sweetly and made all the requisite replies to the incessantly inane conversations that abounded. She would spend her life making just such idle chatter. And she would always feel a stranger.

She didn't belong in the servants' hall either. If she went there, seeking companionship and warmth, the cheerful mood would vanish, and they would stare at her, silent and uneasy, unwelcoming.

But she knew who was back there among those friendly faces. Robert Brennan, Yorkshireman and thief-taker. Someone as foreign to a lady of her position as a Chinese. It didn't matter. She wanted him to smile at her, she wanted his warmth, when her future was doomed to cold politeness. She wanted his strength, his simplicity, his . . .

"You shouldn't be out here alone, lass."

She turned in shock, for a moment convinced she'd conjured him up out of her own longing. He towered over her, and the wind whipped his light, shaggy hair against his high forehead. His jacket was buttoned up tight against the chill night air, and the shadows obscured his expression, but she wasn't afraid.

"It's the countryside, Mr. Brennan," she said, taking another deep, appreciative breath. "Not London. There are no evil creatures ready to leap out of the shadows and do evil."

"That's where you're wrong, miss," he said sternly. "There's evil everywhere, country and city alike. Evil comes from people, not places."

She glanced around her. "Surely there's no evil out on such a beautiful night?"

Brennan glanced back at the house, but it was too dark to read his expression. "Evil's where you least expect it at times, miss. Come back to the house. You shouldn't be out here, and you shouldn't be alone with the likes of me."

"You're not going to tell me you're evil, are you, Mr. Brennan?" she asked in a breathless voice, half shocked at herself. She was almost flirting, and Robert Brennan didn't seem the type to take flirtation lightly. "If you do, I won't believe you."

"No, miss," he said slowly. "I'm not evil. But that doesn't mean I won't hurt you without wanting to. Without meaning to."

"How could you hurt me?" Her question was pitched low, and she could almost feel the longing that spread between them like a fierce, strong length of silk. She didn't know how she recognized it — she'd never felt longing before. But she did, for this man. And she had the melancholy suspicion that it wasn't a changeable thing with her, or the slightest bit fleeting.

He didn't answer her question. "Back to the house with you, miss. My job is to keep the guests safe, and you're not allowing me to see to it. I'd take it as a favor if you were to return to your room. Now."

There was a faint note of strain in his usually cool voice, and Fleur felt suddenly ashamed. She was such a child, imagining things, feelings, where none existed. He was simply doing his job, and she was making it more difficult for him.

"Of course," she said, taking an obedient step back toward the house, only to tread directly on a solid cabbage, twisting her ankle, sending her tumbling toward the ground. . . .

Directly into his arms. He'd moved so quickly, she wouldn't have imagined it possible, and she'd already put out her arms to catch her fall. Instead, she caught him, he caught her, pulling her into his arms against the dark worsted of his jacket.

He was hard, solid as a rock beneath the material, and his arms were impossibly strong as they held her. He was warm as well, heat beneath her chilled hands. For a moment neither of them moved — he simply held her body against him, her breasts pressed against the bright buttons of his coat, her hips against his, and she stared into his eyes breathlessly, waiting, she wasn't sure for what.

She'd never been held by a man, never wanted to be. She wanted this. She wanted him to put his firm, wide mouth against hers and kiss her. Kiss her to distraction.

"Lass," he whispered in despair, still holding her. "You'll be the ruin of me." And before his words had a chance to sink in, his mouth covered hers, his head blotting out the light.

His mouth was wet, hard, open over hers, pushing her lips apart as he used his tongue. He tasted of dark beer and white-hot longing, and Fleur was too shocked to do more than stand there, pressed tight against his body, as he used his mouth on hers.

In the first moment she wasn't sure if she liked it. This was no shy gentleman courting her. This was a man, a real man, kissing her as if she belonged to him. Within the second moment she banished her doubts and slid her arms around his waist, her hands tight on the thick wool of his jacket, holding on for fear she might tumble into the cabbages if he kept kissing her like that.

Her knees were weak, her heart was pounding, her . . . her breasts were tight and hot, and she couldn't breathe. She didn't care. She wanted to die then and there from the sheer raw pleasure of his mouth on hers, his tongue touching hers. She heard a noise, a faint, hungry noise, and knew with a shock that it came from her.

He moved his mouth from hers, dragging in a deep breath of air, and she felt the scrape of his new beard against the

136

softness of her cheek as he moved his lips against her jaw, down the side of her throat. She was trembling, her hands clinging so tightly to his coat, odd, silly tears of need filling her eyes as she swayed toward him, needing more, needing his strength, needing his power, needing his mouth and heaven only knew what else. . . .

And just as suddenly as he'd kissed her, he released her. She didn't fall back among the cabbages, though it was only by the grace of God her legs continued to hold her upright. He'd moved away from her, out of reach, and she could see the way his chest rose and fell in the frosty night as he struggled to control himself.

"Get back to the house, Miss Maitland," he said in a harsh voice.

"But . . ."

"You've no business interfering with the help. If you're looking for a quick tumble, I'm certain you'll find one with the gentry. You're a tasty morsel, and I don't deny I'm tempted, but it would be worth my job if anyone were to find I'd bedded one of the guests."

Fleur could feel the color rush into her face. She didn't move, absorbing the words like the cruel blows that they were, staring at the stranger. "Go back to the house, miss," he said again, cool and harsh. "If you're wanting some rough sport, why don't you ask her ladyship who she could suggest? I'm afraid I won't be available."

She didn't say a word. She could feel the icy wind ripping at her hair, stinging her eyes, burning them. Reddening her cheeks. It was the weather, not shame and despair.

"I'm sorry I disturbed you, Mr. Brennan," she said in a quiet, dignified voice. And then the effect was ruined by a choked sob, and she picked up her skirts and ran as fast as she could, away from him.

* * * * *

He watched her go down the rows of cabbages, veering away from the kitchens and heading toward the main section of the house, where she belonged. Brennan stood still in the moonlight, staring after her. He could still taste her sweetness on his mouth. He could hear the soft sound of longing she'd made in the back of her throat, he could still feel the warm pillow of her breasts as they pressed against his chest, her nipples hard from the cold. A moment later and he would have had his hand down her bodice, or up under her skirts, and there would have been no stopping him. For some mad, wild reason she wanted him as much as he wanted her, and she wouldn't have stopped him, despite the cold, despite the place and time. He would have taken her maidenhead in a bed of cabbage, and neither of them would have noticed.

"She's a randy bitch, isn't she?" Clegg strolled into sight, puffing on one of their host's cigarillos. "Why didn't you take her? She was begging for it."

Brennan stared at his enemy out of hooded eyes. "I like a challenge."

"Hell, we could have shared her. She wouldn't have said anything even if she didn't like it. Sometimes I think you're too picky, m'lad."

"I keep my distance from the quality," Brennan said, controlling his fury with well-practiced effort. "They're not worth the trouble they bring."

"The virgins aren't," Clegg agreed thoughtfully. "Stiff as a board usually, and then they cry until you give them something to cry for. Ah, but the high-class whores — they're something else."

"Out of my league," Brennan murmured.

"Well, if you're not interested in the little slut, mebbe I'll try my luck. If she's got a taste for the rough and ready, I'll be more than happy to oblige her. Always fancied her when I saw her around Spitalfields."

Brennan's hands clenched into fists, but he didn't so much as blink. Clegg was wanting a reaction from him, and anything he said would only make things worse. "Suit yourself," he said with a shrug. "You might think of waiting till she's back in London. No one gives a damn what happens to a girl in Spitalfields. Around here there are all sorts of gentlemen who might feel called upon to look out for her." He said it casually, in an offhand manner. He never made the mistake of under-estimating Clegg's intelligence.

Clegg grinned at him, that friendly man-to-man smile that always made Brennan's skin crawl. "Sure and you've got a point there, me lad. You certain you're not interested in crawling between her legs yourself?"

I won't kill him, Brennan swore to himself. *Not yet.*

"I told you, she's too much of a lady. Kisses like a cold fish. She's more trouble than she's worth."

"So you keep telling me," Clegg said. "I just wonder why I'm having such a difficult time believing you."

"Probably because you wouldn't believe your own mother if she told you the gospel truth," Brennan drawled lazily. "You believe what you want to, Josiah. I'm going back to my pint."

"And what was it that brought you out here on such a cold night? You sure you didn't set up a meeting with the girl during your drive to Kent?"

"With that dragon of a sister watching? Don't be daft, man. I looked outside and saw someone skulking about among the cabbages. We're here to find the Cat, remember. I figured I'd better check on it. What brought you out here?"

"Why, you, Robert. I'm not about to let you or Samuel get the drop on me. That moiety's mine, and I don't intend to share."

139

"Speaking of which, where is Welch?"

"Passed out. He won't be getting in my way. What about you, Robert? Will you be getting in my way?"

"I'll do my best, Josiah." And neither of them had any doubts as to Brennan's meaning.

Jessamine awoke with a start. She had no idea how long she'd dozed, and she cursed herself as she scrambled to her feet. The house was silent, and she could only presume that the other guests had eventually found their beds. All but Fleur.

The noises were faint as she made her way down the dimly lit hall. A muffled laugh from behind one door, a snore from another. And from still another, an odd, rhythmic creaking accompanied by a strange, gasping sound, as if someone were quite ill. For a moment she paused, concerned, wondering if she should ascertain whether someone was in trouble.

But her sister came first. If someone in that bedroom were having a fit, it would doubtless pass sooner or later. They could always ring for a servant. Besides, Jessamine realized belatedly, it was Ermintrude's bedroom. If she were to intrude, she would scarce be thanked for it.

Most of the candles were doused, but enough were left burning that Jessamine could find her way down the winding stairs. She wasn't quite certain where she was going — she had no idea where Fleur could have run off to.

She would check the obvious places first. The library. The music room, though Fleur's talents lay more in appreciating music than in creating it. If all else failed, she would make her way to the kitchen, where if she didn't find her sister, she still might very well find Robert Brennan, the one person who could help her.

That is, if he hadn't arranged an assignation with Fleur.

No, he wouldn't do such a thing, and neither would Fleur.

She trusted her sister, and she trusted her judgment. Robert Brennan was a good man, not the sort to debauch innocent young ladies.

The library was empty, the candles guttered. The music room was harder to find, and she almost discarded the notion. She came across it almost by accident — it was tucked into a corner near the stairs, as if no one in the house had much interest in the arts. The glass doors at the far end looked out over a broad expanse of lawn, and Jessamine crossed the moon-lit room, drawn by the cool silver light.

The door closed behind her with a quiet, definite thunk that echoed icily in Jessamine's heart. She could feel him move toward her silently, and she forced herself to stay still, to wait until the last minute to break for it. She wouldn't let Clegg put his hands on her again, she wouldn't. . . .

"Found your sister?" Alistair murmured in a soft voice.

Twelve

For a moment Jessamine thought she might have preferred Clegg. After all, she had already encountered him once that night, and managed her escape. But the Earl of Glenshiel was a different matter entirely.

He had an almost unearthly beauty in the silver moonlight. She'd done her best to avoid him earlier that evening, not even glancing in his direction, but now she had no choice. His hair was unpowdered, black, his face narrow and pale, and in the shifting shadows he seemed a creature of night, of extremes, of pale and dark, life and death. Extremes that he seemed to view with detached amusement. A card began to form in her mind, but she banished it in sudden fear. She didn't want to see his life, his cards, in her mind or anywhere else.

"How did you know I was looking for my sister?" She made her voice deliberately mundane. "Have you seen her?"

"What else would draw you out, alone and unprotected, at this hour of the night?" he murmured, venturing closer. His gracefulness unnerved her. She was used to men being big, rough, clumsy creatures. Glenshiel was none of that. He was tall, but with a lean, wiry strength very different from the brute force she was used to. His very elegance, his mocking airs and graces, were unlike anything she had ever known, and his movements were sleek and silent, stealthy, like a prideful cat.

It wasn't the first time she'd thought of him in terms of a cat, and she forced herself to look at him with new eyes, considering the unimaginable before discarding the notion. He couldn't possibly be the Cat. What in heaven's name would a peer of the realm be doing stealing jewels? The notion was patently absurd.

"Why should I worry about being alone and unprotected?" she countered. "This isn't a London street. There's no one in this house who wishes me ill. No one who could do me harm."

As he moved closer he disappeared into the shadows, his voice cool and disembodied. For some reason that seemed almost more intimate than facing him in the moonlit dark, and she turned back toward the silvered landscape, doing her best to ignore him.

"For someone who's been forced to rely on herself for so long, you're remarkably naive," he said softly. "I suspect you're in more danger here than you are in that depressing little house. First you have your hostess, who resents treating you as anything more than a servant and would most likely put you over the kitchens if she thought she could get away with it. Then there's the unpleasant Ermintrude, who's eaten up with jealousy over you and your sister. They're not dangerous per se, more of an irritation. But I'm certain you wouldn't be too happy to run afoul of Mr. Clegg."

Jessamine froze. "Mr. Clegg?" she echoed after a moment in a marvelous semblance of confusion. "I have no idea who you're talking about. Who's Mr. Clegg?"

"The Bow Street runner you've been assisting with your card readings. Not a wise choice on your part, by the way. His reputation is beyond unsavory. You would have been far better off working with someone like the thief-taker who accompanied you here. He seems possessed of slightly higher values."

"I don't number Bow Street runners among my acquaintance," she said, keeping her face turned out into the moonlight. "And I assure you, I haven't been reading the cards for

143

anyone outside polite society."

He was closer, though still in the shadows. "Really? Then perhaps you're conducting a liaison with him. I can't say much for your taste though."

She turned back to glare at him. He was close enough to touch her now, half in, half out of the shadows. "Don't be ridiculous. You know perfectly well that I'm not!" she snapped, turning away.

"Why should I know that?"

"Because you . . . er . . ." *Why in God's name had she ever brought the subject up?* She stiffened her resolve, refusing to be embarrassed. "Because whether I like it or not, you happen to be in a position to know that I am entirely unused to kisses."

She could feel his breath on the side of her neck, warm, sweet, smelling faintly of mint and brandy. "Dear child," he murmured, "one can conduct a most licentious affair without ever kissing anyone."

She made the mistake of turning again, but this time he was so close, she didn't have the option of turning back. She was effectively trapped between the glass doors and his lean, powerful body. She wondered if she could shove him out of the way. But that would necessitate putting her hands on him, and she had the illogical, melancholy suspicion that if she were to touch him, she would be far more likely to draw him close.

"I don't believe you," she said, knowing that to continue the discussion was dangerous, a small, secret part of her reveling in that danger. "What's the good of a liaison without kissing?"

She amused him. She could see it clearly in his fascinating eyes, and her annoyance should have put a dent in her obsession. It didn't.

He smiled. "Some people don't like to kiss," he said, letting his golden eyes shimmer down over her slender body.

"I can't imagine it," she said flatly.

"That's because you've only been well kissed," Alistair said without false modesty. "I'm very good at it when the spirit moves me. And there seems to be something about you that arouses my . . . er . . . spirit quite effectively."

She tried to back away from him, but the glass was up against her back, and there was nowhere she could run. "I have to find my sister," she said breathlessly.

"Your sister is perfectly safe. She's back in your bedroom, none the worse for her midnight walk in the gardens."

"Is that what she was doing?"

Alistair smiled. It was a singularly wicked smile promising all sorts of dangerous delights. "She was alone on the stairs, her clothing and hair were still in order, and while she'd been crying, she seemed reasonably intact."

"Crying?" Jessamine said, galvanized. "I must go to her." And without thinking she moved forward, expecting Glenshiel to move out of the way.

He didn't. She came flat up against his solid chest, and his arms came around her, loosely imprisoning, but she had no doubt she'd be hard put to escape. "No, you don't," he said. "She's safe and alone and she'll likely cry herself to sleep more easily without you fussing over her."

He was warm in the cool night air, dangerously so. His eyes glittered with malice and desire, and his mouth was too close. "Don't," she said in a small, soft voice that was damnably close to a plea.

"Don't?" he echoed, mocking. "Don't, kind sir! Pray, spare my maiden blushes. Unhand me, sirrah, or I'll — What is it exactly that you would do to stop me, Jessamine? Scream for help?"

"If I must," she said, standing very still in the lightly capturing circle of his arms.

"Ah, but you don't really want to." He dropped his voice

lower still. "I can see it in your eyes. You're as fascinated by me as I am by you."

"You have an inflated sense of self-worth," she shot back.

"You watch me," he said, pressing closer. "You watch me as I watch you, and you think about when I kissed you. And you wonder if I'm going to kiss you again."

She was having trouble controlling her breathing. "You're absolutely mad," she said.

"And you look at the other men, and you wonder whether you'd like their kisses as well," he continued. "You think that perhaps only my kisses will please you, and that thought terrifies you."

"Why should it do that?" she whispered.

"Because you know I'm a wicked, conscienceless rake who'll seduce you, take my pleasure of you, and then go on to other things, other women, when I grow bored."

Jessamine swallowed. "That seems about the truth of it. Or do you deny it?"

"I don't deny that I'm not cut out for faithfulness, loyalty, or any of those tedious noble virtues. But I could show you things that you never imagined existed. A riot of sensation no other man could ever show you."

"That's hardly an incentive," she said in a flat voice. "You're promising me a lifetime of disappointment after a few nights of enjoyable debauchery. I think I'd be far better off never knowing what I was missing."

"How paltry of you," he murmured.

"Sorry to disappoint you. You seem to have some image of me as a brave, adventurous soul. I'm actually quite ordinary, with ordinary wants and needs. I want to see my family settled, I want a quiet place in the country where I can live in relative solitude. I'm not the sort for wildness and passion."

"Are you not?" he said, a faint smile playing around his

146

mouth. "I could convince you otherwise."

"You would be doing me a grave disservice," she warned him.

"Do you think that would bear any weight with me?"

If only he'd release her. The longer he held her, the more she felt her stern resolve slipping away. It was all well and good to insist herself uninterested in the tawdry emotions of mankind. She truly thought she might be able to convince him if only she weren't feeling the press of his legs against her full skirts.

She just didn't think she'd be able to convince herself.

"Please," she said in a small, desperate voice that held a distressing quaver. "If you have any kindness or decency left within you, you'll release me."

He appeared to consider the notion for a moment, his head tipped to one side as he surveyed her out of half-closed eyes. And then he shook his head. "I'm afraid kindness and decency have long since fled, Jessamine," he said softly. "All that's left is mindless lust. A most diverting pastime, I assure you. Shall I demonstrate?"

"My lord . . ." she whispered, quite desperate.

"Alistair," he corrected her, his mouth hovering above hers like a hawk over a wounded sparrow.

"Please," she said.

"Yes. I do please." And he pulled her into his arms, settling her body against his as his mouth captured hers.

She meant to keep her eyes open, to keep her senses in order, but he was too practiced, too clever, and his lips against hers were damp, clinging, tasting her own in soft little bites that pulled and drew her, and her eyelids fluttered closed in the shadowy darkness as she opened her mouth for him.

His arms no longer imprisoned her — she clung to him of her own accord, and his hands were free, free to reach between

147

their bodies and cup her breast. She knew she should protest, pull her mouth away from his in outrage, but she couldn't. He mesmerized her, and she told herself she had no will of her own.

But it wasn't true. She had a very strong will. And her fierce will wanted Alistair MacAlpin's hands on her breasts.

His mouth slid along her jawline, hot and seeking. "Where did you get such a hideous dress?" he murmured. "You should wear silks and lace and diamonds. Or nothing at all."

Her wits seemed to have scattered. "It was my mother's," she murmured, lifting her jaw to give his mouth access to the sensitive line of her neck above the plain dress.

"Your mother has execrable taste," he said, and she could feel his hands tugging at the laces impatiently. "I want you out of it." And she could feel the material part as he tugged it down over her shoulders, and the coolness of the window behind her made her shiver in sudden fear as sanity struggled to return.

She wanted his mouth on hers. She wanted his hands on her breasts. She wanted him to strip her of her ugly clothes and cover her body with his beautiful one, but she knew such wants were wicked and mad. And profoundly dangerous. He would take everything from her, her innocence, her peace of mind . . . and her gift. And leave her empty and aching.

"Release me," she said in a raw voice.

He'd managed to pull her dress down her arms, exposing the top part of her breasts above the corset, and after a moment of silent perusal his eyes met hers. "No," he said.

He would take her, she knew it. He would do as he said he would, strip off her clothes and his and take her on the floor of his hostess's little-used music room with the silver-bright moon their witness, and she would revel in it. And she would risk everything, including her precious gift — for a rare pleasure that would break her heart and ruin her life.

She gave him no warning, simply shoved hard, propelling herself away from him and against the glass doors, which shattered with a loud crack.

For a moment she felt nothing, just coldness and pressure on her exposed back. And then heat and dampness as Alistair yanked her away, cursing underneath his breath.

"You don't have to court defenestration to get away from me," he muttered under his breath in a less passionate voice, turning her around so that she faced away from him. A perfect time to run, except that he held her shoulders in a painful grip that she couldn't wriggle out of. "You've scraped your back."

"You wouldn't let me go," she said, willing herself not to feel faint. She was made of stronger stuff than that, wasn't she? She was brave and bold and strong, wasn't she? To be sure, she'd never been terribly stalwart at the sight of blood, but surely this time she could face it with equanimity. Couldn't she?

He turned her back to face him before she could gather enough strength to make a break for it. "Sit down," he said irritably, "and I'll find something to bandage it."

She looked at him. He had blood on his hand. Her blood. "Of course," she said faintly. And sank to the floor in a graceless heap.

Alistair looked down at her for a moment. He should have known she was about to faint — her color, even in the moonlight, had been ashen. With a resigned sigh he scooped her up, careful to avoid getting her blood on the pale blue satin of his coat. She was heavier than he would have expected, but still no particular burden. He was stronger than most, and he managed to lift her limp body into his arms with only reasonable effort.

She was more rounded than he'd realized, a fact that pleased

149

him. He had every intention of discovering just how rounded she was, and he was going to taste those curves, luxuriate in them — once he managed to wake her up and bandage the scrape along her back.

He'd already investigated the house thoroughly. It was a simple enough matter to make his way back to his own rooms, carrying his burden, with no one watching. He kicked the door shut silently behind him, then laid her facedown on the wide bed. She didn't move, and he had no doubt she was still unconscious. Once she regained her senses she'd be off again, probably screaming bloody murder.

He stripped off his jacket and waistcoat, tossing them aside, and rolled up the lacy sleeves of his shirt. It was simple enough to finish unfastening the back of her plain dress, and if the scrape wasn't still bleeding, he would have concentrated on the laces of her corset. As it was, he fetched a damp towel and carefully washed her back. The scrape wasn't deep but it needed bandaging. And he found himself wondering whether she'd still be able to lie on her back when he made love to her.

She looked utterly delicious lying on the soft feather bed, and he wanted to mount her, take her, and bite her neck as he did it. She brought out a savagely erotic streak that astonished him, and most likely would terrify her. He needed to rein in that fiery need, or she might leap through another bloody window.

Fortunately a gentleman in his line of work came prepared for all eventualities, and he had bandages and basilicum ointment stashed among his clean linen in case some energetic thief-taker might venture a bit too close. It was a simple enough matter to cleanse the wound and bandage it, and if his hands happened to stray perilously close to her breasts, she wasn't conscious enough to be outraged. When he finished she looked so peaceful, he gave in to temptation, not quite certain why.

He couldn't ravish her while she was unconscious, and he suspected the scrape, though not serious, would be uncomfortable enough to distract her from his nefarious designs. He simply stretched out next to her on the soft bed, lying on his side, facing her. He touched her soft skin, loosening her hair so that it slid over his hands. He breathed in her scent, flowers and soap and warm flesh, and he wanted to pull her into his arms and simply hold her. An odd notion, he thought vaguely, resisting the temptation. He contented himself with catching a thick strand of her hair and bringing it to his face, to his mouth. And he closed his eyes, allowing himself to drift into a sweetly erotic dream.

For a moment she didn't know where she was. Her back stung, her right side was chilled, her left side deliciously warm. There was a heavy weight pressing against her in the darkness, a weight she welcomed, and for a moment she thought she was back in her family home in Northumberland with her wolfhound curled up beside her.

But her dog had died when she was fourteen, and the house had been lost two years later. And she was lying in a strange bed, next to a warm body that most definitely did not belong to her sister.

Enough moonlight remained to filter into the room, and as her eyes grew accustomed to it, her memory returned. And she knew whose bed she shared.

She tried to turn her head to verify her suspicions, but something had trapped her long, loose hair. Tentatively, grimacing at the stinging sensation in her back, she reached up to see what had entangled her hair, only to discover a hand wrapped around the long strands.

Alistair slept deeply. She eased her hair free slowly, carefully easing her body from the wickedly soft comfort of the feather bed. Glenshiel slept on, oblivious of her escape.

She was dressed only in her chemise, petticoats, and corset. There was no sign of her mother's dress in the room, and she dared not take the time to search for it. Nor could she wander out in the hallway in her current dishabille.

A white shirt lay tossed across a chair, and Jessamine retrieved it, drawing it around her narrow shoulders. The bottom came down to her knees, the frothy lace of the cuffs spilled down over her hands, but at least it managed to cover her. If it also managed to smell deliciously like Glenshiel, it was a fitting punishment for her having given in to temptation and not running away the moment he'd entered the music room.

She crossed to the bed. She could always reach out and shake him awake and demand to know what he had done with her missing clothes.

He turned then, onto his back, still soundly asleep, and Jessamine drew in a strangled breath. His shirt, a twin to the one she'd purloined and now had wrapped around her, was unfastened and pulled from his satin evening breeches, exposing his chest. His skin was white-gold in the moonlight, and for a brief, mad moment she wanted to crawl back on that bed with him and put her head against the smooth, warm skin of his chest, and have him hold her.

She'd never seen a man's chest before, and she wondered if all of them were quite so . . . disturbing. So well-formed, so beckoning to the touch. Or, as Alistair had warned her, whether she responded so madly only to him.

She was afraid of the answer. His long, dark hair was in his face, and she gave in to the temptation, lifting a strand and smoothing it away from his mouth.

And then she backed away silently, afraid if she lingered for a moment longer she might betray herself even more profoundly.

The door opened beneath her touch, the hall outside was dark, and she hesitated a brief moment.

To hear his voice float toward her. "Aren't you going to kiss me good night, Jessamine?"

She slammed the door behind her and ran.

Thirteen

Alistair hadn't planned to go a-thieving quite so soon. He'd expected to spend a boring few days with Sally Blaine's tedious guests, flirting madly with Jessamine Maitland whenever he got the chance. Unfortunately his little midnight encounter had put a finish to that plan. If he had to spend another day cooped up in the house, he might do something very unwise.

He'd been a fool to let her go. She'd been snuggled up so cozily next to him in that monstrously soft bed, and he'd lain there beside her, watching the rise and fall of her breasts in the moonlight, the pale, soft skin on her cheek. Her eyes were her most noticeable feature, and with them peacefully shut, he would have thought she'd look just like most other women.

She didn't. She looked delicate, though he knew she wasn't, and utterly delicious. Some dark, twisted part of him had enjoyed lying there, watching her, wanting her, letting the need build and grow until he was ready to explode from it. It would have been a simple matter to take her hand and place it on his manhood. A shock to her maidenly senses, no doubt, which made it doubly appealing. But he hadn't. He'd watched her awaken slowly, keeping his own eyelids lowered so she wouldn't know he was acutely aware of everything about her — each indrawn breath, occasionally with a little catch. The pale fullness of her breasts spilling above the corset and chemise, the faint shadow of her nipple against the thin white cotton. He had stared at that shadow for moments, imagining the taste of her skin through the thin lawn.

But she'd slid from his arms, from his bed, and he made no move to stop her. He wasn't quite certain why. Perhaps it was simply that he wanted her to a dangerous extent, wanted her so much, his hands were trembling with it, wanted her so much that he was afraid, once he took her, he'd never want to let her go. And that was a weakness he could ill afford.

In the light of day he realized how absurd such a notion was. Such romantic flights of fantasy were worthy of a gothic novelist, not a pragmatic, amoral creature like himself. He felt no duty, no attachment, no need for anything in his life apart from the occasional excitement of a bit of felony. Gaming bored him, hunting bored him, flirtations bored him, sex bored him. Except for the notion of sex with Miss Jessamine Maitland, which occupied a great deal of his less vigilant hours.

He wondered whether she was a witch. It had been more than fifty years since witches were burned in England, but there were still some narrow-minded, old-fashioned souls who thought the cards were an instrument of the devil, and whoever read them the devil's handmaiden.

He wasn't one to believe in such claptrap, nor to allow anyone or anything, supernatural or human, that much power over him.

But whether he liked to admit it or not, Jessamine Maitland had bewitched him, enchanted him, so that he did things around her that were entirely out of character for a conscience-less rogue. He should have seduced her, deflowered her, instead of letting her escape so easily.

And he shouldn't be wanting to run, to push his plan ahead. If he had any sense whatsoever, he'd bide his time, give the runners a chance to settle in before he tried something startling.

Ah, but he'd never been one to play it safe. His brother had been the safe, perfect gentleman who drank and gamed and lived well . . . and died for it. Alistair was damned if he'd go the same quick, sorry way.

A few wicked games to distract the vigilant runners and bring excitement to the stultifying house party, and then he would set about his avocation in earnest. His blazing career as a thief was drawing to its inevitable conclusion.

The Cat would go out in a blaze of glory, if he had to die. Otherwise he would carry off one final, shocking robbery, one of such monumental outrageousness that London society would never forget it. And then he would retire to the Continent, to live out his days in wicked profligacy in some wondrously decadent spot — perhaps Venice.

And just to prove how soulless he really was, right before he made his escape he would efficiently, thoroughly, conscientiously deflower Miss Jessamine Maitland.

For the third time in two days one of Lady Sally's guests had lost a valuable piece of jewelry, only to have it turn up in another guest's astonished possession.

"Someone's having a game with you, Clegg," Samuel Welch had the misfortune to point out.

Brennan didn't move. The three runners were alone in the estate office, having commandeered the room as a central headquarters. Clegg had taken the seat behind the desk, setting himself in charge even though his length of service and position with the runners was exactly equal to Brennan's. Welch had already realized his mistake, and his swarthy face looked oddly pale in the murky light of a rainy day. As for Brennan, he simply puffed on his pipe, waiting to see what transpired.

He knew it was one of his gifts as a member of Sir John's men. His patience, his willingness to wait things out. He simply took his time and all sorts of interesting things revealed themselves. People had a tendency to say too much; they grew careless with their ill-gotten gains, and when that happened, Brennan was there to set things right.

"You think so, Welch?" Clegg said softly. "There's not many as makes a game of Josiah Clegg and lives to tell the tale."

Welch was beginning to look sick, and Brennan decided to bestir himself. He had a weakness for the downtrodden, and Clegg had been making a concerted effort to keep Welch subservient during the last two days at this godforsaken house party. Brennan felt called upon to interfere.

"They're making cakes out of all of us," he said easily. "I fancy it's just the gentry thinking up a new parlor game. I blame it on the Cat — he's captured their interest far too well, and they're play-acting robbery instead of theatricals."

"What do you know of the gentry and theatricals?" Clegg sneered. "You're nothing but a north-country farmer at heart. I doubt you were called upon to do the pretty with the quality."

Clegg had long since lost the ability to annoy Brennan, despite his best efforts. Brennan simply nodded lazily. "You're right, Josiah," he said in a measured voice. "But I watch and I listen, and I pick up all sorts of information before I make my move. You can learn a lot that way — it's not a bad habit to get into."

"Are you telling me how to do my job?" Clegg demanded in a deceptively affable growl, and for some reason Brennan was reminded of poor Martin's cut throat.

"Wouldn't think of it," he replied, knocking the dottle out of his pipe. "Just pointing out that these robberies are hardly serious. If they were, the missing pretties wouldn't turn up a few hours later in someone's best linen."

"Do you think the Cat's really here?" Welch asked eagerly, breaking in.

"No," said Clegg flatly. "Brennan's right." It looked like it pained him to admit it. "If it were the Cat's doing, then the jewels wouldn't be found so easily. Someone's trying to distract us, and Josiah Clegg is not about to be distracted."

"But if it's not the Cat, and no harm is being done, why should we bother?" Welch demanded.

Brennan concentrated on his pipe. "I simply said the robberies were in the nature of a game, Samuel. I didn't say the Cat wasn't here."

Welch was suddenly all eagerness. "You think he is?"

"I'm beginning to think he won't be coming at all," Clegg said with a sniff. "You never can trust informers, particularly when you've got a knife at their throat. They'll say anything to keep from getting cut. What would the Cat be doing at a house party such as this one? I've hardly seen a jewel worth tempting anyone more than a launderer's apprentice. He wouldn't be wasting his time."

"Unless he had other reasons for being here," Brennan observed.

Clegg glared at him. "And what would that be?"

Brennan gave him the unruffled smile he knew irritated Clegg beyond measure. "To tease us. The game with the missing jewels seems to support that theory. Mrs. Blaine loses a set of garnet earrings, and they appear in Mr. Arbuthnot's dressing gown pocket. Miss Ermintrude Winters misses a diamond bracelet, and the same is discovered in a sugar pot. These are tricks, and I haven't noticed any particular wit in the majority of the guests here."

"You must have a likely candidate for such a harebrained theory," Clegg grumbled.

"Not really. Mr. Arbuthnot is too stupid, Lord Glenshiel is too self-absorbed, our host is too interested in pinching bottoms, and the rest of the gentlemen suffer from the same reservations. Lack of wit or lack of interest."

"A servant, then? Most of the guests brought their own manservants with them."

"There's no way a servant could have had access to the other robbery sites in the last two years," Brennan observed. "Or had you forgotten?"

Clegg's face turned an ugly mottle. "Kind of you to remind me," he said with deceptive cheer. "So now you've made an excellent argument against your theory. Make up your mind — is the Cat here or is he not?"

Brennan shrugged. "I don't know, Josiah. I just figure I'd best keep my eyes open and be prepared for all eventualities."

Clegg looked at him with active dislike above the gold-toothed smile. "You'd be smart to do so."

Welch had been a silent witness to this, clearly missing half the undertones, but he spoke up then. "That still leaves us with Lady Autry's missing ruby brooch. It's probably the most valuable piece taken so far — mebbe the thief was just toying with us until he took the really good stuff."

Clegg gave him a look of approval. "My thought exactly. We find the ruby brooch and we've got our thief."

"That brooch is worth a fraction of the value of what the Cat usually absconds with," Brennan said. "I don't know why he'd bother."

"Maybe he's bored," Welch said facetiously.

But something clicked in Brennan's tidy mind, so at odds with his loose-limbed, untidy body. "An interesting thought, Samuel," he said, moving lazily to his feet. "I think I'll go for a walk. You've given me much to consider."

"Don't be daft, man!" Clegg's voice was rich with contempt. "Thieves don't get bored. They can't afford to."

"Perhaps this one can," Brennan murmured, heading out of the room. "It's worth considering. I'll close the door so no one will eavesdrop."

"Who would bother . . . ?" Clegg's voice terminated in a muffled obscenity as Brennan shut the door behind him, turning to look down the narrow hallway. He'd seen the shadow lurking, just out of sight, and he trusted his instincts implicitly. There was no sign of her now, but she couldn't have gotten far.

The rain had stopped, though the cool dampness of late autumn lingered in the air. Robert Brennan was a man who, for all his pragmatism, relied on his instincts. To the left was an empty stone barn he'd discovered on one of his earlier forays around the estate. Common sense told him whoever had been eavesdropping was now safely back in the house.

Instinct told him she was in that barn, hiding from him, uncertain, in trouble. If he had any sense at all, he'd beat a hasty retreat, as far away from temptation as he could manage, and confront her in a far more public place.

But then, a young lady like Miss Fleur Maitland shouldn't be seen talking to someone who wasn't much more than a servant. She might even be ashamed to have anyone spy them together.

He set his jaw, irritated with himself and his sudden doubts. Like a green schoolboy, he thought with contempt. If Miss Fleur had any reason to talk with him, he'd discover what it was. If not, he'd turn around and leave her be.

She was sitting in a pile of fresh straw, wearing a pale, pretty dress. The light was dim in the barn, scarcely illuminating her, and she looked still, almost serene, damnably, entirely at home in a barn. Brennan stood in the doorway, watching her, breathing in the sweet smell of the hay, overlaid with the faint trace of flowery scent that could come only from her, and he was assailed with such painful longing that his voice was unnecessarily harsh when he spoke.

"You were spying on us," he said.

She jerked, and he realized that she hadn't known he was standing there, watching her, as he'd thought. "I wasn't," she protested in a scratchy voice, and he could see the streak of tears on her face.

"Then why were you there?" He stepped inside the old barn, ignoring the sweetly familiar sense of homecoming that washed over him. He'd missed the countryside, he'd missed the farm, more than he'd ever guessed.

"I . . . I wanted to talk to you," she said, starting to scramble to her feet in the hay. The full, flowery skirts got caught under her knees as she struggled to pull herself up, tugging at the front of her bodice. She had soft, full breasts, made for babies. Made for a man.

He shut that thought out of his brain as well. "About what, miss?" he said formally.

"About this," she said, opening her small fist and displaying a large, ugly ruby brooch.

He crossed the deserted barn, towering over her. He'd come too close, he knew it, but he couldn't back away from her without making it obvious. He took the jewel from her hand. "Lady Autry's missing brooch, I presume," he said, surveying it for a moment before he tucked it into his pocket. "Did you steal it?"

"Of course not!" she said, clearly shocked. "I found it with my watercolors this morning, and I was so horrified, I didn't know what to think. I didn't even tell Jessamine."

"Why not? Doesn't your own sister trust you?" he said coolly, and immediately regretted it.

The look she cast up at him was so full of bewildered pain and hurt that he couldn't bear it. "Have I done something to give you a disgust of me, sir?" she whispered in a broken voice. "Have I somehow caused you injury? I don't understand your dislike of me . . ."

161

Her china-blue eyes swam with tears, and he wasn't a man to be moved by tears. Yet he wanted to lean down and kiss them away. "I don't dislike you," he said stiffly. "I have no opinion of you one way or another."

If he'd wanted to stop her pain, he'd certainly chosen the wrong words. The tears spilled over with a strangled sob, and she pulled away from him, starting toward the door.

He should have let her go. Better to hurt her now than to start something that would spell disaster for them both. But that choked sob was more than he could bear, and when she started past him he reached out and caught her, meaning to do no more than apologize a bit more gently, but somehow she was in his arms, her face pressed up against his jacket, her quiet, heartbroken sobs thrumming against his chest, and he was holding her, pressing her up against him, and he was bending down to kiss her, and she was raising her face to his, and her mouth was damp with her tears, and then damp from his mouth, and he was settling her down into the straw, cradling her against his big body as if to protect her from all the dangers of the world, and she was flowing against him as if she knew that was where she belonged, and duty and class and right and wrong had no place in the stillness of that deserted barn.

Alistair stepped away from doorway of the barn, a faint smile on his face. He was pleased with his latest machinations. There was no question in his mind that Brennan was the smartest of the runners who were after him, and there was nothing more distracting than young, forbidden love.

Besides, Jessamine's pretty little sister was so disarmingly smitten with the thief-taker that Glenshiel couldn't let it pass without interfering. He knew perfectly well his efforts would cause more harm than good. It would also confuse matters gloriously, leaving Jessamine to tend her rebellious, brokenhearted sister, leaving Brennan too frustrated and despairing to put his best efforts into finding the Cat. He was protecting himself, and he refused to count the cost.

Still, they were rather sweet together, the large, untidy runner and the compact, sweetly beautiful girl. It was a shame fate couldn't be kind, that there couldn't be a happy ending for such mismatched lovers.

But fate was a sly trickster, he knew that of old. And even if those two would never have their hearts' desire, at least they'd have the memory of a brief, forbidden taste of it to warm them during the long years.

He strolled back toward the main house, humming a bawdy tune under his breath. He passed no one, and he suspected the two of them would be safe and uninterrupted in the barn for the rest of the afternoon. Perhaps he should have stayed to see whether the stalwart Brennan gave in to temptation and deflowered the flower.

He grinned sourly. It was the sort of thing he would do himself, and the spice of risking an audience would have only added to his pleasure.

But Robert Brennan was a different sort, Nicodemus had informed him. A man with a conscience, with morals, with scruples, none of which afflicted Alistair, praise heaven. He would no more tumble a well-bred virgin in the straw than he would stab his own mother. Fleur Maitland would leave that barn intact, but knowing what she was missing.

And Robert Brennan would be too eaten up with frustration and nobility to be able to think clearly when the Earl of Glenshiel took to his room with a severe case of the stomach gripes, and the Cat went prowling on the London rooftops.

"I love you," Fleur said quite firmly, staring up at him. He'd pulled away from her, as she knew he would. He'd kissed her with fierce abandon, and then sanity had returned. He sat in the straw beside her, arms on his knees, breathing deeply, refusing to look at her, and she knew he would push her away again. "I love you," she said again.

He turned to glance down at her. "Don't say that, lass," he said heavily. "You know there's no future for us. You don't want a tumble in the straw from a farmer's son, and don't be telling yourself that you do. You're not that kind."

"I love you."

"Stop it. You don't know what love is — you're a milk-fed babe with no knowledge of what the real world is like," he said angrily. "You're untried and innocent and you'll bring us both to disaster with your fancies."

She pushed herself up on her elbows, suddenly angry herself. "No knowledge of what the real world is like?" she echoed. "I've lived in Spitalfields for the last three years. I went from a life of protection and privilege to not much better than life on the streets."

"Don't be daft! You have no notion what life on the streets of London is like."

"Don't interrupt me," she said, too angry to be cautious, she who never got angry. "I spent fifteen years of my life in safety, in peace, in the country, and then I was taken off to live in a filthy city, surrounded by strangers. Jessamine tried to protect me, but she couldn't be with me all the time. I've seen people lying dead in the gutter. I've seen men with their throats cut. Whores servicing their customers with their mouths in an alleyway. Rats and disease and filth and death. I've seen all those things and more. I know how a woman can take a man standing up, I know how a child can pick a pocket so quickly no one would even notice. I know there are men who come in their fancy carriages to the streets of Spitalfields to find children for their twisted desires. I know all those things and more. I wish to God I didn't. So don't tell me I have no knowledge of what life is all about. I know too much about filth and despair and poverty."

"You don't know the ways of society. . . ."

"I do, dammit," she said, horrified at herself for cursing. "I know they'll disapprove of us, try to keep us apart. And I don't care. I love you, Robert Brennan. I want to be with you."

"Lass," he said in a gentler voice, "how can you think you love me? You barely know me. Go back to your sister. She'll see you safe with your own kind. I'm not the man for you, and when you're older and wiser, you'll be glad of it."

She stared at him for a silent moment. Her mouth still felt damp and tingling from the kisses she wished more of, and she could still feel his hard, strong hands on her waist.

But he would kiss her no more. She rose to her feet, brushing the straw out of her skirts, disdaining his scramble to assist her. "And when you're older and wiser, Robert Brennan, you'll regret you weren't brave enough to fight for what you wanted," she said.

Keeping her back straight, she left the barn with all the dignity of a duchess.

Fourteen

There was only a light mist falling that evening, but the wind whipped Jessamine's hair free from her demure arrangement, flinging it against her face. If she had any sense at all, she would get out of the rain and the wind, back to the relative quiet of her room at Blaine Manor.

But it was an uncharacteristically quiet night at the raucous house party. Several of the more daring couples had gone off to the races and weren't expected back till late. Still others had opted for a quiet night of whist, while the Earl of Glenshiel was closeted with a vile case of the grippe, according to Freddie Arbuthnot. And Fleur had taken to her bed as well, her eyes huge and red-rimmed in her pale face. Pale, that is, except for the faint rosy rash that blushed her cheeks and chin, a rash that looked like it was caused by a man's whiskers.

Fleur couldn't respond to her sister's questions; she simply turned her face into the pillow and wept, a circumstance that distressed Jessamine tremendously. Fleur was not, by nature, a weeper. She cried over hurt animals and lost children, but the heartfelt depths of her sobs struck an unnamed terror in Jessamine's heart.

She could only blame Glenshiel. She had no particular cause to do so, but she had rapidly come to the conclusion that the Earl of Glenshiel was the author of all her most recent misfortunes, and if he hadn't somehow managed to sneak around Jessamine's careful surveillance and upset her sister, then he doubtless had a hand in it.

Fleur wasn't telling, and Alistair MacAlpin had retired to his room with a highly suspicious illness. And Jessamine, at loose ends, had every intention of finding out just how sick he actually was.

It had been a simple enough matter to breech the fastness of his room. She had retraced her steps from a few days before, making certain there were no helpful witnesses as she rapped on the door.

There was also no answer to her tentative knock. She rapped louder, then placed her ear against the heavy wood. Not a sound echoed from beyond, and she reached down to open the door, when a loud harrumph made her leap backward with a shriek.

"His lordship is indisposed, miss."

It was his sepulchral-looking manservant, Malkin, staring down at her with such stark disapproval that Jessamine almost withered. Almost.

"So I gathered," she said brightly. "I just came by to see how he was. If he needed anything."

"I will convey your concern, miss," he intoned. "Be assured I am more than adequate to the task of looking after my master. Rest and quiet are what he needs now. I doubt you'll see him till midday tomorrow."

"He's quite ill, is he?" Jessamine said. "Exactly what are his symptoms? I have some talent with herbs, and I might be able to brew him a tisane that would put him in better heart."

"He has the bloody flux."

"How very unpleasant," she said faintly.

"Quite."

Neither of them moved, and Jessamine wondered which of them was the more stubborn. It didn't take her long to realize she was no match for a superior manservant, and she contented herself with a faint smile. "Give his lordship my best wishes for his speedy recovery," she said, relinquishing the field of battle. "Certainly, miss."

But he did no such thing. The moment Jessamine turned the corner of the cavernous hallway she stopped, leaning against the wall, listening for the sound of the door opening, listening for Glenshiel's faint voice.

When she dared risk a peek it was only to discover that the manservant was retreating, not even bothering to check on his deathly ill master. Which served to convince Jessamine of one thing. Alistair MacAlpin was not in his room.

She doubted she'd have the chance to check. His guard dog wouldn't have retreated far, and if she tried to enter the bed-chamber once more, he'd doubtless stop her just as swiftly.

She wouldn't find much more of a welcome in her own room. And there was no peace to be found in the elegant house of her hostess. She didn't need to read the cards to know that something was afoot, something dark and dangerous and infinitely exciting.

And it involved Alistair MacAlpin.

The music room was still deserted in that singularly unmusical household. Outside, the rain was falling, but inside the one branch of candelabra she'd pilfered from the hallway sent streams of flickering light over the small room. The glass door still held a crack, proof that no one had breached the fastness of the place.

Jessamine averted her gaze deliberately. The scrape on her back was no more than a faint irritation on her body, but the memory of Glenshiel was a burning brand on her soul. He'd managed to distract and confound her at every turn, threatening everything she held dear.

She cleared off the top of the harpsichord, blew away a faint layer of dust, and set her reticule atop the painted lid. The cards felt warm, living in her hands as she pulled them out, and she was aware of a sudden sweep of misgiving. She knew the cards too well — they seldom kept secrets from her. From the moment she had first set eyes on the disturbingly charming Earl of Glenshiel, she had fought the temptation to do a reading. It was a temptation she could resist no longer. Not when the cards called to her with the answers.

She let her mind go completely blank as she let the well-worn pasteboard cards shuffle against one another. The colors and symbols flashed by, and she closed her eyes for a moment, picturing him. The narrow, clever, dangerously handsome face. The mouth that could curve in a mocking smile or one of devastating sweetness. The mouth that had touched hers, wooed hers . . .

She laid the cards out in front of her by feel, the warmth of them tingling her fingers. Then she stared in growing apprehension.

The Prince of Swords. Who else would he be? Bold to the point of foolhardiness, a man who toyed with right and wrong. What would a man like Glenshiel know about wrong?

One card followed another, none a surprise. In truth, she hadn't even needed to lay the cards out, she knew so well the truth that she'd been fighting. The Lovers were expected, as the Tower of Destruction.

Only the High Priestess surprised her, and she stared at it, perplexed. She seldom drew the High Priestess — its power was immutable and frightening. She looked down into the ancient seeress's painted face and saw her own eyes looking back. And reflected in those eyes was the silhouette of a black cat.

It might have been a sound, or her own highly tuned senses. She looked up at the moment, past the cracked window, and saw a dark figure skirting the outer wall, moving with a feline grace. It was too dark to see more than a shadow, and the creature blended with the night, but she knew who it was. Who it had to be.

She didn't hesitate. The rain had stopped for the moment, the door opened silently beneath her hand. A minute later she was out in the night air, heading after the shadowy, catlike figure.

It was cooler than she'd expected, and damper, and the wind pulled her hair from its tight arrangement, lashing it against her face. For once she could thank fate that she was forced to wear the high-necked, heavy dresses she and Fleur had cut down from their mother's wardrobe. She would have frozen in one of Fleur's low-cut, diaphanous gowns.

He was heading for the stables, slipping through the night like a wraith. She followed him, hoping she was equally as circumspect, that her wind-tossed skirt and hair would blend with the darkness.

The stables were deserted at that hour, and in the distance Jessamine could hear the sounds of the servants in the hall. They must be eating — the Cat had timed his escape well.

She slipped into the stables after him, blinking as her eyes grew accustomed to the murky light. He seemed to have disappeared, and she stood motionless, peering through shifting shadows, breathing in the scent of hay and horses and leather, comforting scents from her childhood.

It took her a moment to recognize the muffled sounds she was hearing, the crisp clapping of hooves that told her that her nemesis had already made his escape, taking his horse and leaving the back way.

There must be madness in the air, Jessamine thought almost abstractedly, for her to even entertain the notion that the elegant Earl of Glenshiel was a common thief, that he would sneak out of the house and take off into the night on nefarious business.

And she had every intention of following him.

Madness, perhaps, but this time she was giving in to it. Glenshiel was a threat, the Cat was a threat, and she had the ability to neutralize both that night. If she went tamely back to bed, her self-disgust would know no bounds.

Besides, what did she have to lose? There would be no place in society for the likes of her, an eccentric who would never marry. No matter how wealthy Fleur's future husband, it was unlikely his fortune would extend to making Jessamine a welcome member of society.

Most important of all, she was wildly curious.

She rode well, and even though it had been two years since she'd been on a horse, she had little doubt she could keep pace with any man. It was sheer luck that Marilla had seen to it that she knew how to saddle and bridle her own mounts, or she would have been helpless in the deserted stables.

As it was, it took precious time to ready one of the sleek, beautiful mares, and by the time she'd managed to scramble onto her back and head out of the stables, it should have been too late to follow him.

She paused, her hands on the reins, feeling the grace and power of the creature beneath her, and closed her eyes, focusing on the cards. The Prince of Swords, playing with right and wrong. She nudged the horse with her knee and let her take the lead.

It should have come as no surprise that they were heading out toward the London road. She kicked the horse into a faster trot, leaning forward to encourage her, whispering in her ear. Her gift with cards extended to animals as well, and the responsive creature moved faster, her sleek, strong body blending with hers.

She had no sense of time or place. She wore no gloves, and her hands were icy and chilled on the reins. Her hair had tumbled free, a witch's tangle down her back, and the night

171

was cold and damp. She didn't care. She didn't even care where she was going or what she would find. She had turned her will over to the fates, letting them, and the horse, take her where they wished. God only knew what she would find at the end of her destination. Alistair MacAlpin? Or the Cat? Or both?

It came at her out of the night sky, dark and smothering and immensely powerful, like a blanket of death, knocking her off the horse so that she landed, hard, on the deserted roadway, stunned, breathless, knowing only smothering blackness as she felt the huge weight that pinned her down.

She struggled for breath, for sight. Her breath came back to her in a choking rush, but the heavy folds of whatever covered her offered little in the way of fresh air, and she fought more wildly, kicking out, connecting quite solidly with bone and muscle.

"Bitch," came Alistair MacAlpin's pleasant drawl. "Do that again and you'll regret it."

Jessamine froze. She knew who it was — she'd been certain that was who she'd been following. Yet the reality off his body on top of hers, pressing her down, shocked her into temporary acquiescence.

There was a sharp stone beneath one shoulder blade, another beneath her hip. His weight was solid, flesh and bone, atop her, and she felt annoyance, discomfort, and a strange, dangerous stirring.

"Get off me, Glenshiel," she said through whatever muffled her face. "You weigh a ton."

"That's my sweet-tongued lass," he said, rolling off her. He flipped the enveloping cover from her body, and she could see him sitting next to her on the deserted roadway, looking abominably pleased with himself.

He was dressed entirely in black. Tight-fitting black breeches, black boots, a black shirt with nary a ruffle on it.

Belatedly she realized the blanket that covered her was an inky black cloak, and she shoved it away from her with impressive disdain.

"What are you doing out here dressed like that?" she demanded in her archest voice.

He was clearly unimpressed. Despite the thin sliver of moonlight she could see him quite well, and the look in his eyes boded ill. "I could ask the same of you," he countered pleasantly enough.

"I was following you."

"Rather foolhardy, don't you think? And it could be quite embarrassing. I've probably gone to meet a lover, and if you happened to sneak up on us while we were otherwise . . . occupied I imagine your sweet little virgin eyes would go blind with shock and horror."

"I doubt it. And you haven't come out to meet a lover."

"You wound me, Jessamine. Most women find me well-nigh irresistible. Only you seem curiously immune to my somewhat tarnished charm. I wonder why? I've gone out of my way to seduce you, and no matter how diligently I apply myself, you still seem to despise me. I wonder, do you hold something against men in particular, or is it just me?"

"You aren't trying to seduce me," she said flatly. "You're just trying to keep me from discovering who you really are."

There was a sudden ominous silence. "What a very foolish little girl you are," Alistair purred after a moment. "For one so very bright, you are alarmingly obtuse. Assume you've actually discovered my deep, dark secret. I have little doubt that no one knows you're out here — no groom would have allowed you to take that horse, and no guest would have let you go unaccompanied. So what's to keep me from strangling you and disposing of your body in some deserted spot?"

A trickle of fear slid down her spine. "You wouldn't," she

173

said, more a guess than a certainty.

He rose on his knees in the dirt, towering over her. "Tell me, my pet. Exactly what do you suspect I am?"

Now was her time to back down, to come up with an easy lie so that she might escape from this man, who suddenly seemed entirely capable of doing her grave harm. He was no longer the useless, elegant creature from the drawing rooms who watched her as she read the cards. Nor was he the seductive rogue who'd backed her into far too many corners and come dangerously close to making her forget all that was most important to her.

Tonight he was dark and cold and fierce, and he frightened her. If she had any sense, she'd make up some airy excuse.

But she looked into his hypnotic eyes, and sense abandoned her. "You're the Cat," she said.

His faint smile was chilling. "And did the cards tell you that, my pet?"

"The cards don't lie."

"And you work with the runners, don't you? A little-known fact, but I make it my business to be apprised of all apparently extraneous details. You feed information to Josiah Clegg, and in return he gives you money. That's how you've been able to support your family these last years, isn't it?"

She wanted to deny it as she'd denied it before. It was her social ruin, the end to all her dreams and plans for Fleur's security. But she sensed it would be useless. Besides, it might not matter. If he were to kill her, how she'd spent her last few years would be unlikely to matter.

"It would be a waste of time to deny it," she said. "But consider this. If I were working with one of the most powerful thief-takers in the country and I were to disappear, don't you think Clegg would put his considerable resources to finding out what happened to me, and bringing the wrongdoer to justice?"

"No. Clegg doesn't care about anything but his purse, and you know it. You were better to have allied yourself with someone like Robert Brennan."

He rose then, towering over her, lithe and fluid. Reaching down, he pulled her up beside him, dangerously close. "I'm afraid you've come too far to go back, sweet Jessamine. I have business in London tonight, and I don't have time to see you safely home."

"I got this far without incident — I can find my way back," she said, trying to still the spurt of hope that filled her.

"I'm afraid not," he said with real sorrow. "You'll accompany me."

"Don't be ridiculous . . ." She started to back away, but he caught her arm, and his grip, though gentle, was utterly inescapable. He wore thin black gloves, but she could feel the warmth of his skin through the leather, through her layers of clothing, and it chilled and burned her.

"You'll come with me," he said again, "and I'll show you just who and what the Cat is. Come along, sweet Jess."

She tried to yank her arm away from him, to escape, but it was useless. His grip was iron. "Don't call me that!"

Her horse hadn't run far. She was grazing near Glenshiel's mount, dulcet and peaceful, waiting for her. "Why not?" Alistair murmured, releasing her arm and settling his hands on her narrow waist. "It's your name, is it not? What about tender Jess? Loving Jess? Stalwart Jess?" His voice was a low, seductive purr.

"What about excessively angry Jess, who will see your hide nailed to the wall if you don't let her go?" she shot back.

The hands tightened around her waist, lifting her, and in a moment she was back on the horse, staring down at him. His hands were still on her waist, and she could feel every finger pressing against her.

"They won't nail my hide to a wall, Jess. They'll hang me at Tyburn, and thousands of people will come to watch a peer die, and they'll be selling apples and tracts of my so-called confession, and ladies will bid over articles of my clothing, and if you tell them you once bedded me, you'll be the toast of that motley society."

She shivered in the night air. "I wouldn't be there to watch," she said. "And I haven't . . . bedded you."

His smile was ineffably sweet as he looked up at her. "Ah, but you will, Jess. You'll be there to watch me die, and you'll weep hot tears of remorse."

"I doubt it."

"And you'll remember the night I took you over the rooftops of London," he continued, undaunted, as he vaulted onto his own horse, the reins to Jessamine's mount held tightly in one gloved hand so she couldn't escape. "And the night you gave yourself to me."

"Never."

He leaned across the saddle, caught her chin in one gloved hand, and kissed her, a brief, deep, erotic claiming of her mouth that she was powerless to resist. "Tonight," he said.

And a moment later they were thundering down the London road, Jessamine clinging to the pommel to keep her balance as Alistair, the Cat, led her onward.

Fifteen

Robert Brennan was in a suitably foul mood. Frustration had something to do with it, sheer physical need that he thought he'd mastered a decade before. He was like a randy school lad consumed with lust for an errant barmaid. Except that Fleur Maitland was no barmaid, she was a lady. And he was no boy, he was a man with a man's responsibilities and self-control.

Guilt had something to do with it as well. The look on Fleur's face, the sheen of tears in her eyes, ate into his soul like acid. He'd done his best to keep away from her — she was temptation pure and simple, and resistance was becoming more and more difficult.

Anger had something to do with it. Someone was making a May game of the runners, and it angered him as little else could. The Cat was there at Blaine Manor, he had no doubt of that whatsoever. The tricks with the jewelry were just that, tricks to annoy and confuse the keepers of the peace. But he wasn't fool enough to think things were going to stop at that.

It was a quiet night. Mrs. Blaine and most of her guests were out. The rest had retired early, and once again Brennan's guilt and frustration surfaced. Not that Fleur would welcome his comfort. Just then she was probably sobbing her heart out on her sister's shoulder.

Except that he didn't think so. His instincts, usually infallible, were telling him things were afoot. Clegg and Samuel had gone into the nearby village to spend the evening at a pub, but

Brennan had declined their invitation to join them. Something was going to happen, his very blood told him so. He just wasn't sure what.

He'd half decided that Freddie Arbuthnot was the infamous Cat. To be sure, he seemed to have neither the wit nor the daring to pull off some of the crimes attributed to the Cat, but looks could be deceiving. He had the entree to the very top of society, and he was in need of money. So desperate was his need, as a matter of fact, that he was busy courting the singularly unpleasant Miss Ermintrude Winters.

The only other choice was the seemingly indolent Earl of Glenshiel. He'd seen the man from a distance, listened to his drawling, faintly sarcastic conversation, and come to the conclusion that he was more interested in the cut of his satin coat than exerting himself for the sake of larceny.

But there was something in Glenshiel's odd golden eyes that hinted at more than appearances suggested. Something mocking, derisive, and devious. Wit was there as well, lurking. And he seemed far too interested in Jessamine Maitland.

Brennan had no idea whether he believed in her putative powers. To be able to track a criminal by the fall of a card seemed alien to his deliberately practical nature, but there was little doubt that Clegg's success, and his fortunes, had risen astonishingly in the past year. Josiah Clegg was essentially a lazy man, far more ready to earn an easy penny than to exert himself for the larger reward, yet that was exactly what had been happening. It would make a great deal of sense if he were getting supernatural help.

If such a thing could be considered anywhere in the realm of sensible, Brennan reminded himself wryly. He looked toward the main wing of the house, the windows lit against the stormy night sky. Fleur lay behind one of those squares of golden light, probably cursing his soul. He told himself that that was what he wanted, and he almost believed it.

The Earl of Glenshiel lay behind another of those windows, suffering the grippe, too miserably ill from a surfeit of oysters to see anyone. Or so he said.

And there was no way Brennan could find his way into that portion of the house. Reserved for the quality, those pretty, useless creatures who knew nothing about hard work or real life. It was damnable — there was nothing he could do but bide his time. And watch.

Sooner or later the Cat would expose himself. Sooner or later he would make one fatal mistake, and then Brennan would pounce. He had no intention of letting Clegg claim that generous reward. Brennan wanted it, needed it. And Josiah Clegg's nefarious ways deserved no more rich rewards.

Jessamine was cold. She hadn't dressed warmly enough, she had no gloves, and the tearing ride across the countryside was jarring and absolutely terrifying in the utter darkness. She couldn't see where they were going, but Glenshiel had no such problem. Like a cat, he could see in the dark, and his hand on her reins kept her horse close behind.

When he finally drew to a halt, it was so abrupt she almost tumbled forward over the pommel of the saddle. The closed carriage that awaited them was black and somber, more like a funeral coach than a private phaeton, but Jessamine had no illusions. It would be light and very fast.

Glenshiel was already beside her, reaching up to help her dismount. "Come along, Jessamine," he ordered.

She stared down at him through her tangled curtain of hair, glaring, unwilling to move. "If you think I'm going anywhere further with you . . ."

His hands were hard on her waist, and he hauled her down from the horse with nothing short of brute force. She fell against

179

him, and if she'd had the presence of mind, she would have tried to knock him over.

It wouldn't have done any good. He was in dangerous control of the situation, and of her, and there was little she could do for the time being but go along with him.

"What the 'ell is that?" a coarse voice, followed by a pungent odor, demanded. Both emanated from a small, swarthy creature dressed in improbable black.

"This is my partner in crime, Nic. Miss Jessamine Maitland, about to embark on a night of larceny. This, dear Jess, is Nicodemus Bottom, my mentor and accomplice. He disposes of the purloined jewels for me and takes a share."

"Are you out of your bleedin' mind?" the man exploded. "Your bleedin' lordship might have a bleedin' death wish, but I hopes to live a long and happy life without being turned over to the likes of Josiah Clegg. What made you bring her along? She'll be the death of both of us."

"It wasn't my idea. She followed me," Alistair said mildly enough. "I couldn't very well let her go back to the house and raise the alarm."

Nicodemus glared up at her. "I'll have to kill her, I s'pose," he said grudgingly. "I don't hold with killing females, but if it's a choice between her and me . . ."

"If anyone kills her, I'll do the honors," Alistair drawled. "She'd probably prefer that. In the meantime, we have an appointment in London."

"I'd prefer that you didn't discuss me as if I weren't even here," Jessamine said.

"Lass, I wish to God you weren't here," Nicodemus said. "And you aren't going to have any say in what happens to you. You're a nasty complication, that's what you are."

"And you're a nasty little man," she replied.

"Not as bad as his lordship here," the man called Nicodemus

said cheerfully enough. "And not near as bad as your bosom buddy Clegg."

"Everything set in the carriage, Nic?" Alistair had already moved away, opening the door and peering in.

"You can count on me, yer worship. You wants I should hit the lass over the head and tie her to a tree? It would make things a mort easier."

"No," he said. "I want her with me."

He was a good ten feet away, holding on to the door of the carriage. Nicodemus was even farther away, and with those bandy legs he wouldn't be able to keep up with her. Jessamine waited a moment longer, until Alistair leaned into the darkened interior of the carriage, and then she took off, picking up her heavy skirts and running toward the woods in mindless panic, sensible of nothing but her need to escape, and fast, from these two conscienceless villains.

She heard the explosion behind her, accompanied by a harsh whizzing noise. The quiet thunk, the spit of bark from the tree not two feet away from her path, convinced her immediately of the unbelievable, and her shock was so great, she tripped over her skirts, sprawling onto the forest floor.

He took his time reaching her, obviously unconcerned with the possibility that she might decide to run again. He towered over her, and she simply lay there in a tangle, glaring up at him. "You shot at me," she said faintly. "Didn't you?"

"Yes."

"You could have killed me!"

"Yes," he said again in a thoroughly pleasant voice. "And I'm not in the mood for target practice. You have three choices. You can get up and run again, and this time I won't deliberately miss. You can lie where you are, and I'll let Nicodemus put a bullet in that addled brain of yours. Or you can get on your feet, walk back to the carriage, and climb inside without any further fuss."

She didn't move. She couldn't see his expression in the darkness, but she had little doubt it was completely cold and ruthless. "I don't suppose I have a fourth choice," she asked in a remarkably docile tone of voice. "You could leave me here, and I could walk back to the manor, and I could promise not to say a word to anyone. . . ."

"No," he said. "Make up your mind."

She felt oddly shaken, though she wasn't about to let him see it as she scrambled to her feet without his assistance, brushing the twigs and loose dirt from her dress. Her dress had a wide rip under one arm, and her knee hurt, but apart from that she was still in one piece.

"I'm coming with you," she said resignedly.

"A wise child after all," he murmured. He still held a gun, a small, lethal-looking pistol, and it was pointed directly at her midsection. "Come along, then. We have a great deal to accomplish tonight."

The carriage was inky black as Jessamine climbed up into it. Her hope that Glenshiel would drive it was immediately dashed when he climbed up after her, pulling the door shut, closing them in together. He was sitting opposite her, she could tell that much, and when the carriage started with a jerk, she allowed herself the luxury of a horrified shudder.

What Nicodemus lacked in skill as a driver he more than made up for in enthusiasm. The carriage bounded forward at a furious pace, and it was all Jessamine could do to cling to the leather seats to keep from sliding onto the floor.

Alistair seemed to have no such problem with his balance. She could hear him moving around across from her, hear his muffled murmur of gratification. A moment later she was struck in the face with an armful of soft cloth.

"Nicodemus came through again," he said. "He knows my

needs very well, including a change of clothing in case something should go wrong. Tonight that something is you, my pet."

"Sorry to be disobliging," she said in a sulky voice. "What is this?"

"Your working clothes. I can't have you trailing me over housetops wearing full skirts and panniers. Strip."

She clutched the clothes more tightly against her. "I beg your pardon?"

"It's a bit late for that," he drawled. "Take off your clothes, Miss Maitland."

"I'll do no such thing. How dare you suggest —"

"The carriage is pitch black. Your modesty is perfectly safe, but I'm not in the mood to argue further. We're already running late, and I'm going to have to rethink my plans for the night. Take off your clothes and put on the ones I gave you. Or I'll do it for you."

She had no doubt whatsoever that he would do just that. "Very well," she said in a darkly hostile voice, reaching behind her to unfasten the row of tiny silver hooks.

It was hard going. She was used to Fleur assisting her — her mother's cut-down dress was designed to be put on and taken off with the help of a maid. But she wasn't about to ask Glenshiel to put his hands on her, not for a moment. Her fingers, still numb with cold, fumbled, and finally she tore at it, and the sound of the material giving way was shockingly loud despite the thunder of the horses as they hurtled toward London.

She paused, waiting for him to say something, but there was absolute silence from the blackness on the other side of the carriage, and she consoled herself with the knowledge that if she couldn't see him, he couldn't possibly see her.

She pulled the dress off her shoulders, shoving it away from her. The chill in the carriage prickled at her arms and chest

183

above her chemise, but she knew it would be useless to complain. She pushed the dress onto the floor, reaching behind to unfasten the hoop skirt and petticoats. It was a tedious process. The tapes were knotting, her fingers were clumsy, and despite the utter darkness of the carriage, she felt exposed and indecent. When she was finally wearing nothing but her chemise and corset she was shivering, and her hands shook as she tried to ascertain what was what in the pile of clothing he'd flung at her.

"The corset as well." His sepulchral voice came out of the darkness, and she quickly clapped the clothing against her partially exposed chest. "I will not!"

"You can't climb over rooftops in a corset any more than you can in full skirts. Untie it."

She bit her lip, wondering if he was relying on his hearing to assure him she was complying, wondering if she could fake it. Instinct told her it would be a waste of time.

"I can't," she said sullenly.

"Why not?"

"It's knotted. I didn't have time to fix it this morning, and I was counting on Fleur to assist me. . . ."

"Turn around."

"Don't you touch me!"

He muttered a weary curse under his breath. "Turn around, Jessamine, and I will endeavor to touch nothing more than your recalcitrant corset stays."

"I don't want —"

"Haven't you yet discovered that your wants have very little interest to me? I want you out of that corset and into the clothes Nicodemus brought, and I suggest you put all possible haste into the matter. The longer you sit around in your chemise the more I might find ways to entertain myself during this trip. Turn around." His voice was cold and smooth as ice.

Jessamine turned.

184

His hands found her corset with unerring dexterity, his fingertips touching nothing but the heavy linen and whalebone garment that encased her backbone. She could feel the warmth of his breath on her bare shoulder, and that tiny patch of heat was doing odd things to her stomach. He suddenly yanked at the corset, and it came apart just as the carriage hit a bump, sending her back against him in a tangle of arms and legs and loose clothing.

She scrambled away from him with little less than desperation, huddling in the far corner of the carriage as he retreated to his own corner. His hands had brushed the side of her neck, the tops of her breasts, and everywhere they'd glanced her skin heated and burned.

She yanked the ruined corset off, dropped it on the carriage floor, and began to investigate the clothes he'd tossed at her. It didn't take her long to have her worst fears confirmed.

"These are men's clothes," she said.

"Of course. They're mine. But you've already proven that you're not averse to wearing my clothes. I've yet to see the return of the shirt you pilfered when you ran from my bed."

"Don't put it that way!" she protested.

"You don't like being called a pilferer? You'll be guilty of much worse before the night is out."

"I didn't run from your bed. You make it sound as if we were lovers."

He said nothing, but even in the inky darkness she could imagine the look of amusement on his face. She pulled the shirt around her, grateful for its warmth, and began fastening the tiny buttons.

The breeches almost stopped her cold. She wouldn't, she couldn't wear such a thing. . . .

"Are you finished?" he drawled.

She yanked them on, falling against the side of the carriage as she tried to keep her balance and pull the blasted things over her hips. Her chemise was too long, and she tucked it inside the loose breeches.

"They're too big," she said in a sour voice. "They'll fall off."

"Tempting thought," he murmured.

No help from that quarter, she thought sourly, giving in to temptation and sticking her tongue out at him. She sat back against the cushions in her strange apparel, folding her arms across her chest and glaring in his unseen direction, prepared to endure.

Nicodemus was right, he was out of his bleedin' mind, Alistair thought lazily, stretching his legs out in the crowded interior of the carriage, bracing himself against the rocking motion. There were countless times that evening when he could have changed the course of events. When he first realized someone had the temerity to follow him. When he'd lain in wait and realized that the person who had come after him was no thief-taker or any other professional.

And when he'd knocked her to the ground, felt the delicious warmth of her beneath him, he still had the choice. He could have clipped her on the jaw, rendering her unconscious, before she realized who he was. By the time she came to, alone in the woods, she'd have no idea what hit her. Even if she'd suspected who and what she was following, she'd have no proof.

But he'd touched her, felt her, smelled her, and his wild nature had taken over. His decision was immediate and absolute. He'd never been a careful man, and now he was ready to risk everything.

He didn't regret it for a moment. He intended to compromise the so-very-curious Miss Jessamine Maitland, to do so quite thoroughly. He would take her a-thieving with him, across the rooftops of London, so that no one would believe her if she tried to put the blame on him and protested her own innocence.

He would take her to bed then. He had no doubt he could strip away any lingering doubts she had. He knew her curiosity, her needs, her desires far better than she did. He knew what she wanted, and that knowledge would have horrified her.

And he knew how to give it to her. He would take her places she was afraid to go, with her body, with her soul. He would take her through the darkness into the brilliant light of release, and she would never be a threat again.

By the time he brought her back to Blaine Manor she'd be ruined, unless her younger sister managed to cover for her. The hue and cry would be raised, and when she returned, bedraggled, whatever excuse, be it the truth or something utterly fanciful, would never be believed. He would wander from his sickroom, looking pale and properly horrified at Miss Maitland's fall from grace. If she accused him he would faintly deny it, if she said nothing he would shake his head in solemn dismay.

It was cruel of him to destroy her reputation, but he had no choice. It was her fragile plans or his life, and the choice was obvious. He'd come too far along the odd path he'd chosen to turn back, and if Jessamine Maitland had to be sacrificed, so be it. At least he'd make her enjoy it.

He'd almost forgotten why he'd ever started it all. A whim, a moment of greed, a cool anger toward his brother's friends, a boredom with the life presented him, all combined to make him ripe for trouble. He'd jumped into it heartily, and never regretted it, even when there was no escape. He wasn't about to start wasting his time with worthless regrets now, was he?

He stared at Jessamine in the darkness, his cat's eyes perfectly attuned as they had been all evening. Her skin was creamy and pale, and it had taken all his resolve not to push the chemise from her shoulders and find the soft warmth of her breasts with his tongue.

His blood was running high for the danger to come, for the woman who sat opposite him, dressed in his black silk clothes, clinging to the seat of the small carriage as they hurtled through the dark of night.

The risks were enormous. The cost astronomical. And he didn't care. Her legs were long and slender in the black breeches, her hair a wild tangle around her angry face, her breasts a soft swell against the silk shirt.

He would take jewels tonight, and he would take her. And the very real danger was not that he'd be caught.

But that she would mean more to him than the jewels.

Sixteen

Robert Brennan was a light sleeper. This had saved his life on more than one occasion, and would doubtless do so again. He heard the surreptitious footsteps, the soft rustle of clothing, and he was immediately alert. He sat up in the narrow cot that the Blaines had allotted him. Clegg and Samuel were down the hallway, and the noise of snoring was so loud, it could have been caused by an army.

Whoever it was paused outside his door, and Brennan reached down for the pistol he always kept by his side. That too had saved his life numerous times. He'd never used it to kill a fellow thief-taker, but tonight might be the night.

It was closer to morning than night. The light mist had stopped, and outside the air was clear and frosty. Brennan leaned against the wall, waiting, his gun ready as the door began to open.

She was silhouetted in candlelight, and he let the gun drop with a muffled groan of despair. There was a limit to how much temptation he could resist, and he was fast approaching it.

"What the hell are you doing here?" he demanded in a snarl he'd never used with a woman before.

Fleur stood there staring at him, transfixed. Probably never seen a man without a shirt before, he thought sourly. She was pale, though as he expected her eyes were red-rimmed from crying.

"My sister has disappeared," she said in a raw whisper. "It's

189

the middle of the night and she hasn't returned to our room. Her cloak is missing as well, and I'm afraid something terrible has happened. She would never have left me alone, with no word, if it had been up to her. She thinks I can't take care of myself." She managed a travesty of a wry smile. "I'm sorry I bothered you. I was actually looking for Mr. Clegg. Jessamine has helped him on occasion . . ."

She was starting to retreat, but Brennan was already surging out of bed, unmindful of the fact that he wore only knee-length drawers. He caught her arm and pushed the door shut behind her, closing her in with him, only the candlelight illuminating the small, closetlike space. "You keep away from him," he said fiercely. "Josiah Clegg is a dangerous man, and he means you nothing but harm."

"Whereas you want nothing more than my happiness?" she said, the wryness strengthening.

"Aye, lass."

The words fell between them gently, and he could have cursed himself. He was fighting it, Lord, he was fighting it, but fate was conspiring against him. It was a battle he would lose sooner or later, but the stakes, Fleur Maitland's well-being, were too high to risk.

He released her abruptly. She was so small, and he was so big, the discrepancy in their sizes magnified by the tiny room, and he felt huge, overwhelming, protective. He stepped away from her, though there wasn't far to go, and reached for his discarded clothes. "Let me put something on, and you can tell me about your sister," he said in a more neutral voice. "You can trust me to find her far more than you can trust the likes of Josiah Clegg. Why don't you sit?"

The moment the words were out of his mouth he could have kicked himself. The only place to sit in the tiny room was his narrow, rumpled bed. He didn't want her there. He wanted her there more than life itself.

She was wearing her nightgown, a long white lacy thing with layers of fine trim. The shawl she'd pulled around it provided warmth but not much covering, and her hair was loose down her back. In all, she looked like she'd look if she were sharing his bed. Except that she'd be naked.

She sat down gingerly, keeping her shawl pulled tightly around her, her eyes averted as he pulled on his breeches. "I haven't seen her since early evening," she said in a muffled voice. "It's completely unlike her — I'm afraid some harm might have befallen her."

"Did she say where she was going? What her plans for the evening were?" Brennan asked, pulling his shirt on.

She blushed. Even in the dim candlelight he could see the color staining her face. "We didn't have much conversation."

"Were you fighting?"

"I was . . . distressed. She was attempting to comfort me."

It wasn't guilt he felt twisting inside him, he told himself. Just simple pain that he'd had to hurt her.

"All right," he said briskly. "Even so, that would suggest she'd be even less likely to take off. She'd be concerned about you, wouldn't she?"

"Yes. She has a tendency to worry, and to hover."

"Do you have any idea where she might go? Has she made any close friends, or any enemies, among the guests here?"

"She and Ermintrude have never gotten along." She was calmer now, relaxing under his businesslike demeanor, and she pulled her feet up under her on the bed, tucking her bare toes beneath her nightrail. The sight of those small, bare toes almost undid him. "But I doubt Ermintrude would do her any harm. I thought perhaps she might be assisting Mr. Clegg . . ."

"Clegg's asleep," he said flatly. "Dead drunk, and I expect he's alone. Has she said anything about a man? Do you suspect she might be carrying on an assignation?"

She blushed again. He'd taken the candle from her and set it in the deep windowsill, and it threw strange shadows about the room.

"I don't know. She's been keeping something from me, and I haven't wanted to pry, but I suspect it might have something to do with the Earl of Glenshiel."

It was all he needed for it to fall together. His faint suspicions had had no basis — now they did. "Is she in love with him?"

Fleur lifted her head and stared him straight in the eye. "I didn't know you believed in love, Mr. Brennan."

It was a challenge, flung down like a gauntlet, and he took an instinctive step toward her, when Clegg's thick voice tumbled loudly down the hallway.

"Who've you got in there, laddie?" he demanded, crashing against the door. "Having a bit of tasty pie, are you? Why don't you share with your mates, eh?"

Fleur leapt up in utter panic, and Brennan moved swiftly, pulling her against him and clapping a hand over her mouth. "Go away, Josiah," he called out in a sleepy-sounding voice. "You're drunk, man, and hearing things."

"Takes more than the likes of Sammy Welch to drink Josiah Clegg under the table." He pounded against the door once more. "Come on, Robbie, let me in," he wheedled. "You've got a lass in there, I know it, and me John Thomas is in need of snug nest for the night."

Brennan could feel Fleur shudder in his arms, and he held her more tightly, wishing he could stop her ears as well as her mouth. "You'll wake the others, man," he called out. "You don't want the quality being disturbed by the likes of you — think what Sir John would say."

"Bugger the quality. And bugger Sir John," Clegg muttered

192

in a slightly quieter bellow. "Are you going to let me in?"

"No."

"Bugger you too, then. I'll find out who you've got in there. See if I don't. And then I'll have a taste of it meself. I'm not a man who takes no for an answer. Had each of me sisters by the time they were twelve, for all their tears and pleading." His voice trailed away, his footsteps as well, but Brennan made no move to release Fleur.

He'd forgotten he had his hand across her mouth. Forgotten, until he felt the faint pressure of her lips that might almost have been a kiss. He slumped back against the wall, and she sank against him, soft and pliant, seeking warmth and comfort.

Ah, he could comfort her well and truly, he told himself. Love her so well her life would be ruined, and all he could offer her was a hard life in Yorkshire in the mud and dirt and dales.

He caught her face in his big hands, letting his thumbs gently caress her mouth. She was so young, so foolish, so giving. He'd hurt her time and again trying to drive her away, and she still looked at him with love and trust in her eyes.

"Lass," he whispered, "you'll be the death of me." He kissed her very gently on the lips, all he would allow himself this time, and then set her away from him with regret and determination. And she didn't fight him, simply pulled her shawl more tightly around her.

"The servants said Glenshiel's got the stomach grippe," he said in his most prosaic voice. "That's not the time a man uses for flirtation, but things aren't always as they seem. Let me make sure Clegg's gone back to bed, and then you run along to your room while I check on his lordship. I'll try and be discreet — we don't want the entire household knowing if your sister decided to slip the traces for one night."

"She wouldn't do that," Fleur said staunchly.

He sighed. "Lass, I could have you on that bed in two

seconds flat if I wanted. Are you telling me your sister's any different?"

She flinched as if he'd slapped her. "No, Mr. Brennan. We're both whores at heart when we think we're in love."

She didn't say another word, watching him silently as he pulled on his shoes and stockings. It felt oddly domestic, and yet he wondered what else he could do to drive her away, to give her a total and permanent disgust of him. He'd given her as grave an insult as he could imagine, and yet he sensed that she saw through the deliberate cruelty and lies to the truth of matter: That he loved her with all his heart, curse him. And would for the rest of his life.

The hallway was deserted. He took the candle in one hand, put the other around Fleur, and ushered her out into the shadows, shielding her smaller body with his. But as they turned the corner leading to the main section of the house, he thought he heard the quiet closing of a door.

Jessamine kept sliding off the leather seat. There may have been straps to hold on to, but in the darkness she couldn't find any. All she could do was try to brace herself as the coachman called Nicodemus Bottom drove them at a hellish pace toward London.

She wondered whether her companion had fallen asleep. She wouldn't have put it past him — he seemed to have nerves of steel, and the riotous rocking of the carriage probably had little effect on him.

"What would you have done if the bullet had actually hit me?" she asked suddenly. "It was dark — you couldn't have been that sure of your target."

"I see perfectly in the dark," he said in a tranquil voice. "And I'm an excellent shot."

"Still, you couldn't be certain."

"Life is never certain, thank God. One of its few pleasures."

"What would you have done?" she persisted.

"I'm not quite certain. I may have cradled your wounded body in my arms and sat there in the dirt, howling my despair and remorse at the moon."

"There is no moon tonight."

"Well, scratch that notion. Perhaps I might have rushed you back to Blaine Manor in search of medical aid, confessed my sins, and allowed your friend Clegg to carry me off to the hangman."

She shuddered silently, glad he couldn't see her. "I can't see you being quite so self-sacrificing."

"Can't you? You're probably right. If it were a mortal wound, I probably would have had Nicodemus drag your body into the underbrush and cover you with leaves. A slight wound gives me too many unpleasant possibilities," he said with a drawl. "I am a practical man, you know."

"I believe you." She leaned her head back against the hard cushion. "Don't you think our hostess will wonder where we are?"

"I'm in bed with the grippe. As for you, I'm afraid you overestimate your importance. In the scheme of things you are more than expendable."

"My sister . . ."

"The thief-taker will look after your sister, I expect."

"No!" Her sudden panic was absolute, and ignoring the reckless speed of the carriage, she lunged for the door.

He stopped her, of course, with his hard hands, and when he thrust her back against the seat, he came with her, crowding her there, too big, too warm, too strong. "Not Clegg," he said, having read her reaction. "Brennan will see that she's safe."

"I'm not convinced that's an improvement," she muttered.

"You can't control everything, Jessamine," he said with a

low purr. "Your sister is young and foolish, and she doesn't give a rap about position or money or any of the practicalities of life. She'd toss them all away for her handsome Bow Street runner, and you won't be able to stop her."

"What do you know about it?"

"I've done my poor best to further the match. You want her to marry a worthless aristocrat like me? She deserves much better."

"Damn you."

"Indeed. If you want to save your family from ruination, you will have to sacrifice yourself on the marriage altar, not your little sister."

"No," she said flatly. "I will never marry."

"Then you can become some rich man's mistress," he said. "Someone who will keep you in diamonds and not much else. Someone who will teach you to appreciate the pleasures of the flesh."

"No," she said again, cold and certain.

"No marriage, no mistress? Are you planning on becoming a nun, then?" he murmured, sounding no more than casually interested. But he was too close, she could feel the warmth of him, and his long legs were too close to her own breeches-clad ones.

"In a manner of speaking."

He laughed then, a soft, infuriating sound, and his hand caught hers before she could slap him. "You weren't made for celibacy, my pet. Allow me to demonstrate."

She wasn't expecting his sudden strength as he pulled her into his arms, across his lap. She struggled, but the rocking, jarring motion of the coach only flung her back against him. His hand caught her chin, holding her face still as he kissed her, but the more she squirmed, the tighter he held her.

He lifted his mouth from hers, and in the darkness she could see the cool glitter of his eyes. "The more you fight me," he murmured, "the more you excite me. Might I suggest passive acquiescence for a while? After all, there's a limit to what I can accomplish in such cramped and active quarters, and if there's no challenge, I might grow quickly bored."

It sounded reasonable enough. Not that she was about to trust him, but how he could manage to lie with her in this tiny space was beyond her limited comprehension. Besides, fighting hadn't worked.

"Go ahead," she muttered gracelessly. "Do your worst."

"Oh, no, my love," he said, reaching for the front of her borrowed shirt. "I intend to do my very best."

His fingers were warm against her chilled flesh as they slid inside the front of the shirt, inside the loose neck of her chemise. She opened her mouth to protest, but he put his lips against hers as his warm hand covered her breast, and the jolt of the carriage sent a strange, unnerving tremor through her body. Through her belly.

"No," she whispered when he moved his mouth down the side of her neck, nibbling lightly, pressing his teeth against the sensitive skin at the base of her throat.

"Yes," he growled, an animal sound of pure hunger, and she tried to will herself to be utterly still. Not to respond to the things his mouth was doing. Not to respond as his fingertips slid over the tight swell of her breast, teasing the nub, so that a strange, burning ache began to spread from where his hand touched her, caressed her, down between her legs.

She shifted, squeezing her knees together, and in the darkness she heard his soft laugh. "It won't do you any good, darling," he said. "I'll get there in a little while."

She didn't know what he was talking about, and she didn't want to. His sensitive fingertips were drawing concentric circles around her breast, and she found she was having faint trouble breathing. It had nothing to do with his mouth at her collarbone, nibbling its way downward. Nothing to do with the muscled legs beneath her, with no thick layer of skirts and petticoats. She might as well have been naked — there were only two thin layers of cloth between them, and she could feel his body heat, his muscles, his . . .

She tried to pull away as the realization hit her that he was fully, frighteningly aroused, but he wasn't about to let her go. He'd somehow managed to unfasten the tiny pearl buttons, and the ribbons of her shift had already come loose. It was simple enough to bare her breasts to the cool night air. Simple enough for him to bend his head and close his mouth over her.

She shrieked, but there was strength beneath his erotic caress, and she couldn't break free from him. He tipped her back against his arm, giving him greater access, and she felt dark, wicked, and oddly pagan as his hot, wet tongue circled her breast, then sucked at it, deep, drawing motions that made her want to weep with confusion and need.

This was what Marilla had warned her against. Jessamine could feel herself being drawn down, down, into some dark, wicked place of longing and delight, where nothing mattered but the dangerous pleasure of his mouth sucking at her breast. Surely this was witchcraft, far more than her simple cards? It was so powerful it frightened her, and she could feel her will draining away. And with her talents, her one defense against a cruel world.

"Stop," she whispered. "Please. I don't want to lose my gift."

"That's the first time I ever heard it called that," Alistair murmured. And he slid his hand between the tightness of her thighs, cupping her.

She was too horrified to do more than moan. His mouth captured her other breast, and if anything, the sensations were even more intense, a depraved delight that echoed in the pressure of his long, elegant fingers against the most private part of herself.

She wanted to tell him to stop, but it would have been a lie tumbling from her mouth. She didn't want him to stop. Marilla had warned her, and now she knew why. She was ready to toss everything away for the sinful pleasure he was giving her, the deft stroke of his fingertips through the indecent breeches, the hungry pull of his mouth at her breasts, the strength of his arm beneath her back.

She wanted, needed, more from him, though she wasn't quite sure what that encompassed. She reached up to push him away, but her hand tangled in his long hair, and she found herself caressing the silken strands, closing her eyes in fading delight as he . . .

The carriage slammed over a bump, tossing the two of them sideways, and never in her life had Jessamine been so grateful for a rocky ride. It didn't matter that she was on the floor of the carriage, tangled with Alistair. What mattered was that his mouth was occupied in cursing, not kissing her, and she was able to regain enough of her scattered senses to push herself free from him and scramble back up to the seat, yanking her shirt back around her exposed breasts.

Her body still tingled, burned, from his caress. Her breasts ached, the place between her legs was on fire, but she pulled her legs up tight against her for protection.

"Don't come near me again," she warned him fiercely.

"I can't get very far in this carriage," he said dryly, his voice making it clear that he was entirely unmoved by what had just transpired between them. Jessamine's fury and shame was complete.

"Just leave me alone."

"If only it were that easy." He moved in the darkness, sinking

199

down beside her once more, and she struck out at him in sudden panic.

He stopped her, ruthlessly, efficiently, catching her flailing fists in his hands and holding them prisoner. "Behave yourself," he snapped.

"Me?" Her outrage was complete.

"We've several hours of traveling time left, even taking Nicodemus's enthusiastic driving into account. I suggest you put your head on my shoulder and go to sleep."

His utter gall rendered her momentarily speechless. But only momentarily. "And I suggest you —" Her extremely clever and rude suggestion was muffled as he slung an arm around her shoulder and drew her against him. Her struggles were absolutely useless — she had no idea such an elegant creature could be possessed of so much strength.

"Have you worn yourself out yet?" he inquired in a mild voice, seemingly untouched by her wild attempts at escape.

It was useless. Jessamine forced herself to go still as a wave of angry emotion washed over her.

"That's right," he murmured against her hair. "Go to sleep, my fierce one. You've a long night ahead of you, and you'll need what rest you can get."

He was right, she was unutterably weary. "I hate you," she mumbled, giving in, letting her body relax in his grip.

"I know you do, my precious one," he said. "After tonight you'll have even greater reason."

"After tonight you'll be in Newgate." It should have come out as a threat, but her extravagant yawn lessened the effect.

It was utterly ridiculous, she thought. She couldn't curl up next to him, trusting enough to fall asleep. She couldn't relax in this jolting, tumultuous carriage. She was being abducted, she hated him, she . . .

Slept.

200

Seventeen

It was a grand night for reiving. Alistair tilted his head back, staring into the clear night sky, and breathed deeply of the crisp autumn air. The rain clouds had finally vanished, the thin sliver of moon had set, and a handful of stars shone brightly against the rich black velvet of the sky. Like a cluster of perfect tiny diamonds, he thought. It was a damned shame that most of the people he robbed had execrable taste in jewelry.

"Where are we?" Jessamine asked.

He turned to glance down at her. Nicodemus had dropped them off in the mews that abutted Curzon Street with the admonition to "watcher back." The night was still, and if any watchmen were on duty, they were in another part of the area.

She looked utterly delicious. Men's clothes suited her — there was something inexplicably arousing about the way the breeches clung to her long legs, the way his shirt flowed over her breasts. But then, he found her arousing no matter what she wore.

"London," he said briefly.

"I know that!" She seemed remarkably uncowed by her experiences so far. In fact, she'd been abducted, almost seduced, threatened, and even shot at. And she was still brave enough to be angry.

"You're going to help me rob that house over there," he said, nodding in the direction of a newly constructed mansion that owed more to money than aesthetics.

"You can't make me," she said. "All I have to do is run, screaming . . ."

"And I'll catch you before one tiny shriek is out of your mouth. And I wouldn't be very happy," he replied in his most gentle voice.

Even in the dark of night he could see her skin blanch. "What makes you think I won't find some way to call attention to us?"

"Because you know perfectly well that no one will believe your innocent involvement. They'll probably try me in the House of Lords and hang me. You they'll simply drag out to the nearest lamppost and hang you right there and then. They do that, you know."

"I know," she said, shuddering.

"You've come this far . . ."

"Not by choice!"

"And you may as well accept your fate. Your wisest course would be to go along with me. I'm a very accomplished thief, my pet. I'll have us in and out of that monstrosity of a house over there in no time at all. We'll meet up with Nicodemus and be back in Kent before sunup, with no one the wiser."

"Why are you doing this?"

"So you won't be able to use your wicked cards to inform on me. If I'm caught, I'll tell them about my charming accomplice the night I robbed Justas Winters's house."

"That's Ermintrude's house!" Her shriek of horror was blessedly muffled.

"Who better deserves our attention?" he countered. "Freddie Arbuthnot happened to mention she has a singularly ugly set of peach-hued diamonds. I think it would only be fitting to deprive her of them, don't you?"

"No one deserves to be robbed."

"Such a little Methodist you are," he murmured. "Still, you must admit, if any soul *did* deserve it, that would be Ermintrude."

"I admit nothing."

"But you'll help me. Since you have no choice in the matter."

"I hope you roast in hell," she said fiercely.

Her hair had come free, and it tumbled down her back, a thick fall of golden brown, a stream of dangerous color. He was standing in front of her, and he reached around her head and caught up the thick waves, tucking them up inside the cap he'd brought for himself. His own hair was dark enough to escape notice.

She stood very still, letting him touch her. His face was close to hers, and he wanted to kiss her again. Indeed, he wanted to kiss her more than he wanted Ermintrude Winters's diamonds, a realization that disturbed him. He stepped away from her, dropping his arms.

"Come along, my love," he said. "The sooner we embark on your life of crime, the sooner you'll be safe in bed."

"That's what I'm afraid of," she muttered, but she trailed along behind him obediently enough.

"You should consider yourself honored," he said, leading her through the side alleyways to the thick iron gate that surrounded the property. "You get to witness an artist at the very peak of his powers. This is no simple place to rob for a variety of reasons. Do you care to hazard a guess?"

"No."

"For one thing," he continued, undaunted, "it sits alone in its little park, with no houses abutting it as is so common in the city. Therefore we can't enter through the roof — there's no way to get up there."

"Too bad. Let's go back," she said.

"Ah, but there are alternatives," he said, ignoring her. "Even if I can't show you the glory of the London rooftops, I can at least initiate you into the pleasures of larceny."

"Kind of you," she muttered.

"First we have to get past this iron gate that surrounds the place. A simple enough matter — I've already discovered a side gate that they seldom bother to check. Once we're on the property, things get a little more difficult. The family is away, and the house is tightly locked."

"But you doubtless have a remedy for that."

"Ah, you're beginning to appreciate me," Glenshiel murmured wryly. "I do indeed. Picklocks."

"I beg your pardon?"

"Tools employed by the uncommon criminal. Delightful little instruments that Nicodemus was able to supply me. Learning to use them was a bit of a challenge, considering I had no mentor, but I confess I've become quite expert at them."

"You must be very proud." Her voice was acid.

They'd reached the side gate to the Winters estate. It opened too easily, no challenge for his skills, and he pushed it free, ushering her onto the grounds. "So now we must decide," he continued, closing the gate behind him, "how best to approach the fortress. If we try to gain entry through the back, we're more likely to be overheard by whatever servants are currently in residence. But if we were to attempt the front door, we would risk being seen by passersby."

"I presume there's a side door, as there was with the gate?" Jessamine suggested in a deliberately bored tone of voice.

"One would expect as much, but in this case there isn't. The house is of recent design, made to be impregnable to the hordes of thieves that wander the city, and the only other doors are on the first floor. They lead on to small stone balconies that I imagine are supposed to be gothic in design."

She peered up at the house. "It does look rather gloomy."

"So what do you suggest we do, Jessamine? How shall we breach this impregnable fortress?"

He waited almost endlessly for an answer. She was beginning to be caught up in it, he could sense that she was. He was attempting to seduce her soul as he planned to seduce her body, and he wanted, needed, a sign that he was succeeding.

"A tree," she said finally. "You could climb a tree and jump over to one of the balconies."

He resisted the impulse to kiss her. "A good thought, but this is too damnably new. There are no trees left standing near the building."

"A ladder?"

"I forgot to bring one."

It managed to coax a smile from her. "We give up and go back to Kent?" she suggested hopefully.

"Don't be so poor-spirited. We have a challenge ahead of us, and we'll meet it. I may not have a ladder, but I have a rope." He drew out the thin, strong length from the satchel he carried with him.

"Convenient," she drawled. "When they catch us, they won't have to search for something to hang us with."

"They won't catch us, my pet. Come along."

She followed him across the frozen ground quite dutifully. "And there's something to be said for the breeches," she continued in a marginally more cheerful voice. "At least my modesty will be preserved as I'm swinging in the breeze."

He glanced back at her. "Ah, Jessamine," he murmured without thinking, "a man could love a tart soul like yours."

And the words fell between them with the shock of a blow.

A man could love a tart soul like yours. The words taunted her unmercifully. *A man could love you.* Not this man, she prayed fervently. Not any man, but most especially not this one. Because this was the one man she didn't think she'd be able to resist.

He seemed almost as horrified by his random words as she was. He said nothing more as he led her toward the huge, dark house, but the knowledge burned in her brain. Beyond the gate in the darkness the city of London continued about its business, the noise muffled as life went on. He was several paces ahead of her — he might not notice she'd taken off until she'd gotten enough of a head start.

He was fast, but he might decide the Winters house was worth more than her unwilling cooperation. The moment he was fully occupied she could seize her chance and abandon him. She'd been alone on the streets of London before at such late hours, and she had faith that she'd be able to make it back to Spitalfields safely. There she could change into her own clothes, spend the very last of her hoarded money on a private coach, and make her way back to Sevenoaks before anyone noticed she was gone.

Except that she doubted a carriage was to be had at that hour. And even her usually somnolent mother might notice the midnight arrival of her elder child and have a few unanswerable questions.

There was always another alternative. She could present herself at Bow Street. Seek out the magistrate himself and inform on the Earl of Glenshiel. The reward would be plentiful, and Josiah Clegg would no longer be a threat.

"Don't even think about." His voice floated back to her. He was standing beneath one of those gothic balconies, the line of his body intent on surveying this latest obstacle.

"Think about what?"

"Running away." He glanced back over his shoulder, his

206

expression unreadable in the dim light. "It's time for you to get to work."

"I'm not . . ."

He picked her up as if she weighed no more than a handful and boosted her up toward the balcony. In her shock she flailed out, catching hold of the stone railing in her panic and kicking out, her foot connecting with something resilient and vulnerable.

Glenshiel cursed in pain, gave her another shove, and she was up and over, sprawling on the hard stone floor of the small balcony.

It hurt. She wasn't about to give him the satisfaction of knowing that, however. She pulled herself to a sitting position, looking down at him through the stone railing. "What do I do now?" she demanded.

"You see if the door is locked."

"Why wouldn't it be?"

"I'm certain it is. However, if by any chance someone forgot to lock it, then it would a simple enough matter for you to get in by yourself and let me in through the front door, thereby saving me a great deal of trouble."

"Aren't you afraid I might go for help instead?"

"No," he said. "You're in too deep already."

He was right. On all accounts. The door was locked, and she wasn't ready to turn him over to the authorities. Not yet, at least.

She leaned over the balcony, peering down at him. "So what do we do now?"

"She speaks. O speak again bright angel . . ."

"Now is not the time for Shakespeare," she said sternly.

"But you make a perfect Juliet."

"More like one of those girls who dress as boys in one of the comedies," she said.

207

The rope landed at her feet with a quiet thwap. "Life isn't a comedy, Jessamine," he said. "Are you any good at tying ropes? I need you to knot that over the banister."

"For your sake, you'd best hope so," she replied, picking up the coiled length. It was thin and seemingly very strong, and she worked swiftly, pulling at it to make sure it would hold his weight. She tossed the end over the side, aiming for his head. It missed him.

"You wouldn't like it if I fell," he said cheerfully enough, pulling at it. "You'd be trapped on that balcony — I doubt you could climb down by yourself without doing yourself some injury, and I'm not sure you'd want to call for help."

"I tied it as best I could," she snapped, stepping back from the railing as he started to pull himself up after her.

It made her nervous to watch for a variety of reasons. He was absolutely right — she'd come too far along the path he'd forced her. If he were to fall, it would be her own disaster as well.

For another, she disliked the eerie, primal awareness she had of his strength, his body, his power, as he pulled himself up the rope and climbed over the balcony. His dark hair was pushed back from his face, and the black clothes clung to his lean, lithe body. He looked dangerous and beautiful, a demon lover.

Except that it was jewels and robbery he loved. Not her. Thank heaven, she reminded herself.

She kept out of his way, a move that didn't escape his notice, and the smile that slashed his face was plainly visible in the darkness as he bent down and began to fiddle with the lock.

It clicked almost immediately. He pushed the door open, then held it for her. Jessamine took one last, longing glance over the side of the stone balcony, at the rope still dangling.

And then she stepped inside the cool darkness of Ermintrude Winters's house.

She didn't scream when Alistair's gloved hand closed around hers. She didn't even hesitate before gripping that hand tightly as he led her through the darkened building with eerily accurate night vision. Her heart was pounding wildly — at any moment she expected servants to rush out of the darkness, demanding to know what business they had in the empty house.

Up the wide stairs they went silently, hand in hand. She held on to him as if he were a lifeline — she had no idea where they were going, but he moved unerringly, and she followed, trusting.

They stopped at the top of the stairs, and Glenshiel's voice was pitched so low it was no more than a whisper. "I don't suppose you know which room belongs to Ermintrude?"

"I've never been here before. Ermintrude considers poverty to be déclassé."

"Somehow that doesn't surprise me," he drawled. "We'll simply have to go by trial and error."

"What makes you think Ermintrude doesn't have the diamonds with her? If they're worth such a great amount, I'd expect her to wear them even in her sleep."

"She went on at great length about leaving them behind. She insisted her father's house was impregnable, and the Cat wouldn't dare attempt to breach it."

"A challenge you couldn't resist," Jessamine whispered dryly.

"Of course not. Especially considering what a ruthless bitch she is." The doors leading to the upper hallway were all closed, and Jessamine couldn't begin to guess which was her erstwhile friend's.

Alistair didn't seem to have any reservations. He began opening doors, silently enough, peering into the darkened interior and then backing out again. Jessamine followed along, saying nothing, until he finally stopped in triumph at one of the last doors. "This is it," he said, pushing her inside and shutting the door behind them.

"How do you know?"

"That cloying perfume she wears," he replied, moving past her toward the window. "I'd know it anywhere."

She tried to follow him, and immediately bumped into some low object that he'd managed to avoid, hurting her shins. She muttered something dire under her breath as her eyes grew accustomed to the dim light. Alistair had already achieved his object, and even in the darkness the jewels sparkled.

"Don't you have any morals at all?" she demanded. "Any code of honor?"

"Certainly." He tucked them in the black satchel he slung over his shoulder. "They just happen to be of my own design. I don't pay any attention to other people's definitions of right and wrong. I don't take from people who can ill afford it, and I don't take from people who don't deserve it."

"And who are you to set yourself up as judge and jury, to decide who deserves to be robbed?" Jessamine demanded. "You hardly seem a decent judge of character. What if you make a mistake? What if Ermintrude is secretly charitable and gives generously to the poor?"

"Highly unlikely. If so, I'd probably feel compelled to return those deliciously gaudy jewels I just purloined."

"Ha! You are a very very bad man," she said sternly.

"True," he said in a mournful voice. "There's no redeeming me. Come along, Jess. We've more to do."

"More?" She choked.

"This was dead easy. We need more of a challenge. Besides, I want to take you over the rooftops. I think your old friend Isolde Plumworthy deserves our attention."

"You're mad!"

"Not in the slightest. Her house is wedged in quite tightly with several others, and we should have a glorious time under the stars."

"What if I told you I don't like heights?"

"I would be desolated to force you to suffer through such torment," he said sweetly.

"But you'd force me anyway."

"Come now, Jess, don't tell me this isn't fun?"

"It isn't right," she said sternly.

"That wasn't my question." He sighed, took her hand again. "I'll make you admit it sooner or later," he said. "I'll show you a London that few people have ever seen. And then I'll dress you in Isolde's jewels and carry you back to Kent."

"I have the melancholy feeling I'm never going to see my sister again," Jess murmured.

"Foolish child. Trust me. I'll keep you safe."

"Trust you?" The notion was so absurd, she laughed out loud. Except that oddly enough, she did trust him. "It's not my safety that's in question."

"Isn't it? Then whose?"

"Yours, my lord."

"Doesn't it seem ridiculous to stand in a darkened bedroom with a jewel thief and call him 'my lord'? *Alistair* will do nicely."

She ignored the comment. "I read your cards, my lord. That's how I knew who you were. You are going to meet with disaster this night. I saw it."

He leaned forward and cupped her face, and his smile was dazzlingly bright in the darkened room. "I met with disaster the day I set eyes on you, my love." And he kissed her, a brief, hard, hungry kiss that left Jessamine's stomach clenching in sudden, wicked longing.

When he pulled away, there was triumph and despair in his eyes. "Sometime, sooner or later, you will kiss me back," he

211

said, taking her unresisting hand in his.

"I will weep at your grave," she said sternly.

"Well, I suppose that's a reasonable alternative." And he drew her back through the darkened hallway.

Fleur leaned against the wall, staring out into the frosty night. She'd lost track of time — Robert Brennan had delivered her to her room like the perfect gentleman he insisted he wasn't, ordering her to get some sleep while he investigated the situation. She'd looked up into his dear, stubborn face and let him believe she'd do just that.

Of course it was impossible. Jessamine was out there somewhere, in trouble, perhaps in danger, and all Fleur could do was pray that Brennan could save her. There was no man she'd more freely put her trust in, despite the fact that he seemed determined to convince her he was dishonorable and heartless. He'd save her sister, if indeed Jessamine needed saving. He'd do everything he could for Fleur. Except love her.

She reached up and rubbed her fingertips against her aching scalp. Life had been a series of disasters since the day her father died and their security vanished. She'd kept hoping that sooner or later things would right themselves. She'd wanted to believe in Jessamine's happy fantasy of a rich, kind, handsome young man to love her and to take care of her family.

But there seemed to be a dearth of rich, kind, handsome young men offering her their hands and hearts. And even if there'd been a gross of them, she wouldn't have wanted them. She wanted Brennan.

And she couldn't have him.

She didn't want London, the great dirty city she'd grown to hate. She didn't want silk gowns and jewels and servants by the score. She wanted clean air, good food, her painting supplies, and a strong, good man to love her.

At this point it seemed as if everything was going to elude her. She shook her head, resolutely banishing her self-pity. As long as Jessamine was all right, they would endure. They'd survived on the very edge of the slums of London for this long; between the two of them they would prevail. Jessamine had been loath to give up control of the family, afraid that no one else could keep them safe.

But the time had clearly passed for Fleur to marry salvation even if she wished to. They would have to find another way to survive.

She must have fallen asleep. She didn't hear the knock on the door, yet she knew Brennan would never enter her bedroom without knocking. She simply opened her eyes to find the first rays of dawn streaking through the bedroom, and Robert Brennan looking down at her out of those clear blue eyes.

"I don't know what to tell you, lass," he said heavily. "She's gone, there's no doubt of it. So is Glenshiel. His bed's not been slept in, and two horses were taken from the stables sometime in the evening."

"Do you think he kidnapped her?" Fleur asked hopefully. "Could you mount a rescue party . . . ?"

"No," he said. "I think she must have gone with him of her own accord. Either they'll be back or no. I can't just take off after him, much as I'd like to."

There was something in his face that broke through Fleur's anxiety. "Why?"

"Why would I want to go after him? Because he's the Cat, that's why. I don't know whether your sister's helping him, or whether she just got caught in his schemes, but there's nothing I'd like better than to catch him in the act. I have no sympathy for gentlemen thieves," he said bitterly.

"Then why don't you go after him?"

He looked down at her, and his wide mouth tightened in

213

frustration. "Because I can't leave you here without protection."

For a moment she felt a surge of hope, one she squashed down immediately. "You don't need to worry about me. After all, you've made it perfectly clear that the notion of anything between us is completely repugnant to you. Besides, Sally Blaine is hardly likely to toss me out in the road if my sister disappears."

"I wouldn't count on it, miss," he said, and she hated when he called her "miss." "And if there's no problem with the likes of them, there's Clegg. He's a dangerous man, and if I'm not here to protect you . . ."

"Then let him go after the Cat."

"Then it's your sister who wouldn't be safe."

"What makes you think she's safe with a notorious thief?" she countered.

"Instinct. To my knowledge, the Cat has never harmed anyone. Never stolen from anyone who couldn't well afford to lose a bauble or two. If it weren't for the fact that he makes a mockery of my work, I'd be half tempted to let him go. But I can't do that — I've made an oath and I intend to keep it."

"Aren't you breaking it by staying here?" She was goading him, she knew it, and she couldn't help it. Her misery was too overwhelming to keep her tongue still.

He ran his big hand through his rumpled mop of shaggy blond hair, and the expression on his face was tender and exasperated. "There are, occasionally, things more important than duty."

She turned her face from him, no longer able to bear looking at him. "What am I going to do, Robert?" she asked in a mournful little voice.

"I'll see you safe, lass. I'll get you back home, and then I'll find your sister and bring her to you. I promise you I will."

She didn't dare turn back. She could almost feel his hand,

near her face, and she thought if he touched her, she would fling herself into his arms and never let him go.

She held herself very still, waiting. But a moment later she heard the quiet closing of the bedroom door, as he left her, alone. And staring at her reflection in the frosty window, she could see the tracery of tears on her pale, ghostly face.

Eighteen

Things had gone reasonably well up to the very moment of disaster, but Jessamine was not fooled into thinking the night would turn out advantageously. She had read the cards, seen the debacle loom over both of them. By the time they reached Lady Plumworthy's house, she knew there was no escape — for either of them.

Alistair moved through the shadows like a cat, silent and unseen, and Jessamine did her best to follow suit. The sight of Isolde Plumworthy's marble mansion was enough to momentarily panic her.

"She's at home," Jessamine hissed.

"Not to worry. I expect she's well occupied with some poor creature like Calderwood," Alistair replied, unmoved, as he surveyed the edifice. Lady Plumworthy's town house harked back to the 1600s, and in the following decades other houses had snuggled up close beside it, so that they abutted one another with barely a few feet between them.

"You aren't planning to simply walk in, are you?"

"Dressed like this?" he countered. "Not likely. Besides, the object of this little exercise is to throw any possible suspicion away from me. While the Cat prowls London, the Earl of Glenshiel lies puking his guts out in Kent."

"Do they suspect you?"

Alistair considered it for a moment. "It wouldn't do to underestimate a man like Robert Brennan. And Clegg has an unfair advantage." He gave her a wicked smile. "Are you truly afraid of heights, my pet?"

"Yes."

"Pity. You'll get over it."

She expected no mercy from him, and he showed her none. The fronts of the houses were stately, inhospitable. At the back was a rabbit warren of outbuildings and sheds of varying height, almost like a staircase leading to the heavens. Alistair scrambled up onto a garden shed, crossed to a stable, then vaulted up an outlying section of one old house. There he paused, looking back at her in the cool night air. "You aren't going to make me come back for you, are you?"

She stood on the ground, looking up at him. He was already halfway to the rooftops beyond, and the very notion made Jessamine's palms sweaty. "You go on ahead," she said with false cheeriness. "I'll wait for you down here."

As she expected, that pig wouldn't fly. "Come along, Jess," he said patiently. "The longer we wait, the greater our chance of being discovered. The garden shed's quite easy, and I'll give you a hand with the barn."

She glanced behind her. She could run, and this time he might not be able to catch up with her. The mews were deserted, not a soul in sight.

"I wouldn't, Jess." His voice floated down from above, obviously reading her intention.

She glared at him. "It seems like an eminently suitable idea to me," she said. "This time you wouldn't be able to catch up with me, and I really doubt you'd shoot me. It would make too much noise, call attention to you."

"A good point." He sank down on the roof, watching her. "So why haven't you run?"

She couldn't get that damnable card out of her head. The Ten of Swords, piercing his back, bringing all to a desperate end.

217

If she ran now, she would never know. He loomed over her from the rooftop, clearly thinking he was invincible, and she knew just how human he really was. And she didn't want him to die.

She wasn't about to examine why. The sudden knowledge was enough, accepted.

Without a word she started up over the garden shed, scrambling at first on the slick wood, then gaining purchase. He made no effort to help her, merely sat on the higher roof and watched as she made the small leap to the stables. Beneath her a horse whinnied nervously in response to the thudding on the roof, and she almost slipped.

The lower section of the house wasn't quite as close as she had thought — there was at least a two-foot gap between them — and the next one was a good three feet taller. She stared at it for a moment, picturing her body smashed onto the cobblestones below.

Alistair had risen with his usual fluid grace and walked to the edge of the rooftop, watching her. "This is the worst section," he said entirely without sympathy. "If you can make this jump, the rest is quite easy."

"You've been up here before?"

"On occasion."

She wasn't quite ready to attempt it. She didn't know whether she ever would be, but she was more than happy to stall. "I thought you plied your trade while you were a guest in people's homes. That you simply wandered into their private rooms and helped yourself to their valuables."

"Not a trade, dear one!" he protested in mock horror. "Peers of the realm do not involve themselves in trade. Let us say it is my avocation. A way to still ennui."

"And fill your pockets."

"It does have that felicitous side effect," he said. "Are you going to stand there all night, or are you going to jump?"

"What if I fall?"

"I imagine it would hurt," he murmured without a great deal of sympathy.

"What if I died?"

He glanced down at the ground below. "I would think that would be highly unlikely. You might break a leg at the absolute worst, but in truth I think all you'd suffer would be a few bumps and bruises. Now, a fall from the heights of the roof would be a different matter. That could kill you quite handily." He smiled at her sweetly. "Come along, my pet, and I promise I won't push you from Isolde's rooftop."

"Were you considering it?"

"The thought entered my mind, I must admit. It would tidy up things."

"Wouldn't my family wonder what I was doing here?"

"Oh, you wouldn't be recognized. I'd see to it that you'd fall facefirst. You'd be smashed up quite nicely."

Jessamine swallowed. "Are you trying to frighten me?"

"You don't frighten very easily, do you?"

"I never have."

"Make up your mind, Jessamine. You've come this far already. Take the final step."

Marilla's voice echoed in her head, warning her. She would lose everything, perhaps even her life. All she had to do was turn and go back.

"I hope you're prepared to catch me," she said.

"Trust me, Jess. You're safe with me."

"No, I'm not," she said. And she leapt straight into his arms.

He caught her. The force of her landing knocked them both over, and they went down on the slanted roof, rolling, heading for the side, when he stopped their almost certain plummet. He was on top of her, his long legs entwined with hers, and the sensation was shockingly intimate in the scant covering of breeches. She might just as well have been naked with him.

He was breathing heavily, as was she, and he stared down at her, a strange expression in his golden eyes. The sky was ink-black overhead, with tiny pinpricks of stars piercing the darkness, and then he moved his head and blotted out the light as his mouth caught hers for a brief moment before he rose, pulling her with him.

"Well done, Jess," he said. "But next time warn me when you're about to leap."

"I thought you said that was the worst of it?"

"I lied," he said cheerfully. He tugged at her, but she held stubbornly still.

"Before I go farther, I want you to answer me one question," she said.

"You are a stubborn thing, aren't you? Ask me anything you like as long as you promise to stop arguing with your fate."

"Why?"

He glanced at her in the darkness. "Why?" he echoed.

"Why would a peer of the realm, no matter how impoverished, become a common thief?"

"Jessamine, you wound me!" he protested. "There's nothing the slightest bit common about my thievery."

"Why?" she persisted. "Does it have something to do with your brother?"

For a moment she thought he wouldn't answer her. Then he laughed, a soft, faintly bitter sound on the night breeze. "You've been reading too many novels, my pet. I'm not haunted by a desperate need for revenge. My brother chose his own fate. I imagine he drank and gamed to while away the intolerable boredom of London society. I choose to steal diamonds instead. It will probably end as badly, but I've enjoyed myself far more than poor James ever did."

"Is that a good enough reason to become a thief?"

"To relieve boredom? Undoubtedly. I have no affection for London society, or for much of anything at all, except pitting my wits against a locked-up house and a pile of priceless jewels. Is that answer enough? Will you come with me now?"

She didn't move. His mockery was in full force, and she believed him when he said he cared for nothing and no one. Or at least she believed that he thought it was true.

What a fool she was to think there was salvation in a man who'd chosen lawlessness. He would die, and he would bring her down with him.

A chill breeze slid across her face, and she could taste the sea and the promise of snow. And suddenly she didn't care. For the next few hours she would do as he bid, and she wouldn't think, wouldn't question. For the next few hours she was his. "Answer enough," she replied.

He moved upward with unerring precision, taking her along with him. Higher and higher they climbed, over rooftops and dormers and odd gables, past windows that were shuttered, darkened, brightly lit. Past sleeping children and active lovers, past crowded ballrooms and empty schoolrooms, until they reached the slate-covered roof.

Alistair pulled her up the last increment, moving a few feet away as she regained her bearings. And for a moment, for one of the few times she'd been in his presence, she forgot about him as she looked at the vast city spread out around her.

It was beautiful, enchanted. Even at that hour, lights were everywhere, like tiny jewels in a velvet cloak. In the distance she could see the river and the Palace of Whitehall, farther on was the rounded dome of St. Paul's Cathedral. Beyond that lay the slums, with Spitalfields on the outskirts, sinking into morass and decay. And to the right stood the great mass of the Tower of London, oddly beckoning.

221

She pulled her gaze back, to the wonder around her, to the stars shining down just for her. "It's rather magical, isn't it?" she whispered hesitantly.

"I didn't know you believed in magic."

She glanced at him. "I read the cards. I know more about magic than most people do."

"Then why are you afraid of it?"

"I'm not afraid of anything."

"You're afraid of me," he said softly.

She was silent, unable to refute him. She glanced up at the stars again, drinking in their brilliance, and she could feel the unaccustomed weight of her unbound hair down her back.

"You still haven't told me why you didn't run," he said. "What did your magic cards tell you? Did they tell you I was your destiny?"

"No."

"No, I'm not your destiny?"

"No, they didn't tell me that," she said irritably. "It's cold up here. Are we simply going to stand around talking?"

"I could warm you," he said. "What did the cards tell you?"

"I don't want to talk about it. . . ." She started past him, not even certain where she was going, but he caught her, bringing her up against him.

"What did the cards tell you, Jess?" he murmured, his mouth hovering over hers. "Am I going to die tonight? Did you come along so that you could watch?"

She stood utterly still in his arms, past the point of dissembling. "I saw disaster. Destruction. It would mean nothing to you, but it was the Ten of Swords, which signals complete chaos. Things will never be the same."

"How delightful," he said, and his lips were unbearably close. Tantalizing. "Are you going to try to save me? Or will you help me to my well-deserved fate?"

If she kissed him, it would be the beginning of the end. Marilla had warned her — you can't serve two masters. The cards need her pure, undefiled energy.

And Alistair MacAlpin would defile her. Most thoroughly, most gloriously. Leaving her with nothing, not even the cards.

She knew it, and she couldn't help it. She rose on tiptoe and brushed her lips against his gently, her hands lightly touching his face. "I'm not going to let you die," she said quite firmly.

She had taken him off guard. He stared at her, too startled to take advantage of her hesitant kiss, and by the time he'd shaken off his bemusement, she had already moved safely out of reach to the edge of the building and the series of houses that lay out in front of them, the copper roofs, the flatter slate ones beckoning in the starlight.

"Which one is Lady Plumworthy's?" she asked when he came up behind her, breathing a silent sigh of relief when he didn't touch her.

"The far one, with the steep copper roof. Lower than the rest, you'll be pleased to note, in case we have to make a hasty exit."

"I'm not a cat — I can't see in the dark," she replied with some asperity. "I'll have to take your word for it."

"You mean you'll trust me? Will wonders never cease? One piece of advice, Jessamine. Don't look down. Don't give in to temptation and glance over the sides of the building. Even cats aren't overly fond of surveying such a drop."

"All right," she said.

"And do exactly as I tell you. Since you've decided to become a willing partner in this little expedition, you need to realize I'm the leader."

"Who says I'm a willing partner?"

"You did. When you didn't run."

She followed him, of course, across the thick slate tiles of one roof, the steep copper panels of another. Past stonework and chimney pots, past flocks of night birds and a chill wind that whipped through Jessamine's thin clothes and tossed her hair in her eyes, climbing up and then down, an obstacle course of architectural wonder, until they ended on a high stone terrace.

Alistair leaned against the balustrade, his long, dark hair tossed back in the night wind, and smiled at her. "Enjoying yourself so far, my love?" he asked in a soft voice.

"Where are we?" She hadn't realized how loud her own voice could sound, or how quickly he could move. Within seconds he'd pressed her tightly against the stone wall of the house, pressing his hand over her mouth. There was laughter and something else in his eyes, and he pressed his body against hers.

"We're thieves, remember?" he whispered. "Housebreakers. We're not supposed to announce our presence to the world. And we're just outside Isolde Plumworthy's bedroom. Fortunately the old bat sleeps like the dead, and I can hear her snoring, so I think we're safe." He lowered his hand from her mouth, but he made no effort to release her. His strong, lean body blocked the wind, and she told herself she welcomed it. Knowing that warmth was the least of her concerns.

"How do you know how deeply she sleeps?" she whispered.

His laugh was silent. "My knowledge isn't firsthand, thank God. I prefer to bed women who aren't old enough to be my grandmother or young enough to be my daughter. As a matter of fact, I suspect you're just about the right age."

She shoved at him, which accomplished absolutely nothing. For all his lighthearted tone, he was immovable. "What do we do now?"

"We can stand here all night, and I can see whether I can deflower you with us both on our feet. I suspect I could manage, but it wouldn't be comfortable and we'd probably freeze. I could take you into Isolde's house, we could filch some of her ugly jewels and divide the proceeds between us."

"No," she said far too loudly, and once more his hand clapped over her mouth.

"You'll see me at Tyburn," he warned her gently. And then he released her, stepping to the edge of the terrace and looking over. "If those two options don't suit, perhaps we might just enjoy the adventure of climbing down from our lofty perch. It looks to be a challenge, but you don't strike me as the type to shy away from a challenge." He'd already flung one long leg over the edge of the balustrade, obviously preparing to abandon her without a second thought.

She rushed to the edge of the terrace. They were above a garden — trees brushed against the stone walls, and there was a series of balconies that might provide a gradual descent. Might, if one were the Cat.

"Alistair!" she gasped as he began to descend. "You can't leave me here."

He paused, considering it. "I don't know, I think it would be vastly entertaining, watching you try to talk your way out of it."

"You wouldn't be there to watch. Lady Plumworthy already thinks I have something to do with the robberies. She'd probably turn me over to one of her nasty manservants."

"You're right." He threw his leg back over the side. "I suppose I'll have to take you with me after all."

"You're a pig, my lord," she said. "You were never going to abandon me, were you?"

"Sooner or later everyone always abandons you, Jessamine. Haven't you discovered that dismal truth yet?"

She stared at him as something dark and warm grew beneath the bleakness of his words, and she didn't stop to think. To think would be a mistake, the words needed to come from her heart, not her brain.

"I wouldn't abandon you," she said so softly she half hoped he wouldn't hear her.

But his hearing was as acute as his night vision. His head jerked around and he stared at her. "What did you say?"

"Alistair . . ."

The door to the bedroom slammed open, the glass smashing against the stone wall. Alistair was still in shadows, perched on the banister, but the light that shone forth illuminated Jessamine perfectly, standing in her black thieves' clothes. It illuminated the cruel, thick-lipped face of Isolde Plumworthy's sinister majordomo, dressed only in a pair of breeches, his body covered with long, red streaks that might have been scratches, might have been whip marks. And it illuminated the gun in his hand.

His cruel, dark eyes narrowed as he surveyed Jessamine, caught like a trapped animal, and his thick lips curled in a smile. "I knew it was you," he said. "I told Herself, but she wasn't quite sure."

He hadn't noticed Alistair lurking in the shadows. He could escape so easily. Jessamine didn't dare give a sign, to tell him to run while he could. She simply stood there, utterly still, terrified by the gun in the man's hand and the cruelty on his face.

"You'll be a prime bit of sport for her ladyship and me," Hawkins continued, the gun never wavering. "It's not like you don't deserve what happens to you. They'll kill you no matter what — might as well provide some pleasure to one of your many victims than give the crown the chance. Unfasten that shirt and let me see your titties."

Jessamine didn't move. "I'd rather take my chances with Bow Street," she said stiffly.

"I don't give a damn what you'd rather. You won't be taking

226

your chances with anyone. Take off your shirt or I'll put a bullet behind your ear."

"But then I wouldn't be much fun, would I?" she demanded caustically.

"Oh, I can still manage to enjoy it once they're already dead. I imagine her ladyship is broad-minded enough to experiment," Hawkins said cheerfully, raising the gun.

The next few seconds were an endless blur. Alistair launched himself across the terrace, and the explosion that followed echoed through the night air. Jessamine blinked with disbelief as Alistair wrapped his long fingers around Hawkins's throat and calmly smashed his head against the stone. The sound was thick, wet, sickening, and when the man slumped to the terrace Jessamine had little doubt he was dead.

And then Alistair came toward her. His face was bleak, shadowed in the darkness, and his hands had blood on them. He put them on her arms and lifted her, pushing her off the balcony so that as she fell she wondered if he was trying to kill her as well. She landed hard in a thick hedge, the branches scratching her face, ripping at her clothes, and she lay there, winded, unable to see, to think, to breathe.

Breath came back to her in a huge aching rush. She struggled from the imprisoning shrubbery, staring up at the high terrace far overhead. Someone was screaming, a loud, angry wail, but no one leaned over the balcony to see who had escaped.

He was lying facedown on the hard ground. No bushes had cushioned his fall, and even in the darkness she could see the black stain of blood on his beautiful face. His eyes were closed, and she rolled him over, putting her head against his chest to see whether he lived.

His heartbeat was weak, irregular. She reached up to brush the hair out of his eyes, and saw her hands were covered in his blood. She knelt beside him in uncomprehending despair, and

227

all she could see was the prostrate body in the card, pierced by swords, as disaster reigned all around.

"Is he dead?"

She never thought the voice of Nicodemus Bottom would be so welcome. She scrambled to her feet and flung her arms around the little man in incoherent joy. "We've got to help him, Mr. Bottom," she said. "He needs care, he needs a doctor. I think he's been shot, and he certainly had a bad fall. . . ."

"I'm not risking meself," Nicodemus said firmly, pulling out of her embrace with a shake. "We had an arrangement, did his lordship and me. If something were to happen, I was to get the hell away from him."

"You can't. I need to get him someplace safe."

"You're to come with me. He made me swear I'd get you safe back to Kent. He's not going to make it, miss, not after a fall like that one. Best cut our losses and see to ourselves."

"No!" She sank back down by Glenshiel's unconscious body. "He's not going to die. Not yet. And I'm not going to leave him. You can run if you want. Just leave me his carriage."

"Lord love you, miss, it ain't *his* carriage," Nicodemus said. "And the sooner I abandon it, the safer we'll all be. I imagine the owner knows it's missing by now, and while my opinion of the London police isn't very high, a coach and four is a difficult thing to hide."

"Then go!" she said fiercely. "I'll drag him to safety if I must."

Nicodemus stood there, clearly torn. "Clarges Street is not far from here," he offered.

"Why should that matter?"

"His house is on Clarges Street. I could help get him there. But that's it. Then I'm off. And if you have any sense at all, you'll come back with me. We're already late as it is. It'll be

228

past sunup when you get back to Kent, and you'd better have a list of excuses."

Her hands were gentle as they touched Alistair's bloody face. "I don't need any excuses," she said quietly. "Because I'm not going back. Help me get him to safety, Nicodemus, and I promise I won't ask anything more of you."

"A likely story," the little man grumbled, leaning down and pulling at Glenshiel's limp body. "I'll need your help as well, miss. He's a bigger man than he appears."

Together they managed to half carry, half drag him to the waiting carriage. Jessamine welcomed each groan as a sign that as long as he still hurt, he still lived. She was beyond conscious thought now, all she could do was pray, a jumbled, mumbled litany that made no sense.

She held him in her lap, pressing his head against her breasts as Nicodemus pulled the stolen carriage into the empty streets of London. He felt cold to the touch, and his breathing was shallow, rapid.

"Don't you dare die on me, Alistair," she hissed at him. "I know it was my fault, and I'm not going to have your death on my conscience. Why in God's name did you have to be noble all of a sudden? Don't die on me, dammit."

She looked down, and in the darkness of the carriage she could see that his eyes were open, unfocused, staring, and for a moment she thought he was dead. And then a mere shadow of a smile twisted his pale mouth.

"Not yet, at any rate," he said. And he closed his eyes once more.

Nineteen

The house on Clarges Street was dark, cold, and empty. Beyond that, Jessamine didn't pay much attention as she struggled with Nicodemus to get Alistair's unconscious, bleeding body up the stairs. Three wretched, hateful flights, narrow ones, with Alistair ominously silent between them as they wrestled him upward, banging him against the steps.

The bedroom was icy cold, the bed stripped of linen. Together they dragged him forward, tipping him onto the bed, where he lay on his back in the darkness, so utterly still that Jessamine had to lean closer to ensure he was still breathing.

"I'm off, then," Nicodemus announced, making no move to leave them.

"Where are the servants?"

"They come in daily, except for Malkin, and he's still guarding the door down in Kent. Come back with me, miss. He's made it this far, he'll be all right until Malkin comes back to look after him."

"Alone in this cold house with a bullet in him?" she said, not bothering to glance at him. "He'll die."

"Lord, miss, he'll die anyway. No need to bring you down with him."

"Light the candles, Mr. Bottom, before you leave us?" she requested in her calmest voice. "I need to see how badly he's been wounded."

His flesh was cold as she pulled the sodden shirt from him.

She knew what the dampness was — blood, soaking through the black silk. She was so intent on her patient that she only gradually noticed that the room grew lighter, concentrated only on how deathly pale Alistair's face was beneath the smear of blood.

He looked far too young to be so wicked, she thought. Far too young to die. She turned, to find Nicodemus standing beside her, a stack of linens in his arms. "You'll be needing bandages," he said in a sour voice. "You get him cleaned up while I build a fire, and then I'm leaving, whether you come with me or not."

She gave him a beatific smile. "Bless you, Nicodemus," she murmured. "We're going to save him."

"Don't count on me for nothing," Nicodemus protested. "I'm here to look after my own hide."

"Yes, Nicodemus," she said, planting a kiss on his swarthy cheek before she turned back to her patient.

In the end she lost track of time. She was a skilled healer — Marilla had taught her what she knew of the healing arts, and she'd been an apt pupil. Some of what she had learned bordered on medical heresy — wounds, and the hands that treat them, should be clean, for one thing. It wasn't until she managed to wash the blood from Alistair's strong, wounded body that she discovered things weren't as bad as she had feared. The bullet had passed through his upper arm, tearing a hole through his flesh, but there was no bullet to dig out and remove. Despite his fall, no bones seemed to be broken, and once she bandaged the wound, he seemed to rest a little easier.

"Let's get some linen on this bed," Nicodemus growled in her ear, and she jumped, startled, realizing for the first time that the room was warm from the fire he'd built, and that the sun had risen.

"Shouldn't you have left by now?" she asked, running a

231

weary hand through her disordered hair.

"We both should have," he responded crankily as he spread a fresh sheet out. "You shouldn't have insisted on staying, and you certainly shouldn't be here now. I can only hope he'll die of his wounds. Otherwise he's going to kill me when he finds out I didn't take you back home."

"Nicodemus . . ."

"Now, you go along with you, miss. Go downstairs and get yourself a cup of tea, if this house possesses any such thing, while I put some decent clothes on his lordship. It ain't proper, a decent young lady like yourself spending time with a naked man!" he announced, his proprieties outraged.

"Is he naked? I was so busy worrying about his wounds that I hadn't realized," Jessamine said, leaning past Nicodemus to get a better look.

Nicodemus pushed her away unceremoniously. "For shame, miss!"

She managed a weary grin as she backed away. "You're putting a damper on my education."

"One you need, miss!"

"If there's tea in the house, I'll find it," she said, starting out into the hallway. "And I'll make you a cup as well, Nicodemus."

"Lord love you, miss, I'd rather find his lordship's brandy. I think it would do the three of us the most good."

"Tea, Nicodemus," she said firmly. "It's too early in the day for spirits."

It was a small house, tidy enough except for the drops of blood marking their passage from the back stairs up to the bedroom. The basement kitchen was dark and cold, and finding tapers and lighting the fire took a maddening amount of time. There was tea all right, but not much else, and Jessamine realized she was ravenously hungry.

She was on her second cup when Nicodemus made his appearance. "He's resting comfortably enough," he grumbled, pouring himself a cup. "If he hadn't fallen, I doubt he would have even lost consciousness. The arm's not that bad, though he lost a powerful lot of blood. As soon as he wakes up, our worries will be over."

"I didn't know you were worried," she said.

"I'm still here, ain't I?" he demanded in a self-righteous tone. "Though if I don't do something about that bloody carriage, we're all in the soup. Speaking of which, is there any food in this place?"

"Not much."

"Then again, you probably can't cook," Nicodemus said with a sniff.

"I'm not the frail aristocrat you seem to think," she replied calmly.

"True enough, miss. You wouldn't have been able to follow the Cat if you were. Are you ready to come back with me? If we hurry, we might make it out of the city without anyone noticing the carriage. You can say you went for a walk last night, lost your way, and only just found the path back to the house."

"And you think they'll believe it? Especially when Glenshiel doesn't return?"

"Who cares what they believe? They can't prove it."

"I'm not leaving, Nicodemus," she said. "It's too late to worry about my reputation, and I think I've known that for quite some time. What I didn't realize is that I'd destroy my family as well." She leaned back in the chair, closing her eyes wearily. "I don't suppose I could ask you to bring my sister back to London? I'm afraid she's in for a rough patch out there in Kent, at Ermintrude's mercy."

The room was silent for a moment, and then Nicodemus

233

spoke, a rough kindness in his voice. "I'll see her safe, miss. You'll look after his lordship, then? He's a very bad man, he is, but he don't deserve to die."

"I'll keep him alive if it kills me," Jessamine said with a faint smile. She opened her eyes to see Nicodemus standing by the door, looking at her with an odd expression on his face.

"I'll take your sister back to Spitalfields so your mum can look after her," he said. "I'm older than you, miss, and I've seen a lot more. Don't expect disaster until it falls in your lap. We might be able to get out this mess right and tight."

"I hope so," Jessamine said faintly. "I dearly hope so."

"Your sister, Miss Maitland, is a whore!"

Fleur let the embroidery drop into her lap. All morning she'd been awaiting such a denunciation, though perhaps not quite so baldly. She'd spent the day in her room, and up until that point no one had even bothered to inquire after her. No servant had come to make up the fire or bring her early morning chocolate. No one inquired after her welfare.

But now Sally Blaine stood in the doorway, Ermintrude smiling smugly beside her, and the accusing finger she pointed was trembling with rage. Behind the two sisters Fleur could see an entire crowd of interested bystanders, and it took all her self-possession to simply pick up her embroidery once more.

"What are you talking about, Sally?" she managed to say with deceptive calm.

"It's Mrs. Blaine to you," Sally snapped back, her artful coiffure quivering with indignation. "Your sister has taken off with the Earl of Glenshiel, and you may be sure an elopement was never a possibility. She has betrayed my hospitality and my honor, and I expect you're no better than she is. I want you to leave here. Immediately!"

It was as Brennan had suspected, Fleur thought miserably

234

as Josiah Clegg elbowed his way past the two angry women with an admirable combination of deference and swagger. And where was Robert Brennan when she most needed him?

"Now, now, Mrs. Blaine," he said blandly. "You can't blame the little miss for her sister's transgression. Not that I blame you for being upset. Why, it's an outrage, pure and simple. And being an officer of the court and sworn to uphold decency and protect the citizenry, I'll see to it that Miss Maitland is returned back to London all safe and sound." He followed this magnanimous offer with a bland smile, and his gold front tooth flashed brightly.

Fleur's temporary calm vanished as she leapt from the chair, knocking it over in the process. "No!" she cried, but Clegg had already clamped one slightly grimy hand on her forearm.

"You don't have any say in the matter, miss!" Ermintrude said sharply. "You've trespassed on our hospitality and you're not welcome here. You either leave with the Bow Street runners or you leave by foot. Either way, I have every intention of having your bags searched to make certain you haven't stolen anything from us."

"Miss Winters." It was Brennan's voice, broad, calm, authoritative, that broke through the tension. "I'm sure you weren't really suggesting any such thing. Not of an old family friend whom you were instrumental in inviting into your sister's home."

Ermintrude looked faintly flustered by Brennan's commanding presence. "Er . . . I suppose not. But her sister . . ."

"Miss Maitland's mother is ill. She was called away unexpectedly and she left her younger sister in my care. I promised I'd see her safely home, being as how I was the one who brought her here in the first place." He cast a slow, meaningful glance at Clegg.

Clegg made no effort to release her. "I can take care of her,

Robbie," he said. "And maybe you'll be explaining what happened to the Earl of Glenshiel?"

"He went back to London to consult his physician, and he was kind enough to give Miss Maitland a ride in his coach. Why don't you release Miss Fleur, Josiah? I'm sure you didn't realize you were still holding on to her."

Clegg glared at him, but after a moment relaxed his crushing grip. Fleur stumbled away from him, toward Brennan, then halted. For a moment it seemed there was no ally, no help anywhere. The other guests were staring at her with every expression imaginable, from lecherous smirks to disapproving frowns. Only Brennan seemed calm and unmoved.

"And how did you know all this, Mr. Brennan?" Mrs. Blaine demanded.

"Aye, you've been a busy lad this morning," Clegg added. "What made it your business to find all this out? Seems to me you spent last night otherwise occupied. You had a woman in your room, don't deny it, and I'm wondering whether it was this little girl right here. Was it?"

The other guests were enjoying the melodrama immensely. Clegg's accusation drew shocked gasps from the hordes of people crowding in her door, and Fleur could feel the color rise to her face like a damning flag of slutdom.

"Look at her!" Mrs. Blaine trumpeted. "She doesn't even try to deny it! I have been grievously misled and betrayed in my efforts to help those less fortunate. Mr. Clegg, I want you to remove this creature from my house immediately."

"No, Mrs. Blaine." Brennan's voice was quiet, commanding, halting Clegg in his tracks as he lurched toward Fleur.

"I beg your pardon?" Sally Blaine seemed astounded that a lesser mortal like Brennan would dare disagree with her.

"Come now, Robbie," Clegg murmured. "You're not thinking clearly. I'll take over the care of Miss Fleur."

"You'll keep your hands off her, Josiah," Brennan said pleasantly, "or I'll cut out your heart."

There was no missing the look that darkened Clegg's affable eyes. It was a brief shiver of pure, mad rage, and for the first time Fleur began to understand Brennan's worries.

"What did you say, Robbie?" His voice was deceptively mild.

Fleur finally moved. "He told you to keep your hands off me," she said firmly. "Yes, I spent the night in his room last night, yes, I'm a slut and a whore. But I'm Brennan's whore."

The look on Robert Brennan's face would have been comical if it weren't so aghast. He opened his mouth to deny it, then shut it again, defeated. There was nothing he could say to rescue the situation, or her reputation, and he knew it.

"Well," Mrs. Blaine said. "Well."

"Not well at all," Brennan muttered.

"You will take your . . . your strumpet and depart," their hostess declaimed with impressive majesty. "And don't expect any remuneration from my husband for your work these past few days. It seems as if you've been too preoccupied to keep my guests safe. It's no wonder things have been pilfered right and left."

Fleur met Brennan's gaze. He was solemn, angry, and slightly dangerous, and for the first time Fleur began to question her unusual bravado. Perhaps this hadn't been the best time to develop her self-assurance and her tongue.

He took her arm, putting his big body between her and Clegg, shielding her from the curious onlookers, and for a moment there was a look of great sadness in his blue eyes. "Lass," he whispered so softly no one else could hear, "you've done for it now."

"I know," she said, smiling up at him quite brightly. "I know."

237

* * * * *

The house was miserably cold. Jessamine rubbed her arms briskly, but it did little good. The Earl of Glenshiel's residence was charmingly compact, but compared to the tiny house in Spitalfields, it was a rambling mansion. There was no way Jessamine could keep enough fires going to warm the place. The kitchen was cavernous and dank, and no sooner had the fire begun to penetrate the icy recesses of the house then she had to race upstairs to replenish the bedroom fire and check on her sleeping patient. By the time all that was settled and she trudged the three flights back downstairs, the fire in the stove would be out.

At least Nicodemus had proved to be a fairy godmother before he disappeared. On one of her many treks to the kitchen she'd found a box of food — half a smoked ham, five eggs, fresh milk and butter, and even a loaf of thick brown bread.

He also brought her discarded clothing. She'd looked at the garments with a mixture of relief and dislike. There was something beguiling about breeches, about going without a corset, about running wild and free with her hair hanging long and tangled down her back.

But those times were over. Disaster pure and simple had befallen the Maitland family for sure. The final coup de grâce had fallen, and Jessamine could see no way out of it. She put on her corset, her petticoats, her thick wool dress with the huge rip under the arm. She draped herself in an old shawl she found hanging in the kitchen, a discard from one of the servants no doubt. And she bound her hair back as tightly as she could, welcoming the pain as a form of punishment for her many sins.

Pride, for one. Thinking only she could save her family, when it was she who had brought the final disaster upon them all. Self-indulgence. The wildness in her nature had been hidden for so long, and had broken free last night, so that when she followed Alistair across the rooftops of London she'd reveled in it, glorying in the very danger and excitement of it all.

Sloth and greed were minor flaws, but envy almost ate her alive. And worst of all, the greatest, most troubling sin had overtaken her. Lust.

She looked at Alistair MacAlpin with fascination and fear, but beneath it all was a sheer physical need that should have horrified her. But it was too powerful even for that. She could remember every touch of his hand, his mouth, and her body shook. She sat in the chair by the fire in his second floor bedroom as the winter darkness fell all around the city, and she longed for him. He slept on and on, and she wondered if his injuries were far worse than she imagined. She wondered if he'd never wake up, if he'd die. And she thought she would want to die as well.

"Damn you, Alistair," she whispered to the crackling fire. "What have you done to me?"

And still he slept, and she wondered if he was slipping toward death.

She awoke with a start. The room was cold, and almost pitch black. The fire had burned out — only a bank of glowing coals remained, sending out a feeble heat into the shadowy room. Jessamine had no idea what time it was, and she was past caring "Hell and damnation," she muttered, getting down on her knees to work on the dying fire.

It took far too long. By the time it was crackling, she rose, aching and weary, and turned to look at her patient — only to realize that the bed was empty.

"Oh, no!" she moaned, panic slicing through her. She was halfway to the door when it opened, and she screamed.

Alistair's reaction was immediate. His hand clamped across her mouth, her body was pressed against his, and she could feel the racing of his heart against hers. He was cold, wet, and angry, and he glared down at her with a rage that should have been awe-inspiring. Except that Jessamine was way past feeling awe.

"What the bloody hell are you doing here?" he demanded.

Unfortunately he kept his hand over her mouth, so there was nothing she could do but stand there, more and more aware of a number of disconcerting physical facts. Alistair was shirtless. He smelled of soap and brandy, and he'd obviously regained consciousness and taken care of the necessities of life, never realizing Jessamine lay sleeping in the chair by the fire.

"Mmmph," she replied, glaring at him.

He dropped his hand, releasing her with unflattering haste. "I'm going to kill Nicodemus," he said in a low, dangerous voice. "I told him to get you back safely. I won't be having you on my conscience. Not that I have one, mind you, but introducing you to a life of crime was quite enough debauchery for one night. You were supposed to be safe with your sister."

"You told me you weren't going to let me go until you seduced me," she replied, the words coming out of nowhere. "You might as well — I'm ruined already."

"I changed my mind," he said, moving past her toward the rumpled bed.

"Why?" It sounded damnably plaintive, and Jessamine brought herself up short. For all her romantic madness, this was the enemy. The creature who could steal everything from her — her heart, her happiness, her hope, and her one real talent. And he'd made it more than clear he'd leave her with nothing. Nothing at all.

He looked down at her. His dark hair was loose around his face. He'd washed, but he hadn't bothered to shave, and the dark stubble on his chin made him look particularly piratical. But he was no dream pirate of a romantic girl's fantasy.

"Not worth the trouble," he said after a moment in a lazy

240

voice. "Virgins are unimaginative and far too weepy. And you, my dear, have been a thorn in my side since I first saw you."

"Then why haven't you simply left me alone?" she demanded, telling herself that it was relief crushing her heart, and nothing more.

"Damned if I know," he said, reaching for a discarded shirt and pulling it carefully over his wounded arm. "Maybe I'm entranced by pain."

"If you like, I'd be more than happy to smack you on the arm," she said sweetly.

"That won't be necessary. Much as I appreciate your willingness to sacrifice your fair body, I believe I'll decline the offer. We need to get you back home safely to your family and concoct a believable excuse for your absence. The alternative is unthinkable."

"What's the alternative?"

"The world, dear heart, would expect me to marry you to salvage your reputation. And that's something I'm not prepared to do."

"Neither am I," she snapped. "In the first place, I have no intention of getting married to anyone. I dislike most men, and I loathe you."

"Do you now?" She could see the faint smile play about his mouth, and her temper rose higher.

"And if I were fool enough to care about you, or to think my situation would be remedied by something as conventional as marriage, it would hardly be salvaged by marriage to a man who's doing his absolute best to get himself hanged."

"True enough," he murmured. "But you're not foolish enough to care about me?"

"No."

"And you have no desire to marry anyone?"

"No."

241

He was coming closer. He'd forgotten that he was buttoning his shirt, forgotten that he was about to drive her away. "And you loathe me completely?" he said softly.

"Yes." She was backing away from him. The floor was still cold beneath her stocking feet, but the fire was beginning to warm the room once more. And Alistair didn't look like a man who'd just returned from death's door. He looked far too healthy. Far too dangerous. Far too determined.

"Despise me, in fact?" he murmured.

"Yes."

"Don't want me to even touch you?" He caught a loose strand of hair between his long fingers and rubbed it slowly as his eyes met hers.

"Yes," she said. "Er . . . no. I mean . . ."

"What do you mean, Jess? My Jess. You want to go to your grave untouched? Unsullied by brutish hands?"

"Yes," she said, quivering, waiting for his hands to touch her, waiting for his hands to take her.

"And you think I'll let that happen, Jess?"

"You just said you would."

He leaned forward, his mouth so close she could almost taste the tang of brandy. "Oh, Jess," he whispered, brushing his hard lips against her soft, trembling ones. "I'm afraid I've changed my mind."

Twenty

She was looking up at him, Alistair thought, with a combination of despair and resignation. As if she knew all her running was at an end, the time had come, and he would have her. She knew it, and oddly enough she accepted it. But he couldn't be sure if it was because she wanted it too, or she was simply worn out.

"I hate that dress," he said in a conversational tone, reaching toward the modest neckline. He had strong hands, and it was easy enough to rip it open, the tearing sound oddly provocative in the shadowy room. He pushed the torn clothes off her shoulders and they fell to the floor, leaving her standing in front of him, dressed only in her underclothing.

"It's the only one I have," she said in a calm voice. Like a virgin martyr, he thought, going to her hideous fate.

"I'll buy you another one."

It was almost enough to stir some emotion in her. For a moment her blue-green eyes flashed, and then went dull again. "No."

"We're back to that game, are we? Yes." He'd already dealt with her corset once, in the carriage that brought them to London, and the chemise beneath it was plain cotton, unadorned with even a stitch of lace. "And I'll replace your underclothing as well. These look like they came from a convent." He kept his tone easygoing as he deftly reached behind her and unfastened the corset strings.

243

"I don't believe nuns wear corsets." Her voice squeaked slightly when his fingers brushed against her breasts as he pulled the corset off her. He loved her breasts. He'd always been fond of well-endowed women, yet Jessamine's small, warm handful seemed absolutely perfect to him. He wanted to taste her again.

But not yet. He had no intention of moving too fast, hurrying things. He'd thought about this moment for a long time, and it needed to be savored. And she needed to stop looking like a damned tortured saint and show a little more enthusiasm.

"I wouldn't know," he said, untying the tapes that held her moderate hoops in place. "I've never undressed a nun. Until now," he added.

It didn't work. She refused to look at him, refused to respond. The hoops and petticoats fell in a pool at her feet, leaving her standing only in her shift. The room was cold, and he could see her nipples through the plain linen material. He wanted to warm her up.

"I like your hair when it's loose," he said, reaching his arms around her to unfasten it. It brought her face deliciously close to his chest, and he could feel the warmth of her breath even though she tried to hold it as he made short work of the hairpins. The fact that he was aroused seemed barely worth noticing. He'd been in almost a constant state of arousal since he'd first seen her, and he'd grown used to the situation. And to the sad fact that no one else appealed to him as a means to relieve that condition.

Her hair tumbled freely down her back, a shimmering tawny curtain, and he wanted to bury his face in it. He didn't.

"You look like Joan of Arc, condemned to the flames," he said softly.

It accomplished what nothing else had so far. She looked up at him, her eyes huge and luminous. "Am I?"

"Condemned? Yes. There's no escape. Tell me, Jess. Do

you really want to?" He bent down low, his voice soft and beguiling. He could see the rapid rise and fall of her breathing, but he couldn't quite read her reactions. Was it fear and dislike, or was she feeling the same all-consuming need that he was?

"I wish I'd never met you," she said in a low voice.

"That's not an option. Do you want to escape, Jess? Say the word, and I'll send you back home, unsullied."

She closed her eyes for a moment, and when she opened them again they were bright with anger and frustration. "Would you make up your mind, Alistair?" she said in a furious voice. "First you tell me you're going to have your wicked way with me, then you say you don't want me. Then you insist you'll take me, then you offer me a way out. I don't believe you have any idea of what you want, but whatever it is, it's probably not me, thank God."

She was delightfully furious. He took her hand in his, pulled it toward him, and placed it over his erection, holding her there as she tried to pull away. "That means, dear Jess, that I want you. Very badly." She was still squirming, trying to free herself, but he wouldn't release her. "It means I can take you whether you fight me, whether you're as passive as a holy saint enduring the torments of the damned, or whether you want it, too. It means I'm a man, Jess. And right now I don't care about honor and decency and a virgin's reputation. All I want is your body beneath mine, your legs wrapped around me, your heart beating with mine. I want to be inside you. I need you."

It was too late to call back that final damning phrase, but he could only hope she hadn't noticed. She'd stopped trying to free her hand, and instead she cupped him loosely, her fingers curling gently around him.

He slid his other hand behind her neck, beneath the heavy sheath of hair, tilting her face toward his. "What's the answer, Jessamine?"

She licked her lips, and he could feel himself surge against her hand. "What was the question?"

"Do I let you go?"

"No," she said.

"Why not?"

"Because I want to feel the flames," she said. "And I need you, too." And she leaned forward and put her mouth against his.

For a first real kiss it was off center and awkward, and so unexpectedly erotic, he nearly came in her hand. Her lips were soft, pliant, seeking against his mouth, and he angled his head, letting her taste him, letting her learn the contours of his mouth before he opened it, luring her inside.

The touch of his tongue against hers startled her, as it always did. But this time she didn't pull back, she moved closer, and her tongue touched his in shy flirtation.

He groaned, back in his throat. So much for his intention of stretching this into an all-night seduction. At the rate she was going, it would be over in a matter of minutes. And he was a man who never, ever lost control.

The bed was behind them, high, large, rumpled. Too far away, but the floor would be hard, and she'd be lying beneath him. He pulled back just slightly, and he felt as if he'd been running for miles. "I'll burn you alive," he said, kissing the side of her neck. And he caught her up in his arms, ignoring the pain from his wound, and carried her toward the bed.

She wasn't frightened, Jessamine told herself, trembling as he laid her down on the soft mattress. The bedhangings were dark and smothering, the faint glow from the fire barely penetrated the cavernous recesses of the bed, and Alistair was silhouetted in darkness, standing over her.

He was right, the time for running was past. He would break

her heart and he would die, and she would stand at his scaffold and watch him, weep for him. But at that moment nothing mattered. It was too late, the cards had been read. She lay there and waited for her lover to claim her.

His hands were gentle at the loose neckline of her shift, loosening the drawstring. He pulled it off her, tossing it away with his usual elegant disdain, and she lay, naked and vulnerable, beneath his gaze, hoping the darkness would spare her modesty.

But she had forgotten that cats can see in the dark. Alistair climbed on the bed, straddling her, his hands resting on either side of her body, and he leaned over her, his long hair brushing against her face. And then he purred, low and deep in his throat, as he rubbed his face against hers.

She lifted her hands to touch him, to slide up the length of his warm, bare chest. She could feel the bone and sinew and lean, muscled strength of him. The faint, crinkly texture of hair on his chest that she hadn't even seen. The tension in his muscles as he held himself above her. And her hands trembled.

She pushed him gently. He fell back on the bed beside her, reaching for his breeches, but she was already up on her elbows leaning over him in the darkness. She felt wicked and wanton, a wild, magical creature, naked in the darkness. No one could see her, she was free to do what she wanted.

She kissed his mouth slowly, tasting the contours of his lips, biting him lightly. He tried to reach for her, but she put his hands back on the bed. "Let me," she said, kneeling over him. And he did.

She nuzzled his neck, letting her long hair drift across him. She rubbed against his neck, and his hand came up under her hair, kneading her scalp in a slow, delicious caress. And she moved her mouth down to his chest and put her tongue against his flat nipple, tasting him.

His reaction was so intense, she thought for a moment she'd hurt him. He growled, a deep, groaning sound, and his hand tightened on the back of her head. But he held her against him, and she swirled her tongue around him as he had done to her in the carriage, a lifetime ago.

He was reaching for his breeches, freeing himself into the night air, and for a moment she faltered, suddenly unsure. Her eyes had grown accustomed to the dark, and he was nothing like her limited experience in male anatomy.

He must have sensed her uncertainty. His hands cupped her face, his thumbs gently caressing her cheeks, and she sank back onto the bed, closing her eyes and bracing herself for what she knew would happen.

It didn't. Eventually she opened her eyes, to see him leaning over her, watching her, an amused expression on his dark face. She glanced downward to see whether he might have lost interest, but he was still as noticeably aroused as before. Perhaps even more so.

"That's better," he murmured. "You had that holy martyr look on your face again."

"I don't think this is going to work," she said in a doubtful little voice.

"Trust me," he said. "Just lie back and think of absolutely nothing at all. I'll let you know when I'm ready."

She looked at him doubtfully, certain he was mocking her. But she did as she was told, closing her eyes, thinking of clear blue skies and green fields and lovely summer. . . .

His mouth was between her legs. She let out a shriek of outrage, trying to sit up, to push him away, but he was too strong, holding her hips still as he put his lips against her most private part. She tried to kick at him, but he simply pinched her, and all her struggles were a waste of time. She sank back against the bed, panting, furious, horrified at the depraved thing he was doing to her with his mouth, his tongue. His long hair was spread out over her thighs, and she reached down to pull at it, to try to stop him. But instead, her fingers slid through the long strands, stroking him as his head moved.

It was unimaginable sin. It was torment of the most wicked kind, and she deserved the frightening, fiery ache that was building within her, sending shivers of unknown longings racing down her body. He no longer had to hold her hips captive — she couldn't escape even if she'd wanted to. She was hot and cold, trembling, afraid she might fly apart in a thousand different directions, afraid she might go to some dark place and never return. The dark, burning emptiness grew, possessing her body, and she thrashed back and forth in a mindless effort to loosen it.

"Don't fight it, Jess," he whispered against her belly. "Come for me."

She didn't know what he was talking about. She tried to pull away, but he set his mouth against her once more, and she clutched the tangled bedsheet, digging her heels into the mattress, desperate, lost, wanting only to escape.

And then she did. He touched her with his hand and his mouth, and the combination shattered her, tearing away her last tenuous hold on safety, flinging her into that dark void that frightened her so much. Her entire body seemed to convulse, ignite, as the world stopped for a desperate eternity.

She was drenched with sweat, her heart pounding so loudly she was certain it might explode, and every nerve and fiber in her body shivered and trembled as he rose up over her, between her legs, resting against her.

He cupped her face and kissed her. "Are you still in there?" he whispered with a strained smile.

"I'm not sure," she said in a weak voice.

"I'll find out."

She was too benumbed to realize what he was doing until he'd already started, sliding into her slowly, careful not to force her, not to hurt her. She was right, it was never going to work, he was far too big, she was far too small.

He was right, it worked very well indeed. Until he suddenly halted, and she wanted more. Needed more.

"This is the part you're not going to like," he murmured, but she was past paying attention. She wasn't convinced she liked any of this. She wasn't convinced she hadn't died and gone to heaven.

He withdrew, then thrust again, a little more forcefully, coming to a halt once more. She whimpered, raising her hips, clutching at his shoulders, uncertain what she wanted, knowing only that she wanted it more than life.

He withdrew again, and his hands reached up and caught hers, pushing them down against the bed, twining his fingers with hers. And when he thrust this time, he didn't stop, breaking through the frail barrier of her virginity until he rested deep inside her.

It hurt. It tore at her, and she reveled in the pain. It was part of the claiming, it made her belong to him just as he belonged to her. For however long he kept alive.

He stayed very still inside her, letting her grow accustomed to the size of him, the fierce invasion of her body and soul, and his hands stroked the sides of her face gently, a silent comfort and question. She turned her head and caught his hand with her mouth, kissing him.

He groaned, starting to pull away from her, and for a moment she panicked, afraid that he was leaving her, afraid he was disgusted with her virginity, with her pain, with her need.

But instead he thrust again, deeper now, past the shattered barrier of her innocence, filling her so deeply, she thought she would dissolve from the joy of it.

"Again," she whispered into his shoulder, and she felt his body shake with silent laughter.

"Hold on," he said, a promise and a warning. He took her hands and placed them on his sweat-slick shoulders. He was iron hard, every muscle in his body taut, and she wanted to engulf him, devour him. She wanted to go up in flames and take him with her.

He began to thrust deep inside her, a slow, decadent rhythm that almost lulled her into a peacefulness. Except that she found she wanted more from him, found she was arching her hips to meet his thrusts, and they were faster now, harder, pushing her against the bed, and her fingernails dug into his shoulders as she tried to hold on, but she was slipping, slipping away, and he was thrusting, thrusting, so deep inside her. She didn't want to lose it, she didn't want to let go, but the storm hit her with sudden violence, wrenching her away from any safety she had ever known, and she was aflame, burning, a tight spasm of pure sensation that sent her spinning into darkness.

And he was with her, suddenly rigid, and she heard a muffled cry as he buried his face in her hair, flooding her with heat and life and endless desire.

She wasn't quite sure what happened next. How he managed to pull himself free from her clinging body, from the bed, only to return moments later with a wet cloth. He washed her tear-stained cheeks, he washed between her legs, and she trembled with longing again. And then he caught her in his arms and pulled her up tight against him, pushing her tangled hair back from her tear-streaked face.

"You were right," she whispered, half astonished that her voice hadn't left her entirely.

"I'm always right," he said. "Which moment of wisdom were you referring to? When I told you it would work?"

She shook her head, knocking against his chin. "You said

251

virgins were tediously weepy and unimaginative," she said with a watery little sob. "You must hate me."

"I find you utterly charming, my Jess," he said, stroking her. "You may weep all over me if you wish."

She looked up at him, mindful of how completely pathetic she must appear. "Why?"

"Because I love —" He seemed to catch himself. "Because I love making young women cry. It's my mean streak, I suppose. I can't resist the urge to torment them."

She managed a faint smile. "And I thought you reserved your worst behavior just for my benefit."

"Oh, but I do, my Jess. You inspire me to new heights of wickedness." He touched her face lightly, then grimaced. "I think my arm is bleeding again."

Jess shot up. "I'll find the bandages. . . ."

He shoved her back down again. "You'll stay put. It'll be fine. It wasn't much more than a scratch. A little more blood will cleanse it."

"You should have been resting!" she said, aghast. "You shouldn't have exerted yourself . . ."

"If you don't stop wiggling, I'm going to exert myself again, and I think you'd be better off with a rest."

"Again?" she said, astonished.

"Again," he said firmly. "But you're going to need your strength. Go to sleep, Jess."

"But your arm . . . ?"

"Bugger my arm. Go to sleep, or I'll do something that'll make it bleed even more."

She could see him quite clearly in the darkness. Translucent amber eyes, so guarded against everything and everyone. His wide, wicked mouth. His beautiful, lost face.

"You'll die," she said hopelessly.

He didn't even blink. "Not before I have you every way I

can think of. By then you'll be glad to see me go."

Dark, wicked thoughts danced through her sleepy brain, fantasies and visions and half-remembered stories told among giggling schoolgirls. "Every way?" she whispered sleepily, curling up against him with more trust than she had any sense in showing.

"And more."

She slid her hand up his chest, covering his heart. It beat steadily, slowed down from the desperate pace that had matched her own. Steady and true, as if death weren't waiting to claim him.

She closed her eyes, drifting. And in her dreams the cards danced, and the Prince of Swords lay cold and bleeding beneath her feet.

Twenty-one

When she awoke she was alone, as she'd always known she would be. She guessed it was late morning, from the angle of the sunlight coming in the window, and the banked fire sent out waves of delicious heat. His clothes were gone. So, in fact, were hers.

Jessamine sat up in bed, pulling the thick linen sheet around her. She was aching all over, in places she never expected to ache. She was exhausted, sticky, and bereft. And in desperate need of a necessary.

She climbed down from the bed, draping the sheet around her like a Roman toga. The house was absolutely silent — from the street beyond she could hear the usual city noises, but inside all was still. She had no doubt at all that the building was completely empty.

In a small closet several doors down from Alistair's bedroom she found a bath waiting for her, still steaming, and new clothes laid out. Frilly underclothing, with costly enough lace to feed her family for a week. A rose-colored dress that was so pretty she wanted to weep. But she was past weeping.

She dropped the sheet onto the floor and stepped in the gloriously scented warmth of the tub, sinking down in the water's comforting embrace. Years ago Marilla had told her stories of fairies and magical beings, and she remembered a tale of an enchanted castle, where unseen servants fed the fires, drew the baths, and cooked elaborate meals. But this was no enchantment, and far from a happy ending.

She dressed by the fire slowly, willing Alistair to return and face her when she knew he wouldn't. Her hair was still damp when she pinned it up, and even the rose slippers fit her feet. And then she descended the stairs to find her true love, to find a meal cooked by fairies, to find the answer to her future.

What she found was Nicodemus Bottom.

"Don't you look a sight!" he said admiringly, hopping down from the kitchen table, where he'd perched himself. "I outdid myself this time. His lordship told me to find you something pretty, and I bloody well did. You're a real treat for these peepers."

"I should have known you'd be my fairy godmother," she said. "Did you carry the water upstairs and heat my bath as well?"

"I'm no servant!" he protested. "There's a limit to what his lordship can expect from me."

"Where are the servants?"

"Not back yet. Won't be either, according to his lordship. He said he didn't expect to be spending much time here."

"I see." The kitchen was cold and dark. So was her heart. "Do you know where my sister is?"

"Lord love you, miss, she's back home. Which is where I'm to take you. And no arguments about it," he said, forestalling her. "Glenshiel said I was to takes you home, and this time I'll do me duty. He'll have my head if I fail him."

"What if I don't want to go?" she asked very quietly.

There was sorrow and pity on Nicodemus's face. "Ah, miss, you don't want to be saying that. He don't want you here. It's a cruel fact, but the way of the world, and you've lived in Spitalfields long enough to know it. He's had you, and now he's on to other things that interest him more. Such as thievery. There wouldn't be any happiness with a man like that, and you

255

know it. Be thankful he's sending you on your way before too much harm's been done."

"Sending me on my way?" Jessamine echoed in a hollow voice. She closed her eyes, trying to force the cards into her mind, to call forth some guidance, some explanation. But there was nothing. They were gone, as vanished as her innocence. She opened her eyes again. "I'm going to murder him myself," she said pleasantly.

Nicodemus had been watching her anxiously, pity on his face. At her words, he beamed. "That's me girl," he said. "He ain't worth your tears, bless you. He's a worthless blackguard who'll end his days on the scaffold, and you're far better off without him."

"Of course I am, Nicodemus," she said. "Now take me home, if you please. My family must be worried about me."

He must have hit his head when he fell, Alistair thought coolly, sitting back and sipping at the rich coffee that Freddie Arbuthnot thoughtfully provided. Something that knocked the sense out of him entirely, and it hadn't yet returned.

He never should have touched her. Never should have bedded her. For that matter, he never should have taken her thieving, but that was before his fall, so he couldn't blame that particular insanity on a head injury.

Laying eyes on Jessamine Maitland had been far more dangerous than any tumble off a balcony, any bullet hole in the arm. And he was a man who'd reveled in danger.

He wondered what she was doing now. Had Nicodemus taken her back home yet? Had she refused to go? Had Nicodemus presented her with the carefully composed letter that would finish any tender feelings she might have?

He'd labored over it, searching for just the right tone. Mocking enough to infuriate her without demoralizing her.

Condescending enough to make her hate him. Practical enough to make her accept the velvet sack of gold coins.

Oh, he'd been devilishly clever. Complimenting her on her awkward enthusiasm in the sport of love. Offering to recommend her to any of his elderly friends in need of a mistress.

She would never speak to him again, never go near him. He'd severed any feeling she might have quite cleverly, and it had been no more than what was absolutely necessary.

So why did it feel as if he'd severed his own arm?

Freddie appeared from his bedroom, freshly washed and shaved and groomed by his excellent manservant, though his temper seemed uncertain. "You have an incredible amount of gall, Alistair," he said, flinging himself into a chair. "First you disappear from Kent, leaving me behind without a means of returning, and you carry off the Maitland girl as well, so that the entire house is in an uproar, accusations flying back and forth, and then you waltz in here at the crack of dawn with no explanations and no apologies and expect me to welcome you."

"Of course, Freddie," he said cheerfully. "It wasn't the crack of dawn, it was eleven in the morning. And despite what you think, I was desperately ill, I came back to London to consult my quack, and I delivered Miss Maitland to her mother's door that very night. And no one can prove otherwise."

"Why would someone want to?" Freddie said, a little less dull-witted than usual.

"I can't imagine," he said with a seraphic smile. "Eat your breakfast, man. We have business today."

At this Freddie brightened noticeably. "A cockfight?" he demanded. "A boxing match? An auction of prime horseflesh?"

"None of those excellent choices, Freddie. We're going to the Tower of London."

"Bloody hell," said Freddie, deflated.

"Indeed."

257

Spitalfields looked even more dreary than before, though Jessamine wouldn't have thought that was possible. It was a cold, gray day, and the ice penetrated her very heart as she climbed up the front steps, her back straight, her shoulders squared. Behind her Nicodemus sat in the hired carriage, the gold pieces that she'd flung at him littering the seats and floors.

She still held Alistair's letter in one gloved hand, crumpled in a tight little ball. She would hold on to it forever, to remind herself of how very foolish she had been. As if she might ever forget.

Fleur had already flung open the door by the time she reached it, and she threw her arms around her sister, weeping. "Where have you been, Jessamine? I've been so worried!"

Jessamine didn't even look back. She stepped inside the plain, dark parlor and closed the door behind her. Closing the past out of her life.

And then her bravado collapsed. She leaned against the door and closed her eyes as a vast shudder washed over her body. *I will not cry,* she told herself fiercely. *I will not.*

Fleur put her arms around her very gently, drawing her into the parlor. She settled her by the fire, murmuring soothing, meaningless phrases, tucked a lap robe around the beautiful rose-colored dress, and disappeared, leaving Jessamine staring sightlessly into the fire. Only moments later she returned with strong tea and biscuits, and Jessamine ate methodically, keeping her mind determinedly blank.

"Oh, Jessamine," Fleur said softly. "What did he do to you?"

At that Jessamine looked up, startled out of her self-absorption. And she managed to smile. "Nothing I won't recover from, Fleur," she said. "I'm sorry I dragged you into this. I should have been watching out for you . . ."

"I can watch out for myself, Jessamine. I've tried to tell you that over the years. You don't have to do it all alone."

"If I do, I make a botch of it," Jessamine said. "Where's Mama?"

"Prostrate."

"Any particular reason this time?"

"Two ruined daughters."

"Oh, no, Fleur!" Jessamine dropped her teacup with a noisy crash. "I couldn't have ruined you as well."

"Of course you couldn't have," Fleur said with some asperity. "It takes a man to do that. Congratulate me, Jess. I'm to be married. Today."

"No."

Fleur looked at her blankly. "I beg your pardon?"

"I said no. I won't have you throwing yourself away on a rich idiot you despise. The money doesn't matter — we've managed this far and we'll continue to manage. I want you to marry for love."

"I didn't know you believed in love, Jessamine."

"I don't," she said briskly. "Not for me. But you're different, Fleur. You deserve love. You deserve all the good things in this life."

"And you don't?"

"We're not talking about me. Who is it? Not that idiot Freddie Arbuthnot? Or that disgusting old lecher Lord Edison? You didn't let them touch you?"

"I'm afraid I'm marrying for neither love nor money. I'm to marry Robert Brennan this afternoon at the Church of St. Giles. I'm glad you've returned in time to be there. If you will."

Something was dreadfully wrong. Jessamine had only to look carefully at Fleur's pale, determined face to realize it, and for the moment her own despair vanished. "You're marrying the runner," she said flatly. "And you say it's not for love."

"I forced him, Jess," she said. "I announced to the world

259

that I spent the night with him at Blaine Manor, and he was left with no choice. He hates me."

"You spent the night with him?" Jessamine shrieked, blithely ignoring her own fall from grace.

"No. I simply said I did."

"Why?" she asked finally.

"Because he's too wretchedly honorable. Because I was angry. Because I'm a fool, and I thought if I was ruined, he might be willing to take me."

"And clearly he is."

"Not willing. Resigned. I've made a miserable botch of things, Jess," Fleur said. "And I love him."

She burst into tears, sinking to the floor and burying her head in her sister's lap. Jessamine looked down at her golden head, smoothing the curls. "We've both made a proper mess of our lives, haven't we, Fleur?" she murmured, stroking her. "What are we going to do about it?"

"I'm going to marry Robert Brennan," Fleur said. "Even if he hates me for the rest of his life, he'll have me. And I'll be a good wife to him, Jess. A much better wife than I'd be to some rich lord."

"You're right, Fleur. And I should have seen it." She caught her sister's shoulders and drew her back, looking into her tear-streaked face. "You can't go to the altar looking like a bedraggled kitten, my love. If you're going to be married, we should make you the loveliest bride in Christendom. Let Brennan appreciate what he's getting. What are you going to wear?"

"I hadn't thought."

"Your wedding day, and you don't know what you're wearing? For shame." Jessamine rose, all determination. "This is the last time I can arrange your life, Fleur. Come with me, and I'll take care of everything."

"Mama refuses to come to the wedding," Fleur said, sniffling. "She says I've ruined her life and broken her heart."

"Just as well." Jessamine's voice was brisk. "We'll have more fun without her. Come along, my pet. We've work to do."

Her wedding day passed in a blur. Sir John Fielding himself had sent a carriage to escort the bride and her party to St. Giles, and when it arrived she was ready, dressed in pale pink silk, bathed and perfumed and coiffed. Somewhere Jessamine had found small pink roses to fashion a bouquet, with a few left over to tuck into her hair, and Fleur had sat patiently while her sister fussed over her.

At the church she almost lost her nerve. It would be simple enough, she had always known it. She could refuse to marry Robert Brennan. No one would force her, and he would be free from the burden of responsibility she'd saddled him with.

She'd been cruelly selfish, she knew that, and if she had any core of decency, she'd free him. She saw him standing at the front of the church, waiting for her, a grim, cool expression on his face, and her determination faltered.

Jessamine was beside her, her hand on her arm as Fleur came to an abrupt halt halfway down the aisle. The church was deserted except for one other man, an elderly gentleman with a bandage across his eyes. She could easily turn and run, putting an end to this farce, freeing Brennan. But Jessamine held her tightly, as if sensing her confusion.

"I'm afraid, Jess," she whispered.

"I know," Jessamine said, her voice deep with sorrow. "Do you love him, Fleur?"

"God help me, yes." She stared at him, blinking back the tears, telling herself that the best thing she could ever do would be to turn and run. But Jessamine was holding her too tightly.

"Do you want him, Fleur?"

"Yes," she said hopelessly.

261

"Then fight for him. This is your wedding day, Fleur. Take him."

When Fleur reached his side, she didn't dare look at him. Her hand was trembling, icy cold beneath the thin kid glove when he took it in his large, workman's hands. The disparity between them was never so clear. He was a man of the people, with big, strong, square hands that knew how to do a day's work. Hers were fragile, delicate, adept at watercolors and stitching a fine line and little else. She would ruin his life. She didn't care.

It was over so quickly. A few words mumbled and repeated. Their names in a register, his a rough scrawl, hers a flowery script. And then out into the early autumn evening with Robert Brennan's hand on her arm.

She didn't remember taking leave of her sister. She didn't remember anything at all as they walked through the darkening streets, his large, untidy body beside her, protecting her.

He stopped by a cheerful, noisy pub, and she stole a quick, worried glance up at him. His expression was unreadable. "Where are we?" she asked in a very small voice.

"Where I live."

"In a public house?"

"Above it. It suits me. I can always find a hot meal, and I don't mind the noise. One of the barmaids mucks out my rooms every now and then. If you want, she can come in and help you."

"Did you sleep with her?" The question came from out of the blue, shocking her.

She waited for his scathing response. Instead, he merely glanced down at her, his expression enigmatic. "No," he said.

She wasn't sure what she was expecting. There were three rooms, a bedroom, a sitting room, and a kitchen, though the last didn't appear to get much use. Everything was tidy, and someone had been in to light a fire in the fireplaces, so that it was warm and light and welcoming.

But the man beside her wasn't welcoming. He stayed at the door, and when she turned to face him he looked stern and forbidding. "I'll have them send you up some dinner in a bit. You might want to take a rest."

"Where will you be?"

"Out. I have work to do."

"When will you be back?"

"I don't know."

His words couldn't have been more clear. She had forced her way into his life against his will, and he was going to do his best to ignore her.

"I'll wait up for you," she said with one last trace of hope.

"Don't bother. I'm going after the Cat. With the reward on him, I'll have enough to return to Yorkshire."

"Will you take me with you?"

He seemed astonished that she would ask. "You're my wife, aren't you? Whether I like it or no, you belong to me. You'll come with me."

Relief swamped her. For a moment she thought he'd planned to walk away that night and never return. "I like the country," she said tentatively.

There was no softening in his bleak expression. "It matters little to me. You've made your bed and you'll lie in it."

"Alone?" she asked, shocked at her own boldness.

Something flared in his eyes, some emotion that she couldn't read. "No," he said. And without another word he left her, alone in the warm, cozy rooms, alone on her wedding night.

It was himself he was wanting to punish, Brennan thought fiercely, striding through the city streets at a breakneck pace. She stood there in the midst of his shabby rooms looking like a fairy princess, her heart in her eyes, and all he wanted to do was wrap her up in his arms and carry her into his bed. He was half afraid to touch her. She was so beautiful, so delicate, so exquisitely formed, and he was a great hulking brute of a man. A rough man, born a farmer and he'd die one as well. He wasn't used to ladies. He wasn't used to a lady who'd destroy her reputation on a whim. An innocent who looked at him with hurt and love in her eyes, when he was the one who was causing the pain.

He could have found a way out of the tangle, he knew he could. He could have applied to Sir John, and something could have been arranged. But instead he'd accepted his duty, he'd married her, angrily, reluctantly, all the while reveling in the fact that fate had forced his hand, and she belonged to him.

And he couldn't even be honest enough with himself and with her to admit it. He'd abandoned her in a strange place, alone on her wedding night, because he was too angry and too proud. Too angry with himself.

And yet she was the one being punished.

They were wed legally, permanently, the bond sealed. Even if laws could break it apart, nothing would make him go back on his vows. He had promised to love and cherish, honor and protect her throughout all the days of their lives. And he was a man who never broke his word.

He was doing a bloody poor job of loving her, he thought angrily. He was so caught up in trying to honor and protect her that he couldn't see straight. All he could think about was the look on her face when he left her. The scent of the roses in her hair.

He'd spent a fortune on those flowers, and they'd been worth every penny. He couldn't buy his young wife jewels or silks, but he could buy her perfect roses. He would somehow have to swallow his pride and accept that.

He wondered if she was crying. If she was frightened. If she regretted her rash gesture that had bound her to him. He wondered if she hated him now. He wouldn't blame her if she did.

He had work to do. The Earl of Glenshiel was about town, and Brennan had every intention of catching the Cat in the act. The obvious thing to do was to watch his house on Clarges Street.

But it was a cold night. A woman waited for him. A woman who loved him.

And there were times when duty could wait.

"Enjoying your wedding night?"

Brennan whirled around in shock. Josiah Clegg had materialized out of the darkness, picking his teeth with a thin, elegant dagger that looked far too expensive for the likes of a Bow Street runner.

"Duty comes first," he said stiffly.

"Not when we were at Blaine House, it didn't. That sort of thing gives runners a bad name. I wonder what Sir John thinks of his precious protégé seducing a high-bred young lady when he should have been working."

Brennan summoned a bland smile. "He stood up for me at my wedding," he said.

Clegg stiffened. "Well, ain't that cozy?" he snarled. "You may be more interested in what's between her legs, but I've got work to do. The Cat's planning something big."

"What makes you say that?"

"I have my sources," he said loftily. "As a matter of fact, Samuel Welch got wind of something. Told me a bit, but now he's disappeared."

"Disappeared?" Brennan said sharply.

"I expect the Cat's gotten to him."

"Why are you telling me this, Josiah? You've never been

265

interested in helping me. You want the thief-taker's share for yourself."

"Half the sum is better than none," Clegg said with a reasonableness that was almost believable. "The Cat's too tricky for me. You know who he is, don't you?"

"Do you?"

"Mebbe I do, mebbe I don't. But I expect he's done for poor old Sammy, and I hate to see his sort get away with it. Especially when you consider what he's after this time."

"What is it?"

"You wouldn't believe me if I told you. I can scarce believe it myself, but the facts don't lie. An insult to all of England. And I intend to stop him, with or without your help."

Brennan just stared at him. Josiah Clegg was playing him like a pair of loaded dice, but Brennan had no intention of falling.

"You do that, Josiah," he said evenly. "I've already given Sir John my notice. I'm no longer a runner. I'm taking my wife back to Yorkshire."

"You mean you'll just walk away? With the Cat still on the prowl?"

"You'll see to him, Josiah," Brennan said. "I know I can leave the safety of London in your capable hands. In the meantime, I need to be getting home."

"Back to the bit o' crumpet?"

"Back to the woman I love, Josiah. Back to my wife."

266

Twenty-two

The house in Spitalfields had never felt so cold and empty when Jessamine returned that night. The meager fire in the parlor could barely begin to warm even that small room, and the cheap tallow tapers sent out a wavering light. Jessamine sat alone, staring sightlessly at the cards laid out in front of her.

They meant nothing. Pasteboard pictures as old as time, but they no longer spoke to her. She picked them up and shuffled them once more, laying them out in a random pattern, trying to concentrate. But Marilla's warnings came back to her tenfold. All she could see was Glenshiel — his haughty, mischievous face, his elegant body. His wicked smile.

"Having a spot of trouble, are we?" The voice, low and evil, slid out of the shadows like some nasty, dark thing. Clegg was standing, watching her, and she had no idea how long he'd been there.

She was beyond fear. She glanced up at him, in perfect control, surveying him icily. "What are you doing here?"

"Now, what do you think, missy? We have an arrangement, you and me, and that arrangement stands until I choose to end it. You're all ready to help me, I can see that. Look at your cards and tell me where I'll find the Cat."

She swept the cards up into a pile. "I can't."

The look on Clegg's face in the flickering candlelight was not reassuring. "You've spent too much time with the toffs," he said. "You've forgotten that I don't take no for an answer."

267

"I told you I can't. I've lost whatever talent I had."

He came up to her, standing too close, and he smelled of beer and dirt and something evil. "I don't give a bloody shit about your talent," he said. "Tell me where I can find the Cat."

"I don't know. . . ."

He slapped her backhanded across the face, so hard that her head whipped around. He was wearing a heavy jeweled ring and it cut her. She could feel the dampness of blood on her stinging face, and she had the strange, remote thought that she didn't want to bleed on her beautiful new dress.

"Where is he?" Clegg shoved his face into hers, breathing rank fumes. "I'll give you your share once he's strung up and dancing the hangman's jig, but I'm not about to wait any longer. Brennan knows what's up as well, and he'll try to cut me out. I won't let that happen. Right now he's lying between your sister's legs, but sooner or later he'll remember what's important. And I mean to see that it's too late for him. Where is the Cat?"

"I don't —"

He slapped her again. Her eyes stung, and she found she'd bit her lip. She stared up at him mutely.

"I'll ask you one more time. If you don't answer me, I'll have to hurt you. Where is the Cat?"

She thought of the handful of gold coins she'd thrown back at Nicodemus. She thought of the crumpled letter that lay hidden beneath her pillow, the cruel, dismissive words. Revenge would be gloriously simple. Defiance would mean pain.

"I . . . don't . . . know . . ." She spat out each word at him.

He put his thick-fingered hands around her neck, pressing tightly. "You know you're pretty in that dress," he cooed. "I never fancied you much — you have too sharp a tongue on you. It's your sister I wanted, and I'll have her after I've finished with Brennan. But mebbe I'll show you what a real man is like, first. Not one of your fancy lords, to diddle you in a great fancy bed."

She didn't move. She couldn't, she could barely breathe. He was pressing just hard enough to hurt, just hard enough to restrict her breathing, not enough to cut it off entirely. She stared up at him in silent scorn, waiting, willing him to hurt her.

He pressed harder, and her breath constricted. The room was growing darker, colder, and she realized she would die. It was an unappealing thought, but she could see no way out of it. At least if he strangled her she'd be unable to tell him what he so wanted to know.

The sudden banging overhead startled him into releasing her. It was Mrs. Maitland, her plaintive voice echoing down the stairs, calling for a hot posset.

"Who's that?" he demanded.

She was struggling to get her breath back. She couldn't talk, she could only cough and choke, a fact that amused him. "I remember. It's your mother. Mebbe she'd like to learn what her daughter's doing on the side with the Earl of Glenshiel? Climbing over rooftops and robbing innocent people?"

Jessamine looked up at him with mute horror.

"Oh, yes," Clegg said with a foul smirk. "I know who he is. I just want to know where. He hasn't been back to his house all day. I means to capture him, and I don't care how I have to go about doing it. Now, where is he?"

"I haven't seen him." She braced herself for another blow, but instead he caught her chin in his hand, holding it in a painful grip.

"He'll die, missy. And I'll be the one to see to it." He put his wet mouth on hers, forcing a great, slobbering kiss against her unwilling mouth. "And then I'll be back to deal with you."

It took all her remaining strength to drag herself from the

chair. He'd left the front door gaping into the winter night, and she closed it, locking it, though it would do little good. It had been locked and barred before.

She scrubbed her mouth, washing the foul taste of him away, and then she looked at herself in the mirror. She had never been a beauty, but at the moment she looked positively horrifying. Her eyes were huge in her pale face. The cut from his ring had congealed, and with luck could be covered by her hair. The darkening bruises would be more difficult to disguise, but it was night, and no one would look too closely, either at her face, or the marks of fingers around her pale throat.

Her mother pounded with her cane once more, her querulous voice drifting down. Jessamine didn't hesitate. Her cloak was old, but still serviceable, thick, and concealing. She pulled it over her head, grabbed her reticule, and headed out into the dark London night.

It was past midnight when Brennan finally returned home. The tavern beneath his rooms was raucous, and he winced, wondering what his bride would think, lying alone upstairs, listening to the carousing below.

But perhaps she was no longer there. He might finally have succeeded in driving her away. She knew her way around the streets of London — for the past few weeks he'd done nothing but worry about her when he wasn't able to keep an eye on her. And now that he'd deliberately left her, she'd probably taken off, and she'd be lying in some alleyway, her throat slashed, and . . .

She was lying in his bed, asleep. The candle beside the bed had burned low, casting strange shadows across the room, and he stood over her, caught in a spell. She looked like a princess, delicate and fragile, far too beautiful for a man like him. He could see shadows beneath her eyes, the faint trace of dried tears. He looked at her, and he gave in.

He hadn't made a sound, but suddenly her eyes flew open, and she looked up at him with a wariness that cut him deeply. And was no more than he deserved.

"I didn't know if you were coming back," she said.

"This is my home." It came out more gruffly than he wanted, but he didn't know how to use the sweet words. How to be gentle, when he was nothing more than a rough farmer.

"Yes," she said. "I'm glad you went out. It gave me time to think."

He stripped off his heavy overcoat, hanging it on the hook. Beside her discarded wedding dress, he realized with a start. "And what did you think about?"

"That I have done you a grave disservice," she said, her voice solemn. "I ignored your warnings, I was selfishly unmindful of what I was doing, and I have ruined your life. I have thought about it, Robert, and I have decided that the only fair thing would be to release you from your vows."

He took off his jacket, sat in the chair, and began to pull off his boots. "Lass," he said, "I made my vows to God, not to you. And unless you've suddenly turned into the Almighty, you're not the one to release me from them."

She looked stricken, and he cursed himself. "Then I will simply go away," she said. "I will join a convent, and you can pretend I'm dead. . . ."

"You aren't a Catholic."

"I can convert," she said desperately.

"And I'm no bigamist. I'll take no other woman to wife."

"I'll kill myself. . . ."

"Stop it!" His voice rose to a shout, and she flinched beneath its power. "Stop it," he repeated more quietly, standing up and sliding his braces off his shoulders. "I won't deny that I did everything to keep you away from me. I wanted to save you. I

271

wanted you to have everything you deserve, not a life of hard work and no elegance. I'm the one who's ruined your life, lass. And the damnable thing about it is, I'm glad."

For a moment his words didn't seem to make sense. She stared at him in confusion. "You're glad? You mean you want me? Just a little?"

He sighed. She was beautiful and shy and delicate. Clever and gifted and thick as a brick on occasion. He came to the bed and knelt on it, sliding his hands behind her head, lifting her face toward his. "Fleur," he said, for the first time using her given name, "I love you with all my heart and soul. I love you so much, I was willing to give you up rather than cause you pain. But you stopped me at every turn, and it's too late now. Today I promised God that I would love you until death. I promise you now that I'll love you even beyond that. I'll love you forever."

"Robert," she said with a tremulous smile, "I think I knew that."

He was afraid he'd crush her with his huge, strong body. She was so fragile, he was so big. But she was stronger than he gave her credit for, and her slenderness had nothing to do with frailty. She took him and held him, as she would hold their babies, and he knew there was no going back. He would plant his seed in her this very night, another Yorkshire farmer who, God willing, wouldn't be lured away to the city like his da.

She cried a bit when he hurt her, smiling at him through her tears as she took him into her body. She cried even more when he brought her pleasure, her entire body suffused with it.

And she cried in his arms afterward, wrapped tight against him, fitting perfectly beneath his heart. And he held her there, knowing he would never let her go.

* * * * *

The house on Clarges Street was dark and deserted. It came as no surprise to Jessamine — Clegg had already told her that Alistair had disappeared. If he had any sense at all, any notion of self-preservation, he would guess that they might suspect him and he would make himself suitably scarce.

But then, wisdom and self-preservation seemed to be in short order in Alistair's makeup. He was entirely capable of swaggering back home in the small hours of the morning, oblivious of the fact that he was in danger.

All she could do was wait. The other alternative, to go in search of him, was unacceptable. She wouldn't be welcome in polite society, not after her disappearance from Sally Blaine's miserable house party. And there was no way she could find Nicodemus, her most likely ally.

Her only hope was to wait for him. To warn him to run as far and as fast as he could.

He would doubtless laugh in her face.

The kitchen was just as she had left it that morning, cold and dark and unwelcoming. She stood just inside the door, listening carefully for any sign of life. Not a sound.

She didn't dare light a taper. It hadn't appeared as if anyone was watching the house, but she couldn't be sure. She didn't want to do anything to alert the runners.

The scrubbed wood floor was icy cold to her feet, even through her thin slippers, and she tiptoed toward the pantry, suddenly famished. If she had to settle down for a long wait, she'd try not to do so with an empty stomach. There was no way in heaven that she would venture upstairs. Alistair wouldn't come home to find her asleep in his bed, waiting for him. He'd find her awake in his kitchen, with a carving knife in her hand in case she needed to make her point.

The pantry was pitch black. No light penetrated its inky

273

recesses, and she put her hands out in front of her to guide her way. Only to have them touch something warm. Something solid. Something breathing.

It happened very quickly. He caught her arms, spinning her around and pushing her up against the wall, hard. A strong body covered hers, but she knew that this time it wasn't Clegg. It was someone far more dangerous to her very soul.

It was Alistair.

"It's you," he said after a moment, sounding surprised.

"Who did you think it was?" she responded with commendable asperity. She was getting mortally tired of being pushed around by men. Alistair hadn't hurt her physically, but neither had he released her.

"I thought you had more pride." He was nuzzling her neck, his body pressed up close behind hers. Even through her layers of skirts she could feel him wanting her, and the knowledge made her furious.

She slammed her elbow back, aiming for his ribs, but he must have felt her muscles tense in anticipation, for he simply whirled her around before she could connect. Even in the darkness she could see his eyes glittering down into hers.

"I didn't come back to bed you," she said bitterly.

"Did you think twice about the money you threw in Nicodemus's face?"

She tried to stomp on his instep, but he was too adept for her, pinning her against the wall again, with his hips pressing her, his arms imprisoning hers.

"I came to warn you."

"Generous of you, given the circumstances."

"Don't play games with me, Alistair! I may despise you, but I don't want to see you die. Clegg knows who you are. So does Brennan, and God knows how many other people. You need to leave London before they arrest you."

"If they had any proof, I'd be in Newgate," he said evenly. "Did you tell them who I was?"

"No."

"Then how did your good friend Clegg find out? For that matter, why did he confide that knowledge in you? But then, you're his confederate, are you not? You take a share of his prize money. Most likely it seems cleaner than the money I tried to give you."

"I didn't earn that money on my back."

Curse his soul, he laughed at her. "Trust me, my pet, if that was remuneration for your services, you were vastly overpaid. And if I remember correctly, you weren't always on your back. You were on top, once, and . . ."

He was too strong, and she couldn't stop his hateful words. "Why are you doing this?" she said, torn between fury and helplessness. "What have I done that you should torment me?"

"Am I tormenting you? I promise you, I could do far worse. We didn't really try everything last night. Come upstairs with me, and you can tell me what you told your good friend Clegg."

"Go to hell."

"You shock me, Jessamine. Such language from a gently bred girl," he murmured lightly. "I could take you from the back. You'd like that, my pet. I could touch you when you found your release, make it last even longer."

"Stop it!" The more she squirmed against him, the stronger and harder his body seemed to grow. The images his words were conjuring up were powerful and demoralizing. He knew she was growing heated despite her rage, and he leaned down and bit her lightly on the side of the neck. "I find I'm quite overcome with lust, my pet, which is not a usual case for me. But then, you tend to have that deleterious effect on my sangfroid. I should send you on your way, but self-control has never been my strong suit. I want to come in your body, love. And you want me to. I can feel it in the tiny quiver that dances down you."

How could he guess? The unbearable knowledge shamed her. "Leave me alone," she said furiously.

"Or you could take me in your mouth, sweet Jess," he whispered. "And then you could go back to Clegg and tell him where to find me."

It was more than she could take. This time when she shoved him he fell back, though she knew it had to be willingly on his part. She almost made it as far as the kitchen door when he caught her, and they went down on the wood floor together, his body covering hers.

For a moment she lay still beneath him. And then he shoved her skirts up with rough haste, and she let him, unwilling and unable to stop him. Needing him. Putting his arm under her waist, he pulled her to her knees, and she could hear him fumbling with his breeches. She didn't care. She cared too much. He thrust inside her, and she immediately shattered, convulsing around him in hateful, mindless delight. He moved his hand down between her legs and stroked her hard, prolonging it, and she was sobbing, begging for heaven only knew what, and when he filled her with his seed she cried out, torn with love and anger.

He pulled away from her, leaving her, and she collapsed on the floor, her face buried in her arms, trying to still the sobs that shook her. She had never felt so lost, so abandoned, in her entire life, and the worst knowledge of all was that her despair wasn't in his taking of her. It was in his leaving.

"Get up," he said when she thought he'd left.

She didn't move. She had little recourse against him but sheer stubbornness, and she held on to it fiercely.

He put his hands on her shoulders, and she tensed, expecting him to haul her to her feet.

276

Instead, he was oddly gentle. "Get up, Jessamine," he said in a quiet voice. "The floor is cold."

She didn't want his gentleness. She managed to pull herself into a sitting position, wrapping her arms around her legs and burying her face against her knees. "Leave me alone, please," she asked in her most polite voice.

"As you wish." He opened the door, letting in a shaft of moonlight that surrounded her in a silvery pool. He paused, turning back to look at her, and she knew he could probably see the glitter of unshed tears in her eyes. She didn't care.

"I doubt it's much consolation to you," he said in a perfectly amiable voice, "but no matter how much you despise me right now, it's nothing compared to how much I despise myself."

She lifted her head to stare at him coldly. "You're right," she said. "It's no consolation whatsoever."

He was halfway through the door when he stopped again, and this time when he came back he closed it behind them, shutting them in the darkness once more.

Jessamine had reached the end of her tether. "Go away!" she said, her voice breaking into a sob.

But he was kneeling beside her on the cold floor, and his hands were unbearably tender. "What happened to your face, Jess?" he whispered.

"Nothing."

"Someone hit you."

"I ran into a door."

The moonlight betrayed her, spreading across the kitchen with the brightness of candleglow. He touched her neck, and she knew there must be marks there as well. "Clegg," he said simply. "Did he give you a reason for this?"

"He wanted to know where you were."

Alistair shook his head. "He's smarter than I realized. He could have found me if he really wanted to. Instead, he did this. You're a pawn, Jess. Nothing more. He knew if he hurt you I'd become careless. And that's what he wanted."

"Why would you become careless?"

"Because now I'll do anything to kill him. And rage makes a man vulnerable."

"The bruises will fade," she said.

"My anger won't." He cupped her face, looking down at her with an odd sort of longing. "I'm sorry I dragged you into this. It's too late now, there's no escape for either of us. You'll be ruined, I'll be dead. It's like some damned melodrama." He managed a crooked smile. "Come upstairs with me, Jess. I'll love you properly, not like a rutting beast. You deserve to be loved, you know. Despite your sharp tongue. I hope you find someone worthy of you."

"Don't!"

"Come upstairs with me, love, and let me heal your pain."

And she put her hand in his, letting him draw her up the stairs.

Twenty-three

When Jessamine opened her eyes, the room was dark and cold. She burrowed deeper under the covers, unconsciously seeking a source of warmth. There was none to be found.

She didn't want to wake up. It was still too early, and as long as she lay cocooned in sleep, she wouldn't have to face what she had done. What she had allowed him to do, knowing he would abandon her once more.

The light was an odd bluish murk, strange for dawn, she thought, opening one eye reluctantly. From somewhere below she heard the clanging noise, as if someone had knocked into something, and she sat up, suddenly hopeful. And just as suddenly her hopes vanished. Alistair was the most graceful creature she had ever seen. He wouldn't stumble into anything.

She heard footsteps on the stairs, and she held very still, wondering if Clegg was coming to finish the job he'd started on her. She had no time to search for a weapon, she could only sit there with icy calm, prepared to meet her doom.

Her doom was Freddie Arbuthnot. He stuck his head in the door, spied her in bed with the sheet clutched around her, and promptly ducked back out again with a strangled gasp. "I do beg your pardon, Miss Maitland," he stuttered. "I've been sitting here in this demmed house for hours, waiting for you to wake up, and I just thought I'd check on you. Forgive the intrusion."

She scrambled out of bed, pulling her clothes on as quickly

279

as she could. "For hours, Mr. Arbuthnot? But it's not even dawn yet."

"It's past dusk, Miss Maitland. You've slept the clock around. Alistair said I wasn't to wake you, I was to sit here and wait until you were ready to depart, but it's miserably cold in this demmed house, and I wouldn't have done it for anyone else."

She didn't bother with her corset, fastening the rose-colored dress with careless haste. "You may come in, Mr. Arbuthnot."

He peered around the door doubtfully. "I say, you're a deal speedier than any female I've ever met," he said. "Are you ready to go home, then? Promised Alistair I'd see you back there. Always mean to keep my promises."

"Where is Glenshiel?"

"Can't tell you, Miss Maitland."

"Can't?" she said. "Or won't?"

"Can't," Freddie said promptly. "I haven't the faintest idea where he's gone, though I expect it's far away. He said he didn't expect to see me again."

Jessamine didn't move. With any luck Alistair had decided to head for the Continent, one step ahead of the Bow Street runners. They wouldn't catch him, and even though she would never see him again, he would be alive and well.

Unless, of course, he hadn't gone anywhere. Unless he'd simply embarked on a task that he didn't expect to survive.

She squeezed her eyes tight shut, searching for the face of a card, for a hint, a clue, a tiny ray of reassurance. Only to be rewarded with the same miserably frustrating blankness over everything.

"You all right, Miss Maitland?" Freddie said with proper solicitude. "Promised Alistair I'd make sure you were settled properly."

She managed a shaky smile. "I'm fine, Mr. Arbuthnot." There was one place she could check. His black thieving clothes were in the cupboard in the far room — if they were still there, then he had truly made a run for it. "I just need to . . . er . . . attend to a few matters."

Freddie blushed a deep crimson. "Absolutely, Miss Maitland. I'll wait for you downstairs, shall I? You won't try to run off on me, now, will you? Alistair warned me that you were a very tricky young woman, but I told him he had maggots in his brain."

"Indeed," Jessamine said sweetly.

The black clothes were in the far room, lying in a pile at the bottom of the cupboard. She picked up the shirt, staring at it. It smelled of soot and fire, and her hands were black when she dropped it. Once more she closed her eyes, searching for an answer. There was none.

Freddie was pacing the kitchen, and his kind, foolish face brightened when she appeared. "Knew I could count on you, Miss Maitland," he said cheerfully. "I've called for a carriage. It won't be but a moment."

"Thank you, Mr. Arbuthnot."

"Now, Miss Maitland," he chided. "Don't sound so sad. I'll miss the old boy just as much as you will, but he'll be back, I'm sure of it. Not that he ever liked London much. Always told me if things had been different, he'd prefer to live in that plaguey cold house of his up in Scotland. Can't imagine a civilized person wanting to do anything in Scotland other than hunt. And I can't abide hunting."

"Maybe he's gone back there."

"Doubt it. Said he'd never go back. Still, he's a damnable fellow, Alistair is. You know what he had me do this week?"

"I can't imagine," she said faintly.

"Took me to the Tower of London. Can you imagine such

281

a thing? Told me he wanted to see the crown jewels. I told him they were great trumpery things, and why should we bother. It ain't like in the old days, when you could actually try the demmed things on, don't you know."

Jessamine froze. "He took you to see the crown jewels?" she said in a strangled voice.

"He did indeed. Typical of Alistair's luck. That very night there was a fire in Martin's Tower, and they had to put the jewels in storage until they could repair the place. If he'd waited one day, he wouldn't have been able to see them. But then, he seemed more interested in the room and the bars than in the jewels themselves. Alistair's a strange fellow, but the best of all chaps, don't you know."

She didn't need to close her eyes. The card flashed in front of her, the Tower of Destruction. Flames and fire and disaster, and Alistair was in the midst of them.

He was going to steal the crown jewels.

"We can't wait for your carriage," Jessamine said, flinging her cloak around her and heading for the door.

Freddie stood still, dumbfounded. "Why not?"

"Because I have to get to the Tower of London. Immediately!"

"Not you too," Freddie moaned. "I tell you, those things aren't worth looking at. Too gaudy by half. Besides, it's after hours and no one would be allowed in. Damned drawbridge is probably up. And didn't I tell you there'd been a fire?"

"You told me, Freddie," she said, dispensing with formalities. "I'm still going."

"I promised Alistair I'd see you home," he said stubbornly, blocking the door.

He was a slight man, a foolish, well-meaning man, but he was big enough to stop her if his limited mind was set on it. And it was. The Fool danced through her mind, one foot over a precipice. She wanted to push him.

"You don't understand, Freddie," she said with perfect reasonableness. "I live at the Tower of London."

"Oh. That's different. I thought Alistair said you lived in Spitalfields, but I knew he must have been mistaken. No lady would live in that area. That explains it!" he said, suddenly excited. "He must have been looking for you. He certainly wasn't that interested in those blasted jewels."

"Wasn't he?" Jessamine said. "I'm going to Tower Hill, Freddie, and I'm going now. You can come with me if you want."

"Promised Alistair," Freddie mumbled resignedly. "Always keep my promise."

Domestic bliss at the Brennan residence lasted for exactly sixteen hours. Until Robert Brennan stepped outside his door to find Samuel Welch's body stretched across the landing, his throat slashed from ear to ear.

"Get back in the room," he ordered Fleur, blocking her view of the grisly sight. "Stay there, and don't come out."

It took less than a moment to ascertain that poor Samuel was well and truly dead. He'd been killed elsewhere — there wasn't enough blood on the landing for it to have been done there. Besides, Brennan would have heard the struggle; Samuel would have put up one hell of a fight. Unless, of course, the knife came from the hands of a trusted friend and colleague.

He rose, looking down the narrow stairs to the street below. Clegg was long gone — he'd left his warning like a taunt. One that he knew Brennan wouldn't ignore.

He was no longer a runner, but he still had a duty he couldn't ignore. Clegg was going after the Cat, and for some reason he wanted Brennan in at the kill.

Brennan would face two bad men that night — the Cat and

the Bow Street runner. And he had no doubt as to which man was truly evil. Which man he most needed to stop.

But where were they? What could a renegade aristocrat be planning to steal that would be considered an insult to all of England?

The answer was blindingly simple. The Cat stole jewelry. And there were no more fabulous jewels than those belonging to the royal family. The nefarious Earl of Glenshiel must be after the crown jewels.

Fleur was sitting by the fire, her face pale. "I want you to go back to Spitalfields," he said abruptly, searching for his pistol.

"You're sending me away?" Her voice was low and stricken, pulling him out of his temporary absorption, and he crossed the room in two wide strides, pulling her into his arms.

"Only for a day, lass. To keep you safe. I've a criminal to stop. A man to kill. And I need to know that you're out of harm's way while I do it."

She pulled herself out of his arms. "You're not going to kill the Earl of Glenshiel!" she said, horrified.

"If I have to, I will," he said.

"My sister loves him."

"Your family has strange taste in the men they choose to love," Brennan said wryly. "If I can, I'll let him live. But it might not be up to me."

"But you said you had a man to *kill*."

"Josiah Clegg." His voice was grim. "His time is long past due." He kissed her hard and briefly. "Don't look so worried, love. Nothing's going to happen to me. I'll stop his thieving lordship, and I'll put a halt to Josiah Clegg's wickedness. And then I'll teach you how to be a farmer's wife."

Doubt and hope danced in her beautiful blue eyes. "I would like that, Robert. Above all things, I would like that."

284

★ ★ ★ ★ ★

It was rather like being impotent, Alistair imagined. No matter how far one went, to what extremes one was willing to go, it was more and more difficult to get it up.

He was finding the heist of a lifetime to be, in fact, a dead bore.

For one thing, it was too damned easy. Setting the fire had been outrageously simple, and the idiot guards had simply jumbled the various royal headgear and weaponry in a large wooden crate tucked in the back of storeroom. Heaven only knew what else resided in that cavernous space, but he'd already espied a pile of moldering dull red uniforms, the mummified corpses of several rats, broken pieces of armor, and even a few instruments of torture and execution, including thumbscrews and a nasty-looking headman's ax.

The lock on the door had been abominably flimsy. Obviously the keepers of the royal treasure seemed to think no one would dare attempt such a combination of treason and sacrilege. They'd forgotten Thomas Blood's ill-fated attempt less than a century before.

But Alistair meant to get away with it. The only problem was, he could no longer remember exactly why.

At first it had seemed the final remedy to boredom. The ultimate challenge to his reiving skills, and a fitting crime for the descendant of William Wallace and generation upon generation of Scottish rebels. It was merely a more sophisticated variant of border thieving, and his great-great-grandfather would be duly proud of him.

But he'd never been interested in politics, and his family had intermarried with the Sassenachs so often that half the time he didn't know whether he was Scots or English. His father had supported the Pretender in his fight for the throne, but discreetly enough that in the ensuing debacle he'd still managed to retain his lands and his fortune. And Alistair, watching the workings of political maneuverings from a cynical distance, had nothing but contempt for both sides.

Snatching the crown that Bonnie Prince Charlie had so coveted was an amusing notion when he'd first thought of it. But by the time he stood alone in the darkened storeroom at the very edge of Tower Green, the torch in his hand illuminating the bright gold of the jewels, he was beginning to find that nothing amused him at all anymore.

Several of the crowns were already denuded — as if a magpie or a discerning thief had been there before him. He'd heard rumors that some of the jewels were merely hired for the occasion, and this seemed to prove him right. He picked up a particularly delicate crown studded with pearls and great empty places that should have held sapphires at the very least. He dropped it back into the crate, then picked up another, a jewel-studded coronet that had probably sat atop German George's wig. He grinned at the notion, slipping it into the bag at his feet.

His grin vanished at the scraping sound coming from the far end of the room. It might possibly be a live rat. It might also be the human variety.

He rather hoped so. This was all dismally tame, and he found himself wishing he'd stayed in bed with Jessamine. Not that she would have let him. He'd managed to get past her defenses twice, but it was unlikely he'd manage it again.

"You don't really want to be doing that, your lordship."

Robert Brennan stepped out of the shadows. He had a small gun trained at Alistair's heart, and Alistair had no doubts about his ability to use it.

"Call me Alistair," he said blandly. "There's no need for formality."

"Put the crown down nice and easy. You don't want to be

damaging a bit of England's heritage, now, do you?"

"I don't know if I'd call it England's heritage," Alistair drawled. "After all, none of this is much more than a hundred years old. Cromwell had all the old stuff melted down."

"I remember my history, your lordship."

"How did you happen to find me? Not that I made it that difficult, but the thief-takers have been alarmingly obtuse during my short, colorful career. I was expecting much more of a challenge from you all."

"You weren't my concern," Brennan said. "Someone who pilfers baubles from people who can well afford to lose them isn't likely to cause me to lose any sleep. But when you threaten the very treasure of England, and murder a good man in the bargain, then I have to take notice."

He'd managed to jar Alistair out of his mocking complacency. "I didn't murder anyone!" he snapped. "Unless you're talking about Isolde Plumworthy's majordomo, but I'd consider that more of a boon to society than a crime."

"I'm talking about Sammy Welch. A good friend of mine."

"I didn't murder your Mr. Welch," Alistair said haughtily. "I'd have neither the stomach for it nor the reason."

Brennan peered at him for a moment, then nodded. "No," he said. "I didn't really think you had. But I wanted to make certain. You'll be coming with me, your lordship. Sir John would like a word with you."

"Told him I was coming, did you? How'd he take to the notion of hanging a peer of the realm?" He picked up one of the heavy ceremonial maces, fondling it affectionately.

"I haven't had a chance to speak with Sir John. He doesn't know who you are."

Alistair lifted the heavy mace, holding it in both hands. "Then I still have a fighting chance," he said. "If I killed you, no one would know what I'd been doing. I could get away with it. And I must confess, my friend, that I do very much want to get away with it. To prove to myself that I can walk away from the Tower of London with one of the royal crowns in my satchel."

"You could try to kill me," Brennan said. "Though I should tell you I'm not a man who's easily killed. And my wife wouldn't like it above half. Nor would her sister."

"I hadn't realized you were married."

"Today, sir."

"I offer you my felicitations," Alistair said politely. "Who's the lucky bride?"

"Fleur Maitland."

"Oh," said Alistair. He glanced at the mace. It would be a simple enough matter to fling it at Brennan's head and then duck to avoid being shot. Whether he could manage to duck in time was questionable, but it might be worth a try.

However, then he'd have to finish off the Bow Street runner. And Brennan was right, Jessamine would be most displeased with him. For some reason, Jessamine's pleasure seemed of utmost importance.

It was probably because he'd made the very grave, unthinkable mistake of falling in love with her. Trapped in a cavernous storeroom with a gun trained on his heart, he was suddenly unable to avoid that wretched conviction any longer. It was difficult to lie to yourself when you were staring death in the face.

"Then I suppose I can't kill you," Alistair said pleasantly, dropping the mace back into the crate with a loud crash.

"I'd advise against it, sir."

"Pity," he murmured. "This theft would have been a glorious escapade. A fitting cap to my criminal career."

"Your escapades are done, my lord."

"I rather suspect you are right," Alistair said sadly. There was a shadow against the far wall, behind Brennan. A shadow that was definitely moving. "Then again, you might possibly be mistaken."

"I beg your pardon?"

"I have a confederate."

Brennan glanced around, only for a moment, but it was enough. The mace made a satisfying thunk as it connected with Brennan's well-padded skull, and he went down in a large, untidy heap.

Jessamine stormed across the room in a flurry of rose-colored silk, falling at Brennan's side. "If you've killed him . . ." she said fiercely.

"I haven't." He dropped the mace. "He's a Yorkshireman — they have very hard heads. What are you doing here, Jessamine? And where the hell is Freddie?"

"Freddie's sitting in a boat beneath Traitor's Gate, freezing his hindquarters off. And I'm here to stop you, of course."

"Of course," Alistair said faintly. "You're abominably difficult to get rid of, my pet."

She looked up at him through the shadows. "Are you so very certain you want to get rid of me?"

He couldn't meet that steady gaze. Instead, he glanced back into the crate, poking among the glittering gold with a desultory hand. "Jessamine, I care for nothing and no one. Haven't I succeeded in proving that to you?"

"No."

"I'm a thief. A conscienceless, arrogant wastrel with nothing useful to do with my time. Why don't you marry Freddie? He's pleasant, amenable, and while his fortune isn't large, it's a great deal better than what you're currently living on."

"I don't want to marry Freddie."

"Not even knowing it would annoy Ermintrude Winters exceedingly?" he said.

289

"I don't want to marry anyone."

That startled him. "Not even me?"

"I don't want to be a widow," she said. "I don't want to stand at your gallows and weep."

"Then stand at my gallows and dance," he suggested cheerfully.

She rose, glaring at him. "I hate you."

"Of course you do, my pet. I truly wish I could say I return the sentiment. Is your brother-in-law beginning to rouse? I expect I didn't hit him as hard as I should have."

"Yes," she said. "Put the crown back and run, Alistair. You can make it out of the country before they catch you. What possible benefit could there be in dying?"

"None," he said. "Unless I'd get to see whether you'd really cry for me."

"I've cried too much for you already."

He reached down and picked up the satchel. It was light, with only the denuded crown within, but it was good enough. "Why?" he asked, curiosity stalling his escape.

"Because I love you, you monstrously selfish, arrogant fop!" she shouted at him.

He didn't move. "I beg your pardon," he said. "I am not a fop."

At her feet Brennan groaned, beginning to move. "Would you please leave!" she begged him, and he could see those tears in her eyes. "Take the crowns, take every damned thing, but just escape before —"

"Too late." Josiah Clegg stepped out of the shadows. "Lovely little party we have here. All nice and friendly like." He looked down at Brennan, then kicked him with his sharp-toed boot. "Did you kill him?"

"He's just unconscious," Jessamine said. "Mr. Clegg, you must realize that Alistair —"

"Shut yer face, Miss Maitland," Clegg said pleasantly. "I'll be shutting it for you before long, but if you want to spend a few more minutes on this earth, then you'll go over there and sit down quietly while I deal with his lordship."

"What are you going to do with me, Clegg?" Alistair asked.

"Why, kill you, your lordship. And me old pal Brennan as well. Can't have anyone taking credit for yer capture, now, can I?"

"And Miss Maitland?"

"Ah, Miss Maitland. I'll give her a taste of what she's been begging for. And then I'll cut her throat."

Twenty-four

Jessamine backed away from him, stumbling over a pile of old tools and antique weaponry, but Josiah Clegg had already dismissed her. That had always been Josiah Clegg's failing, she thought. He couldn't believe a woman could pose any threat to him.

"I think I'll shoot you in the head. It makes a great bloody mess, but it's very satisfying. I've never had the chance to kill a lord before. I think I'll enjoy it."

Brennan groaned again, and in the shadows Jessamine could see him struggle to sit up. Clegg turned to sneer at him, enjoying himself. "Of course you're a different matter, Robbie boy. I've killed plenty of your sort, so there's not much challenge in it. I could shoot you in the crackers. I'm going to tell them his bleedin' lordship did it, of course, and who would expect an earl to have decent aim?" He chuckled, advancing toward his dazed colleague with malicious glee.

"No need to kill him," Alistair drawled. "It's me you want. Why bother with Brennan?"

"Because I don't likes to share," Clegg said with a raspy chuckle. "And I enjoy killing." He raised his gun, aiming it directly at Brennan's groin.

Jessamine scrambled to her feet, grabbing the first metal thing she could find and brandishing it threateningly. It looked like an old ax of some sort. "Leave him alone," she said, moving toward him.

It distracted him for one crucial moment. In the blink of an eye Alistair reached into the crate in front of him and sent a golden object winging toward Clegg's head. Brennan rolled out of the way, ducking under a pile of rubbish, but the golden mace only glanced off Clegg's forehead, falling to the dirt floor with a noisy clatter.

"Bitch," Clegg said, no longer interested in his first two victims. "Bleedin' whore. I'll take care of you first, and let the others watch."

"Keep away from me," she screamed.

She could hear Alistair scrambling behind her. "You want me," he said, his voice desperate. "Leave her alone."

"Make me, boy-o." He made the fatal mistake of turning his back on Jessamine. "You can't stop me in time, and I'm going to put a bullet right between her lovely little —"

Jessamine hoisted the heavy tool over her head, shut her eyes, and slammed it at him as hard as she could. The weight of it threw her off balance. She could feel a solid chunk as it landed, and then she went tumbling to the floor as the weapon took on a life of its own.

For a moment all was eerily silent. Jessamine struggled to her knees, peering through the ill-lit darkness as Alistair suddenly loomed large.

"Holy Mother of God," he said softly. "Remind me never to annoy you when you're near a weapon, dear heart."

"Did I kill him?" she asked, aghast. She could see Clegg's legs sticking out from behind a crate, motionless.

"I'd say so," Alistair murmured.

Brennan had managed to rise to his feet. He was bleeding from the blow to his head, and his color was an ashen green. "Thoroughly," he said.

Jessamine rose, starting to move around the crate to get a better look at her fallen nemesis, when Alistair stopped her with

293

an arm around her waist. "I don't think you want to see, my pet. Do you have any idea what you flung at him?"

"No. I was just trying to stop him."

Brennan reached down and picked up a double-sided ax that was ominously dark on one side. "It's a headman's ax," he said. "Still quite sharp."

"I never realized you had Tudor blood in you, my precious," Alistair said.

"You mean I . . . ?"

"Precisely," Alistair said, drawing a finger across his throat and making a disgustingly cheerful rasping noise. "Severed it completely."

If the room was dark before, those shadows were now closing in on her. "I'm going to be sick," she said quite firmly. "That, or faint."

"Might I suggest the latter?" Alistair said sweetly. "We already have quite a mess to clean up."

It was the finishing touch. The darkness closed in completely, and Jessamine slumped to the hard-packed floor, still remembering the solid thunk as her weapon connected with living flesh.

Alistair caught her, of course. It would probably be his last chance to hold her, he thought, and he had every intention of enjoying it to the fullest. He glanced over at Brennan, who was still staring down at his fallen comrade with an expression of disgust mixed with satisfaction.

"What are you going to do now?" he inquired.

"I'm not sure, sir. One thing I do know — I can't let you get away with the crown jewels."

"I wasn't planning on taking them all," he said with great reasonableness. "For one thing, they're too heavy. I thought one big one might make my point."

"I'm afraid not, sir."

"And how do you intend to stop me? Will you kill me, Mr. Brennan? The man who saved your life? You may not be aware of it, but Clegg was just about to blast your nuts away when I threw that mace at him."

"You're mighty handy with the mace, sir," Brennan said, touching his wounded forehead. "But I appreciate your efforts on my behalf."

"My pleasure."

"Not enough, however, to let you go."

"Brennan, you have a headless Bow Street runner and a fainting woman on your hands. How do you indeed to stop me?"

"I'll shoot you if I must. And I don't have her on my hands."

He regretted it, of course, but there was really no choice. "You do now," he said simply. He tossed Jessamine's semiconscious body toward Brennan, counting on the runner to drop his gun rather than a lady. A second later he knocked over the candle, plunging the room into utter darkness.

"Sorry to leave you like this, Mr. Brennan. But I have my pride to consider." And catching up his rough satchel, he disappeared into the darkness.

There was a moon that night. A half-moon, but a bright one, shining down over Tower Green. No one seemed to have noticed the disturbance in the old storeroom, but then, things had been lax at the Tower since Cromwell's day. Alistair tossed the satchel over his shoulder and walked down the pathway, whistling cheerfully.

A raven swooped by, cawing a wicked note of laughter, and Alistair's whistling came to an abrupt halt. He would have no trouble leaving the way he came, and he had the coronation crown of King George to cheer him on his way.

He paused in the middle of the walkway, momentarily distracted. The crown was heavier than he'd realized, and for the moment he wasn't quite sure what he would do with it. Even Nicodemus might draw the line at turning one of England's priceless treasures into ready cash, and besides, Alistair had no real need of money. The manor house in Scotland had been shored up, in better shape than it had been in centuries. London was no longer a hospitable place for the likes of him, so his house on Clarges Street could be dispensed with.

But where would he go? What would he do?

He considered his options as he strolled aimlessly through the midnight streets of London. The Continent bored him. The thought of exotic, willing foreign women bored him. The thought of pilfering diamonds from the French court bored him.

He didn't want diamonds, he didn't want to climb over rooftops. He didn't want French courtesans or Italian mistresses.

He wanted Jessamine.

He looked down at the satchel, paused, and pulled the crown from its resting spot. It didn't look much the worse for wear — a dent or two perhaps, but nothing that wouldn't be fixed by a jeweler's hammer.

Oliver Cromwell was out of favor even among the German Hanovers. Only one statue remained within the city limits of London, a great bronze monstrosity that had the Lord Protector glaring down at his frivolous countrymen from a public garden near the small Puritan church where Cromwell had once worshipped. "You don't approve of me, do you, old Noll?" he said softly. "Well, I don't approve of you. You need some livening up."

The crown sat quite jauntily atop Cromwell's bronzed pilgrim's hat. Alistair stepped back to survey the effect, then smiled. As a finishing touch it couldn't be bettered. "Wear it in good health, milord Protector," he said. And then he sauntered off into the moonlight, making his escape.

Jessamine took deep, cleansing gulps of the fresh night air. Her brother-in-law stood beside her, one polite, protective arm around her as she slowly regained her senses.

"Are you feeling better?" he asked.

She glanced back at the tightly shut door of the old storehouse. She wasn't even certain how he'd gotten her out of there. She had no idea where Alistair was. She knew only that he'd disappeared. And she told herself she was glad.

"I suppose so," she said. "What are you planning to do?"

"About what?"

"About . . . er . . . that?" she said, gesturing back toward the storeroom. "Mr. Clegg."

"Not a thing," he said. "Someone will find his body soon enough, when they go to return the jewels to Martin Tower. I imagine whoever investigates it will assume there was falling out among thieves."

"Will you investigate it?"

"No."

"What about the Cat?"

"What about him?" Brennan said smoothly. "I imagine he'll be one of those mysteries that never has an answer. He terrorized London society for a few months and then disappeared."

"He didn't terrorize anyone!" Jessamine protested.

"It makes a better story. And that's all he'll be — a whopping good story."

"What about the missing crown?"

"I expect we'll find it. It seems to me his lordship doesn't have a truly larcenous nature. It'll turn up sooner or later, probably when we least expect it. But it won't be my concern.

I've finished my work here. I'm taking my wife back to Yorkshire with me, where all I'll have to worry about is the weather and the price of corn."

Jessamine took a deep breath. "She loves you to distraction, you know."

"I know. You don't mind? It spoiled all your fine plans for her."

"They were my plans, not hers," Jessamine said. "She has what she wants, and what she needs now, and I couldn't be happier."

"There'll always be a place for you and your mother."

"You haven't met our mother," she said wryly. "You may regret the offer. We'll manage, never you fear. But I'll be there in nine months' time to welcome my new niece or nephew into the world."

"That's rushing things a bit, isn't it?" he said, startled.

"You'll find that Fleur can be quite determined in getting her own way."

"I think," said Brennan, "I've already discovered that."

"And you need to get back to her. She's probably worried sick about you. And poor Freddie must be frozen solid." She leaned up and gave him a kiss on the cheek. "Welcome to the family, brother," she said, and then ran off into the nighttime shadows before he could stop her.

Freddie wasn't quite frozen solid, but he was clearly unhappy. Being an obedient soul, he hadn't moved from his spot in the tiny skiff where she'd left him, but he complained, a little too loudly, all the way back to Spitalfields, about her ill treatment of him.

"You've been a savior," she said, leaping down from the hired carriage before he could help her. "Alistair will thank you for it."

Freddie looked suddenly mournful. "Do you think we'll ever

see him again, Miss Maitland?"

It was something she wasn't quite ready to face, but she managed a brave smile. "I doubt it, Mr. Arbuthnot. But we'll have our memories, won't we?"

"Splendid ones," Freddie said soulfully.

"Splendid ones, indeed."

"Wake up, dearest."

Jessamine pushed her face deeper into the pillow, trying to drown out the gentle voice. When Brennan had returned her to the house in Spitalfields, she had taken to her bed and refused to rise for two days. She wasn't about to get up now.

Her sister wasn't taking no for an answer. "Wake up, Jess," she said in a sharper tone, yanking at the covers.

Jessamine flopped over onto her back in the large bed she'd always shared with her younger sister and glared at that evil beast. "I don't wish to wake up," she said firmly. "I don't know if I ever wish to get out of bed again. And what are you doing here? Shouldn't you be with your husband?"

"He's seeing to some last-minute details, so he sent me on ahead here. He thought you would be interested in the news-paper."

"I find that highly unlikely," Jessamine said, sitting up and pushing her hair out of her face. She knew her face would be pale and tear-streaked, but she made no effort to hide it.

"I brought you some tea," Fleur said, perching on the end of the bed with the ease of one who doesn't plan to remove herself any too soon. "Someone tried to steal the crown jewels."

"Fascinating," Jess said carefully. "Did they get away with it?"

"Well, the missing crown was recovered a few miles away in a churchyard. Perched atop a statue of Oliver Cromwell."

Jessamine hadn't thought she'd ever be capable of laughter

again, but she was wrong. "A thief with a sense of humor," she said.

"Apparently. Unfortunately your friend Mr. Clegg was killed. Most unpleasantly too. Someone whacked off his head at the Tower."

Jessamine had just taken her first sip of tea, and she spat it out noisily into the cup. "How unfortunate," she said in a faint voice.

"They say he died in the line of duty. He'll have a hero's funeral. Him and his head."

"Fleur!" Jessamine protested.

"Sorry, dearling. I didn't know you were quite so squeamish," she said with a mischievous smile.

"I don't like severed body parts."

"I don't imagine Mr. Clegg is any too fond of them himself."

Jessamine lay back with a moan. "Have you seen Mother?"

"Only briefly. She was on her way out."

It took a moment for Fleur's words to register. Jessamine opened one eye. "Out?"

"She's gone shopping for a new wardrobe. For some reason the notion of her daughter marrying an earl has cured her of her lingering illness."

"You aren't marrying an earl," Jessamine said.

"No, dear. According to the paper, you are."

"What?" she shrieked, scrambling out of bed, sending the teacups flying.

"Glenshiel must have been very busy."

Jessamine grabbed the paper from her hand. It was already open to the social notes, and there it was in smudged print, the news of her pending marriage to the sixth Earl of Glenshiel.

"I'll kill him," she said fiercely.

"Wait till I leave for Yorkshire," Fleur said in a tranquil voice. "As it is, Mother forgives me for my bad taste in marrying a farmer. I'd rather you didn't commit murder until after I'm gone. Or is it already too late?" she said with a wicked laugh.

"Your husband," Jessamine said sternly, "has a very ill effect on you. It's no laughing matter."

"I'm more interested in seeing what effect your husband will have on you."

Alistair MacAlpin, the sixth Earl of Glenshiel, sat in his bedroom watching the fire eat its way through the pile of black clothing. He'd doused the garments liberally with brandy, but it was still a slow process, one he watched with endless fascination. It was an old way of life, disappearing into soot and ashes. He wondered when his new way of life was going to show up at his door.

He hadn't long to wait. It was midday, the house was empty, and he could hear her furious, pounding footsteps up his back stairs. He settled in his chair, a glass of fine brandy in one long-fingered hand, and prepared to meet his fate.

She slammed open the door, standing there like a perfect harridan, or an avenging angel. She was dressed in one of her plain dresses again, which was probably a good thing, since the rose-colored silk had gotten splashed with Clegg's blood, and her hair was bound tightly behind her head again. It was certain to give her a headache, he thought. No wonder she looked so furious.

"I'm going to kill you," she announced.

He glanced around him. "I'm afraid I'm fresh out of headmen's axes, sweeting. You want to saw away at my neck with a butter knife?"

"How dare you print such a thing in the paper?" she demanded.

He gave her his sweetest smile. It left her stonily unmoved. "It seemed like a good idea. I've given up thieving, and I needed

301

something to occupy my time."

"I don't need a thing to occupy my time, thank you very much. I'm sure I'll find plenty of things to do in Yorkshire while I visit my sister."

He rose, and she backed up a little, her magnificent eyes wary. "Ah, but life with me would be such an adventure, Jessamine," he murmured, moving closer.

"I've had adventures enough," she said. "I don't want any more."

"And what *do* you want?" His voice was suddenly deadly serious as he waited for her reply.

"I want a home," she said. "I want children, lots of them, so many that they drive me to distraction. I want to be far away from the city, so that I never have to smell the city stink again. And most of all, I want a man who loves me."

"Ah, Jess," he murmured, pausing in his approach. "You demand so much, and you don't compromise."

"Never," she said.

"I can give you the home," he said. "In the hills of Scotland, miles away from any city. It's huge and rambling and drafty, but the roof won't fall down anytime soon, and there's a loch with the best salmon in the world.

"And I can give you children. I can quite willingly see that you're eternally pregnant if that's what you want." He paused, oddly frightened.

"Is that all you can give me?" she asked him, calm and clear-eyed.

He raised his eyes to look at her. "I can give you a man who loves you so much that he would likely die without you," he said simply.

For a minute she didn't move. And then a glorious smile lit her face, so bright that it finally melted the ice around his heart, and she was in his arms, and he was kissing her, kissing her, and she was crying, and he might have been too as he picked her up in his arms and carried her toward the bed.

And in the fireplace the brandy-soaked clothing burst into merry flames, sending warmth and light throughout the bedroom. And neither of them noticed.

Author's Note

I've never been one to let historical fact get in the way of an entertaining story. As far as I can ascertain, tarot cards weren't used for divination until the early 1780s, a few years after the book takes place. They were used as a card game, and regular cards were used for fortune-telling, but there's no record of tarot being used for esoteric means until later.

And there probably wasn't a statue of Oliver Cromwell anywhere in the city of London. After all, they'd disinterred his body, hanged it, lopped off his head, and set it on Traitor's Gate at the Tower. It takes a while to recover from such ill usage.

The term *cat burglar* didn't come into usage until the 1920s, but then, I never refer to Alistair as a cat burglar. He simply prowls the fancy houses of London like a cat, stealing whatever takes his fancy.

Everything else is as accurate as I could make it. Special thanks go to my niece, Jennifer Todd Taylor, for having the good sense to visit home from England just as I was finishing this book. Her snippets of information were invaluable.